"What are y

"I'm sorry," the
chattering teeth.

Dillon saw that her scarf had slipped down around
her neck and the thin raincoat she wore was no
protection against the cold. She was near frozen.
"Come with me," he said, watching her thick blond
hair settle around her shoulders. Great hair, he
thought. "Do you live near the feed store?"

"I don't think so."

It was the middle of the night, and he was in no
mood for games. "What do you mean, you don't
think so? Don't you know where you live?"

"I can't remember."

Exasperated, Dillon ran a hand through his thick
black hair. He didn't think for a minute this woman
was telling the truth. At least not all of it. He'd
caught a hint of fear in her expression. But
wouldn't a woman far from everything familiar,
marooned with a stranger, be more fearful if she
couldn't remember her name?

Dear Reader,

This September, four of our beloved authors pen irresistible sagas about lonesome cowboys, hard-luck heroines and love on the range! We've flashed these "Western-themed" romances with a special arch treatment. And additional treasures are provided to our readers by Christine Rimmer—a new JONES GANG book with an excerpt from her wonderful upcoming single title, *The Taming of Billy Jones,* as well as Marilyn Pappano's first Special Edition novel.

In *Every Cowgirl's Dream* by Arlene James, our THAT SPECIAL WOMAN! Kara Detmeyer is one feisty cowgirl who can handle just about anything—except the hard-edged cowboy who escorts her through a dangerous cattle drive. Don't miss this high-spirited adventure.

THE JONES GANG returns to Special Edition! In *A Hero for Sophie Jones,* veteran author Christine Rimmer weaves a poignant story about a ruthless hero who is transformed by love. And wedding bells are chiming in *The Mail-Order Mix-Up* by Pamela Toth, but can this jilted city sophisticate find true love? Speaking of mismatched lovers, a pregnant widow discovers forbidden passion with her late husband's half brother in *The Cowboy Take a Wife* by Lois Faye Dyer.

Rounding out the month, *Stranded on the Ranch* by Pat Warren features a sheltered debutante who finds herself snowbound with an oh-so-sexy rancher. And Marilyn Pappano brings us a bittersweet reunion romance between a reformed temptress and the wary lover she left behind in *Older, Wiser...Pregnant.* I hope you enjoy each and every story to come!

Sincerely,

Karen Taylor Richman
Senior Editor

Please address questions and book requests to:
Silhouette Reader Service
U.S.: 3010 Walden Ave., P.O. Box 1325, Buffalo, NY 14269
Canadian: P.O. Box 609, Fort Erie, Ont. L2A 5X3

PAT WARREN

STRANDED ON THE RANCH

Published by Silhouette Books
America's Publisher of Contemporary Romance

This book is dedicated to Dottie Dely, for happy
memories of trips to Washington and New York, buses
and trains, laughter and friendship.

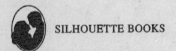 SILHOUETTE BOOKS

ISBN 0-373-24199-2

STRANDED ON THE RANCH

Copyright © 1998 by Pat Warren

PAT WARREN,

mother of four, lives in Arizona with her travel-agent husband and a lazy white cat. She's a former newspaper columnist whose lifetime dream was to become a novelist. A strong romantic streak, a sense of humor and a keen interest in developing relationships led her to try romance novels, with which she feels very much at home.

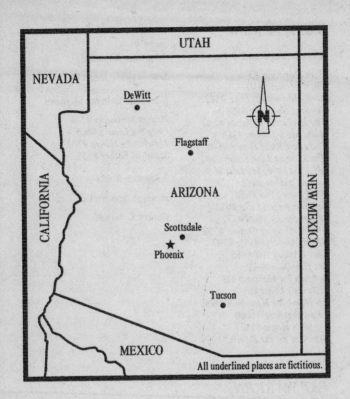

UTAH

NEVADA

DeWitt
•

Flagstaff
•

CALIFORNIA

ARIZONA

NEW MEXICO

Scottsdale
•
★
Phoenix

Tucson
•

MEXICO

All underlined places are fictitious.

Chapter One

Seated on the dais, waiting to make her speech, Kari Sinclair stifled a yawn. It had been a long day, filled with too much smiling and handshaking, culminating in this interminable evening at the Bonaventure Hotel in Phoenix. Dinner on the patio had involved yet another chicken-breast-stuffed-with-rice dinner and an array of lengthy speeches by eager, local politicians. She was the keynote speaker and she was certainly not eager. In fact, if she had to smile much longer, she was sure her cheeks would crack.

The patio area was lovely: tiny lights had been artfully laced throughout delicate tree branches; the moon overhead looked as if it was part of a movie set; and soft, unobtrusive music drifted out through the double doors. There were twenty tables for ten covered in spotless linens, sparkling glassware and fine china, where dozens of the movers and shakers of Arizona politics sat patiently waiting for the youngest daughter of their favorite son to talk to them. It was mid-March, the peak of the reelection campaign for her father, U.S. Senator James Sinclair.

Kari wished she were at home in bed with a good novel. Or even a bad novel.

The book of matches on the table advertised the name of the hotel and city, which was a good thing since Kari wasn't altogether certain where she was. A week of campaigning had done that to her. She did remember that Phoenix was the seventh stop of a twelve-city tour, which meant she had only five more to go after tonight. Thank goodness.

Kari's eyes shifted to a palm tree at her left, where Norma Brice, her aide, stood watching, her ever-present clipboard hugged to her chest. When she'd first started traveling the circuit for her father, straight out of college, Kari had thought it odd that she would need one of his aides. After all, surely she could manage to get herself to the next city and show up on time for her appointments. That was before she'd realized that this gig involved early-morning radio spots, breakfast meetings, guesting on local television shows, luncheons, women's teas, dinners, etc. There were plane schedules to keep track of, and clothes and speeches. It was almost overwhelming *with* Norma; without her, it would be impossible.

Glancing toward the lectern, Kari noticed that Al Rawlings, the party chairman, was really wound up, gesturing, smiling, getting the occasional laugh. He seemed to be thoroughly enjoying himself, so much so that his auburn toupee had slipped slightly lower on the left side, giving him a comical look she was sure he'd find embarrassing. His bushy mustache was real, though, and he stroked it each time he paused for a breath. Who but a politician would think to use facial hair as a prop? Kari wondered, her lips twitching.

She had to look for ways to amuse herself when she was on these two-week blitzes, since overall she found the whole ritual endlessly boring after four years of hitting the trail. Her father, it sometimes seemed, had been in politics forever, twice serving as Arizona's attorney general, moving directly from that to the U.S. Senate and now seeking his fourth term.

Some politicians guarded the privacy of their families zealously, rarely allowing them to be photographed or interviewed. Unfortunately for her, Kari's father was of the opinion that voters related positively to a family man, and his popularity proved him right. Therefore his whole family was involved in getting James reelected, traveling from January to November in an election year.

Her family's obvious and continued enjoyment of the political scene often had Kari wondering if she were adopted. How else to explain why she was the only maverick who hated living in a fishbowl and intensely disliked being asked the most personal questions on live radio or TV? Why did she alone have to force herself to attend these pagan rituals where she was expected to shake hands until her fingers hurt? Perhaps she was missing an important gene.

Kari took a deep breath and immediately wished she hadn't. The flowers and flowering shrubs in this garden setting—hibiscus, azaleas, roses, oleander, poinsettias— each releasing their own special brand of pollen into the evening air, caused her allergies to kick in with a vengeance. Had she known they'd be seated outside for hours, she'd have taken an antihistamine. Groping for a tissue in her small bag, she felt a sneeze coming on.

Just at that moment Kari heard her name announced.

She fumbled with the tissue, scooted her chair back and put on a smile as she walked to the podium amidst enthusiastic applause. Just as she reached the microphone, the sneeze exploded into her tissue. She caught a couple of sympathetic looks, could hear a few nervous snickers and wished she could sink through the floorboards. But, like the good little doobie she'd been raised to be, she blinked her red-rimmed eyes, dabbed at her leaky nose and made a stab at a smile.

Reaching for the sense of humor that had all but abandoned her lately, she gazed out at the sea of faces. ''Dad always told me to start my talks with a bang,'' she said with a self-deprecating laugh. The audience laughed with her and gave her another burst of applause.

Maybe it wouldn't be too bad, Kari thought.

An hour later Kari strolled into their two-bedroom suite as Norma held the door open. Stepping out of her heels, she headed straight for the tissue box next to the bed as another sneezing fit hit her. Four explosions later, she blew her nose somewhat indelicately and fell back on the bed. ''Norma, I hope we packed my antihistamines.''

Norma had already marched into the bath with her long strides and was rummaging through Kari's toiletries. ''Yes, here we are.'' She carried the pill bottle over to Kari along with a glass of water.

After sitting up to take the medication, Kari immediately flopped back. ''I must be a sight with these swollen eyes and runny nose.'' Maybe she could beg off the next leg of their trip. ''Where are we scheduled to go tomorrow?'' she asked, hoping it was some remote little town with only a handful of people who surely wouldn't miss her if she didn't show.

Norma sat in the wing chair near the fireplace and consulted her clipboard. "Tempe. Looks like a heavy day."

Kari almost groaned aloud. "All right, lay it on me."

"You have an early-morning stint on Channel 3's 'Good Morning, Arizona.' Then—"

"How early?"

"The program airs at 6:00 a.m., but they want you there by 5:30."

"Of course they do." Kari closed her eyes.

"Then there's a breakfast meeting at the Tempe Hilton with the political analyst for the *Tribune*. Afterward, there's a spot on KTAR radio, followed by a luncheon with the American Legion Post Number—"

Kari's head shot up. "What? Why them? Why me?"

"They're big supporters of your father."

This time Kari did groan out loud.

Undaunted and used to Kari's surliness on tour, Norma went on. "Then we zig over to the Scottsdale Senior Center, where you'll present several service awards and give a short talk."

"How short?"

"Fifteen, twenty minutes. I have several you can choose from. Then at six there's going to be a rally at America West arena before the Phoenix Suns basketball game. It's a sellout so that should really be something. They've given us front-row seats for the game afterward."

"Don't I have to attend some flag-lowering ceremony at midnight somewhere to culminate such a marvelous fun-filled day?"

Norma's serious gaze scanned her clipboard. "I don't believe so."

"Whoopee." Kari sat up, rubbing her throbbing head.

"Why don't you find a friend and stay for the game. By then, I'll be bleary-eyed."

Norma dropped her gaze to the burgundy carpeting. "But it's you they want to see, Kari, not me."

Not for the first time Kari found herself wondering about Norma's personal life. Dedicated and detail conscious, her long hours working for James Sinclair didn't leave time for much else. She knew that Norma was thirty-two and unmarried, but she'd never heard the woman mention a date. She wasn't bad-looking, her blond hair worn short and straight, and she had nice eyes behind small, granny glasses. Her wardrobe could probably use a little boost since most of her outfits bordered on the boring, running to black suits, navy suits, gray suits, all worn with little white blouses with round collars. She must have a dozen suits in every dull color imaginable.

Kari sighed. Of course, who was she to critique Norma? She hadn't had a date in six months, and that had been with the friend of a friend. Most of the men she met working for her father were either married, too intense or intimidated by James Sinclair to the point of hero worship. Maybe after the election both she and Norma could concentrate on fixing their pitiful social lives.

Rising, Kari slipped off her yellow jacket. "They don't want me, either, Norma. They just want to brush shoulders with someone connected to Dad. You qualify, so stay and enjoy." Walking to the closet, she unzipped her skirt. "I'm going to take a bath. Maybe that pill and a little steam will unclog my head." It had been raining earlier today, and that hadn't helped her sinuses, either. "I've lived in Arizona all my life, yet I can't seem to get used to the climate."

"We can stop in at a health food store tomorrow and get something natural to help you," Norma suggested. "I don't think those pills do much besides dry up your mouth and make you drowsy."

In the bathroom, bending over the big tub to turn on the water, Kari spoke over her shoulder. "From the schedule you just read me, I don't think we have time to take a deep breath, much less squeeze in another stop."

"I'll say good-night, then," Norma said, moving to the door to her room. But the phone rang just then and she stopped to answer it. After a moment she called out to Kari. "It's your father."

Kari found herself smiling as she turned off the water. James Sinclair was a politician through and through, but first and foremost he was a family man. He loved his wife and daughters and rarely went to bed without talking to all three. That was the reason Kari continued the campaigning that she hated, to please the father she adored.

Nodding her thanks to Norma, she took the phone. "Hi, Dad. Are you calling to tell me the polls show you're a shoo-in and I can quit the circuit?"

"Not quite yet, honey." James's voice was a deep baritone that exuded warmth. "How's my girl?"

Kari sat down. "I'm just fine, but my allergies are driving me crazy." She could hear the annoyance in her own voice.

"I can tell you're getting weary, Kari." He knew how his youngest daughter had to force herself to do this for him and loved her all the more for it. But the campaign had barely begun. "After the election you can get away and do exactly as you want for a while."

Dangle that old carrot in front of me, Kari thought. Still, she knew she couldn't let him down. "Okay, how about a trip to Europe? I'd like to rent a car in Italy, drive to the Swiss Alps, see the Berlin Wall, all leisurely, nothing planned out.''

James was frowning. ''Now, honey, that's not safe. Tell you what, I'll have a travel agent friend make up an itinerary, and I'll check with Mom or Dana and maybe they can get away.''

''No. I want to do this myself. Time to cut those old apron strings, Dad. I'm twenty-six.'' And still living at home. After the election, she'd do something about that, too. And this time she wouldn't let her father talk her out of getting her own place.

''Well, we'll see when the time comes. Meanwhile, how's Pinocchio?''

Kari smiled at the catchphrase they'd used for years to let each other know that all really was well. James had one for his wife and Dana, too. ''Pinocchio's just fine.''

''All right, then. I'll talk with you soon. I love you, honey.''

''I love you, too, Dad.'' Kari had barely hung up when another sneezing attack took over. Recovering, she picked up the bottle of antihistamines and read the label. Nothing dangerous in these. What would one more hurt? After all, she was safe in her room. Quickly she swallowed a second pill, then went in to take her bath.

Fragrant from relaxing in the tub and cozily wrapped in her long green robe, Kari brushed out her blond hair, then walked over to gaze out the double windows. From her vantage point, she could see the lights twinkling, hear the music playing. Off in the distance, the contours of a man-made lake curved around the outer perimeter of the hotel grounds. Three gondolas glided through the dark water, the gondoliers singing opera arias in Italian to couples sitting close together. Along the bank, palm trees swayed in a light breeze.

Kari felt a burst of longing, to be out there with those lucky people strolling the weaving pathways, the families dining out under the stars at secluded tables, to be half of a couple embracing under the cover of a fragrant tree. Why couldn't her life be more like that?

Would it ever be? Kari wondered. Already the party had been talking with her father about a possible run for the presidency next national election, or for vice president at the very least. She knew James would love that, but his rise in power would only fence Kari in more.

Her mother would adore being first lady, a role she seemed born to play. Dorothy Sinclair, known to most everyone as Dusty, was still a striking brunette who loved Washington and politics almost as much as her husband. Yes, Mom would be in her element, should she make it to the White House. As would her older sister, Dana, who was as fashionable and outgoing as their mother. Dana thrived on campaigning, and dated only politically correct rising stars, men her father would approve of.

The three of them would be happy as clams living in the fishbowl known as the Capitol, all eyes on them, their every word scribbled down by reporters who even now followed them everywhere. Privacy would be a vague dream, perhaps never recaptured. And then there were the Secret Service men who already were such a part of their lives.

As chairman of the powerful Senate Arms Committee, James had received several death threats. They hadn't slowed him down, but had definitely concerned him. He'd had to accept the Secret Service protection around the clock for himself and similar coverage for his family. While on the one hand Kari appreciated the safety factor, living under constant scrutiny was an unnatural way to exist.

At home in Paradise Valley with the Sinclair house's elaborate security system, it wasn't so bad. But on the road like this, two agents were assigned to her and were always somewhere hovering around, blending in, eyes ever watchful. Hilda Whitney was nearly six feet tall and built solid as a cement pillar, which was why Kari privately referred to her as Brunhilda. Tony Bolognese with his swarthy skin and shifty eyes reminded Kari of someone in a gangster movie. She'd dubbed him Tony Baloney and the tag had stuck. Though he rarely smiled, Tony seemed more amused than offended at his nickname.

They were most likely in their respective rooms by now, one on either side of Kari's suite. It wasn't uncommon for one or both to check on her during the night if they heard something suspicious. She'd told her father that two agents to guard one small daughter was overkill, but he'd stood firm. As always, James Sinclair got his way.

The music grew in volume, drawing Kari to open the window a crack. How lovely the evening was, the night air just a little nippy. She wished she were down there, walking those paths, hearing the music up close. To be free for a few hours, without Norma constantly at her side, without Brunhilda and Tony Baloney dogging her steps—her heart lurched at the very thought.

What would be the harm if she slipped out for just a short time? Norma was probably in bed and fast asleep by now. Her two watchdogs couldn't stay up all night. They had no reason to think she'd sneak out, so they were probably settled in. Excited by the prospect of this small act of rebellion, Kari walked to the closet. She'd have to dress casually, not like a senator's daughter.

If only she'd packed a pair of jeans, but she'd had no reason to. Rummaging through, she found a pair of beige linen slacks and a black cotton shirt. Yes, they would do. Her heart pounding with anticipation, Kari shed her robe and slipped into the casual outfit, sliding her bare feet into leather flats. She wouldn't bother with makeup, since going without would add to her new persona and make her less recognizable.

She found the room key on the end table, then spotted Norma's tan raincoat draped over a chair where she'd tossed it when they'd arrived earlier in the rain. Perfect, she thought as she shrugged into the coat, which was as nondescript as the rest of Norma's wardrobe. In the pockets she found a small amount of loose change and a yellow head scarf.

Hurrying now, Kari quickly pinned up her long hair, then put on the scarf. Gazing at herself in the full-length mirror, she decided she could pass for Norma from a distance. Pocketing the room key, she moved to the door and quietly peeked out. Luck was with her, as no one was in the hallway. Pulse pounding, Kari left her room, walked past the elevators and headed for the stairs.

Finally in the courtyard, she breathed a sigh of relief. She strolled through the lobby and out the double doors and, though a few people glanced at her, no one recognized her. That had been a worry, since her picture had been on the front page of the *Arizona Republic* just this morning. More confident now, Kari meandered along the winding walkways, past the waterfall, down toward the water.

She paused at the lagoon and watched the gondolier help an older couple out and a young couple in. Kari saw

the woman dreamily study the ring on her left hand and
decided they were honeymooners. The gondolier asked if
they had a favorite song and used his large oar to shove
off and away from the pier before he began to sing it.
She was so engrossed in watching the romantic little
scene that she wasn't aware the ticket seller had come
up alongside her.

"Would you like a ride, miss?" he asked.

Startled, Kari looked at the tall, mustached man wearing a white shirt with full billowy sleeves and a red head-
band that held back his dark, curly hair. He was smiling
at her politely, almost flirtatiously, but with no recogni-
tion in his laughing eyes.

"No, thank you," she told him.

"Where is your young man? A lovely woman should
not be alone on a night such as this." His accent was
thick, and his smile widened as he stepped closer.

"I'm meeting him inside," Kari improvised, thinking
it unwise to let anyone know she was wandering about
alone. "Good night." She turned and felt his eyes follow
her as she strolled through the crowd, pleased to be anon-
ymous.

Kari had always loved to walk, and yet for some time
now, it had been impossible to just go for a stroll without
her entourage along. Somehow their presence took the
fun out of it. The Secret Service ruined spontaneity, for
they always wanted to know where she wanted to go,
how long she planned on being gone. Annoying.

At the big front doors she watched the bellman gathering luggage from a cab as two business types stepped
out and headed for the registration desk. Off to the right,
two athletic young men at valet parking retrieved cars for
guests who were leaving. Just a normal evening at a busy

hotel, yet Kari looked at the scene with a different slant, since she was alone.

On her travels she was constantly being hustled in and out of limos, into planes, out of hotels. She rarely had time to really look at people. She did that now, gazing her fill as, with hands in the pockets of the raincoat, she strolled down the three wide steps and along the bricked circular drive.

The brightly lit street beckoned to her with its assortment of shops open evenings for the tourist trade. Kari sauntered past a boutique where mannequins in the window wore the latest spring fashion. Apple green, apparently, was the newest color rage.

Next she came to a fragrant shop specializing in cigars, then a store selling only cheeses and wines, and a travel agency with colorful posters decorating its windows. Paris was the springtime bargain destination. Kari wished she could go in and book a flight for tonight.

The air was cooler now as she strolled unafraid, for there were people on the sidewalks and in the shops. The sky had cleared after the rain, revealing a myriad of stars. She hadn't thought to wear her watch, but she knew it couldn't be too late if all these stores were still open. She walked for block after block, feeling wonderfully free—feeling normal for the first time in months, maybe years.

To think that others were able to do a simple thing such as go for a walk without dragging along two or three people boggled her mind. One day she'd break from the life her family had thrust her into, Kari decided. One day she'd live as a private citizen. She just had to be patient awhile longer.

Swallowing one yawn, then another, she slowed her steps. The excitement of defying her keepers, along with the medication she'd taken, were catching up with her.

She must have walked half a mile or more. Another block and she would turn around, she decided.

The shops on this block were mostly closed, their interiors lit by only one small lamp. Perhaps she'd wandered too far, Kari thought somewhat hazily as she yawned expansively again. Up ahead was a store with lights ablaze, indicating it was probably open. Maybe she should go in there and call a cab. She fingered the change in her pocket, found a quarter. Yes, she mustn't overdo, for she had a very busy schedule the next day.

Walking unsteadily as she reached the shop, Kari narrowed her eyes. The sign read "Wilson's Feed & Grain." Odd, having a store like that not far from a hotel such as the Bonaventure. There was a big red pickup truck, with a horse trailer attached, parked on the driveway right by the entrance. What fool had left that there, making it difficult for customers to go inside? she wondered foggily.

Stepping carefully, she circumvented the truck and stood glaring at it. Rude, Kari decided. Someone was quite rude to inconvenience others like that. Weaving a bit, her thinking process growing hazier, she heard the truck door on the driver's side bang shut. The sudden noise had her flinching, then shivering as she became aware that the night air had turned quite chilly. At the sound of footsteps approaching, she turned.

A man circled the front of the truck, then walked toward her. Even in her lethargic state, she thought he looked like every idea she'd ever had of the working Westerner. She'd seen plenty of them during her travels through Arizona. No frills for this guy. He was wearing scuffy serviceable boots, faded worn jeans, a plaid shirt and a leather belt sporting a silver buckle. Buckles that big were usually handed out as rodeo prizes, weren't they?

As he came closer, she saw that his eyes were a piercing blue and not particularly friendly. His hair was black, just brushing his collar, and his square chin was unshaven. He wore black leather gloves on his big hands. Not a man one would choose to meet in a dark alley, Kari decided, then giggled inexplicably. The man's hard face moved into a frown.

"A cab," Kari managed to say, wondering why her tongue was so thick. "I need to get a cab." Slowly, her movements jerky, she withdrew her hand from her pocket and held out some change. "Gotta call." Shivering now, she wondered if she was getting through to this guy who stood silently studying her.

Dillon Tracy had seen his share of drunks and they disgusted him, especially women. This one was young and slender with nice features. What a waste. She had a grand total of fifty-nine cents in her hand. Just how far did she think a cab would take her for that? Suddenly he saw her sway, her eyes turning glassy.

Quickly he grabbed her shoulders and backed her up to the bench alongside the door. "You better sit down, lady."

Teetering on the bench, she gazed at the truck again. "That yours?" she asked, her words slurring.

"Yeah," he answered, wondering why he was bothering to have a discussion with a drunk.

"Rude. Downright rude, parking it there." She waved an unsteady hand. "Blocks the entrance."

"That's me, rude as the day is long." Maybe someone inside would know her. He'd tell Jack and have him call someone to come get her. Leaving the wobbly woman on the bench, he walked in, spotting the owner toward the back. "Hey, Jack, is my order ready?"

Dillon usually bought his supplies much closer to his Northern Arizona ranch, but he'd been in town arranging to purchase a prize stallion from a Scottsdale rancher and had decided to call Jack with his list, since they'd known each other for years. Jack Wilson's family hailed from Prescott where Dillon's father still ran a grocery store known for miles around for its quality goods and fair prices. Dan Tracy was second-generation Irish and proud, a hard worker who'd raised Dillon and his brother Terry alone after his wife died.

"Sure is," Jack answered, walking forward and drying his hands on his apron. "Did you get what you came for?"

Dillon's craggy face, suntanned from years of working outdoors, broke into a smile. "Sure did. Domino's a prize stud. My ladies back home are all excited about him."

Jack grinned. "I just bet they are. How many horses you got now?"

"A gelding, an Appaloosa, five broodmares, two colts and now the stallion. Those stud fees were killing me. Domino cost a bundle, but I think he'll earn his keep in no time."

Jack clapped his friend on the shoulder. "I believe you're right." He pointed to several large sacks and a big box. "Your order's there. Check it out and I'll help you load."

"Nah, I trust you." Dillon glanced at his watch and saw it was past nine. "I heard on the way over that a storm's brewing up north, and I've got a three-hour drive ahead. The paperwork on Domino took longer than I'd planned." Reaching in his shirt pocket, Dillon pulled out a check and handed it to Jack. "This should cover everything."

"Thanks." Jack bent to hoist the first twenty-five pound sack of feed.

"By the way," Dillon said, picking up another sack, "there's a drunk woman out on your bench."

"The hell you say! Where'd she come from?"

"I don't know, but maybe you'll recognize her. She needs someone to drive her home. She mumbled something about a cab, but she's only got small change."

"Just my luck," Jack said, shoving his door open with a shoulder. Standing outside, he looked toward the bench, then further up the walk. "Where'd you say she was?"

Joining him, Dillon frowned as he gazed around. "Well, she was here, but she's gone now."

"Good riddance, I say." Jack hefted the sack of feed into the pickup and went back for more.

When they were finished loading, Dillon settled the big tarp over all his supplies, grabbed the tie lines and fastened it down. He made a quick check of Domino, then stepped up into the cab. "I'll see you next time," he told Jack as he started the engine.

"Drive safe." Jack waved, then went inside to close up shop.

Dillon merged with the light traffic on the road, heading for I-17 north. For several blocks his eyes scanned the sidewalk, looking for the slight figure in the yellow scarf and raincoat. But after seeing no one resembling the woman, he picked up his speed.

"None of my business," he said to no one in particular.

Chapter Two

Dillon drove well below the speed limit, not wanting to jar Domino. Some horses traveled well, but he didn't know this stallion yet. Traffic wasn't heavy, maybe because word of the pending storm would have most people postponing trips north. Probably only those who lived in that direction were out tonight.

He'd planned on stopping in Prescott to visit his father, but the late hour and the weather had changed his mind. Too bad, because he knew how much Dan Tracy looked forward to his youngest son's visits. For years his father had worked long, hard hours to educate his boys, wanting both of them to have a solid career. Terry had chosen medicine and Dillon the law, perhaps more to please their father than because of any real calling. Terry seemed happy enough practicing medicine in Prescott. Dillon was another story.

Putting the truck on cruise control, he let his mind

wander, remembering what a difficult time he'd had ful-
filling his father's dream. But he'd stuck it out—four
years of college, then four more in law school. Shortly
after passing the bar exam and just before he was to set
himself up in practice, something had happened that had
changed Dillon's life.

Quinn Tracy, his widowed uncle, had died childless
and left him his small ranch in DeWitt, twenty miles
northwest of Flagstaff on the Hennessy River. Dillon had
always been Quinn's favorite, and Quinn had let him
spend his teenage summers helping out with the horses.
He'd lived for those summers, loving ranch life, absorb-
ing everything his uncle could teach him. Yet he'd du-
tifully gone back to school each fall, unwilling to disappoint his father.

But when the ranch became his, Dillon had asked his
father for a three-year grace period to prove he could turn
the ranch back into a moneymaker, which it hadn't been
for some time during Quinn's illness. If Dillon failed,
he'd go back to the law—he'd promised his father. And
Dan had reluctantly agreed.

That had been two and a half years ago and Dillon
knew his time was running out. Quinn hadn't been able
to do much for over two years before he died, and the
place Dillon inherited had been rundown—house, stables
and outbuildings all needing work. The once-proud herd
of thoroughbreds had been reduced to two, an older
chestnut gelding and a gentle Appaloosa mare.

The first year had been the roughest, with Dillon working night and day to fix up the house and almost completely rebuild the stables. He'd survived a drought and
a fierce winter the following year. He'd also gone into
debt increasing his herd, but he'd never lost heart, never
given up. Early on, he'd hired Mac Potts, a crusty old

ranch hand who lived in a trailer on the back of the property. And more recently, he'd taken on Rich Morley, an experienced hand in his mid-thirties who used to work with cattle on a Wilcox spread in Southern Arizona. Rich lived with his sister in town and worked only when Dillon needed him, but Mac was always around, looking after the place and taking care of the horses alone when Dillon was away on a buying or delivery trip.

Things were shaping up. His two yearling colts were training well, and one mare was pregnant, due to foal any day now. Hopefully the others would be pregnant soon, too, thanks to Domino. Dillon was slowly building his reputation for good quality horseflesh, getting to be known for miles around. The hard work was paying off.

Dillon found himself smiling as he thought about his home. He had a love for the place that he'd never been able to muster for the law. The open spaces, the stable smells of leather and hay and horse flesh, the plentiful garden in summer, the nearby Hennessy River, the freedom of being on his own—he loved all of it.

When the day came that his three years were up, he wanted to go to his father and be able to say he was a success in the field he'd chosen, not one someone had picked for him. A man had to be true to himself or he'd never be happy. Dillon knew his father loved him and would come around when he saw the effort he'd made.

The wind had picked up and the temperature was steadily dropping as the red truck climbed to higher elevations. There were clouds in the sky, but they didn't appear to be snow clouds. Maybe he'd get lucky and the storm would hold off, Dillon thought. His eyes on the road, he turned on the radio to try to catch a weather bulletin. Instead, Garth Brooks sang out. A bit off-key, Dillon joined in.

* * *

Kari Sinclair was dreaming. She was on a fast-moving train, in a boxcar, thumping around, her backside landing repeatedly on the hard floor. It was cold and she didn't have warm clothes. The wind was whistling eerily outside, the rumble and rattle causing her to sway. But each time she did, her shoulder bumped into something hard and immovable. Somewhere in the distance she heard music.

A sudden lurching finally awakened her. Feeling disoriented, she opened her eyes but saw only darkness. Tiny patches of dim light raced along both sides of where she lay, but she couldn't determine where they were coming from. A thin covering over a hard metal floor was beneath her, and behind her were high cardboard boxes of some sort. In front of her, rough material covered something, and though it was softer than the boxes, it still wouldn't budge when she pushed against the barrier.

She tried to sit up, but there simply wasn't enough room. She shook her head hard, trying to clear the cobwebs of her memory. It came back slowly as she remembered sneaking out of the hotel in Phoenix, walking past all those shops, then getting drowsy. Of course—the pills. It had to be the allergy medication. She never should have taken that second tablet, especially after not eating much dinner.

There'd been a truck alongside a store and a man who'd looked very forbidding. She hadn't been able to make him understand she needed him to call her a cab. He'd walked inside and left her there shivering on that cold bench. Then suddenly a big dog had appeared out of nowhere, some mixed breed she couldn't identify. He hadn't barked, just moved close to her, his stance threatening.

Kari loved dogs and couldn't imagine why this one

had frightened her. To get away from him, she recalled climbing up into the bed of the red truck and scooting back out of his reach. He'd put his big paws up on the tailgate, but seconds later, he'd lost interest in her and moved on. She'd found a blanket on the floor and a big tarp kept the wind out. She'd thought to lie down just long enough to warm up and clear her head. She must have fallen asleep.

Wiggling and squirming now, she tried to pull herself upright, but the hard edge of a box scraped along her arm and shoulder. Someone had piled more stuff in, blocking her exit. Giving that up, she lay back down, trying to think. If she knew how long ago she'd crawled into the truck, that would be a start. Had the man she'd talked with been the owner of the truck? Yes, she thought so, because she'd scolded him for parking so close to the entrance, and he hadn't taken that well. Since they were moving, it had to be that he hadn't noticed her when he'd loaded more bundles into the truck before fastening the tarp and setting out.

But where was he going?

Maybe if she got his attention, he'd stop and let her off. He'd likely be angry, but surely he wouldn't insist on her remaining. "Hey!" Kari yelled out. "Hey, stop this truck! I want out!" Holding perfectly still, she waited for some response, some sign he'd heard her. Nothing.

Cocking her head, she made out the twang of guitars and a country tune. If she could hear the radio back here, imagine how loud it must be in the cab. And wasn't that a male voice singing along? Well, at least he probably wasn't an ax murderer. Killers rarely sang as they drove off with their victims, did they?

She would force herself to think positively, Kari decided. He was a nicer man than he looked, she assured herself. While he might be a bit annoyed when he discovered her, he would listen to her story and understand.

The day that pigs fly, a small voice inside her said.

All right, so he'd be more than a little angry. It had been a stupid thing to do, to crawl into a stranger's truck. But she'd been woozy from the medication and very cold and so sleepy. Would he believe her story? Would anyone?

Kari tried tugging on the edge of the tarp, but it wouldn't budge. She tried yelling again, but it was like whistling into the wind. And speaking of the wind, it was whipping in and around each small opening, sending shivers throughout her whole body. She'd been dressed just fine for a March evening in Phoenix in the low seventies, but as a native of Arizona, she knew only too well that nights in the desert got progressively colder. Also, if they were traveling north, the temperatures could easily drop to freezing.

The very thought brought about a bone-shattering sneeze, leaving her feeling weak, her throat scratchy. This was all she needed, to get sick on top of being kidnapped by someone who very likely didn't even know he was kidnapping her. Her father, never known for giving his daughters the benefit of the doubt, would certainly hit the roof when he learned what she'd done. She could hear him now, that famous, booming James Sinclair voice that could reverberate throughout the Senate chambers without a microphone. "You did what?" he'd bellow. "You crawled into a stranger's truck and calmly went to sleep?" Ah yes, he, too, would be understanding, the day that pigs danced on the White House lawn.

Funny thing was, Kari rarely did anything resembling adventurous. Dana, especially in her teens, had given their parents more than a few gray hairs with some of her escapades, though fortunately they'd all turned out to be fairly harmless. Harmless was what she'd thought a short walk around the hotel neighborhood would be, just a little stroll, then safely back in bed by ten and no one the wiser. Why was it that the first time she tried something just a bit out of character, nothing went as planned? Kari wondered.

What was that sound? She could have sworn she heard a horse whinny and…of course. She remembered that the truck had been hauling a horse trailer. Too bad she wasn't in there with the horse. Might be warmer. Of course, she'd never been close enough to a horse to even touch one, so that might present a problem.

Enough of this worrying. There was nothing she could do now except wait until the driver stopped and pray he was a decent fellow. Swallowing down a rush of fear and panic, Kari closed her eyes and tried not to think what would happen to her if he wasn't.

Dillon peered out at the murky sky as the first snowflakes fell on the windshield. Slowing down, knowing he couldn't afford to go into a skid on wet pavement with the load he was hauling, he hoped it would stay just flurries. But within ten miles, he saw that the snow was coming down thicker, faster. Setting his teeth, he was glad he had a four-wheel drive and snow tires. Even so, at this slower pace, it would likely be well past midnight when he pulled in to his own driveway.

Actually, it was closer to two as he stopped near the stable door. There was a good four inches of snow already on the ground with no signs of it letting up. Zeus, his German shepherd, hadn't come to greet him as usual, probably because he was in Mac's trailer where it was warm or Mac had left him in the stables, kept heated by the generator. Dillon squirmed into his sheepskin jacket and put his black Stetson firmly on his head, relieved that Mac had remembered to leave the outside lights on for him.

Adjusting his gloves, he was glad he'd prepared for the possibility of bad weather when he'd left home two days ago. Rich had said he thought they wouldn't get any more heavy snow this winter, but Mac had just shaken his head. "Always remember Mother Nature is fickle as a female," the old horse trainer had said, "and she'll turn on you without a moment's notice." Mac had been right.

Dillon needed to get Domino settled in the stall he'd prepared for him on the opposite side of the stables from the mares. And he'd better unload his supplies right after because if this kept up, he might have a worse day of it tomorrow. Zipping up his jacket, he stepped down into ankle-deep snow and slammed the truck door.

Walking back to the horse trailer, he stopped suddenly, thinking he'd heard a muffled sound apart from the wind. Cocking his head, he listened. Yes, there it was again, coming from the direction of the truck bed. Had a cat crawled in while he'd been getting his supplies?

Quickly he untied one end of the tarp and pulled it back, listening harder.

"Help," came a faint voice.

Stunned, Dillon almost jumped back. What the hell! Working fast, he untied the other end and drew back the tarp. Despite the outdoor lights, with the snow cutting down on visibility, all he could see was fair hair and eyes shining. "Is someone in there?"

"Yes," the voice answered, stronger now. "Help me out, please."

Jumping up, Dillon shifted two feed stacks and a box, trying to make an aisle. He reached out a gloved hand

and felt someone grab it. Pulling gently, he eased the
person through the small opening. As she came up
against him hard, he recognized the drunken woman from
Jack's store. Damn! Just what he needed.

"What in hell are you doing in my truck?" he asked,
jumping back down and holding his arms up to assist
her. Funny, close as he was to her, he couldn't smell
liquor.

Her feet in thin leather shoes landed in wet snow, but
she didn't flinch. Yet when she spoke, her teeth were
chattering. "I'm sorry."

He saw that her yellow scarf had slipped down around
her neck and that the thin raincoat she wore was no protection against the cold wind. Snow was dampening her
blond hair already. Out in the light, he saw she was very
pale, her brown eyes wary. He had a lot of questions, but
they'd have to wait until they were in out of the snow.
"Come with me," he said, his temper making it seem
more an order than a request.

Looking this way and that, Kari saw a big horse barn,
a large garage and trees shrouded in snow everywhere
save the small path they'd driven in on. There was a large
fenced area, probably for the horse in the trailer. They
seemed to be in the middle of nowhere in the middle of
a winter storm. Her stomach lurched as she followed the
stranger to the lone house, realizing that she was totally
at his mercy.

Stomping his boots on the covered wooden porch, Dillon found his key and opened the door, then stepped in
and turned on a table lamp. Turning, he saw that she was
just standing on the porch, visibly shaking and looking
lost. No, he sure as hell didn't need this, but it seemed
he was stuck with her, at least for tonight. "Come on in
out of the cold," he invited, softening his tone a bit.

Kari walked in slowly, her feet almost numb with cold, her thin pant legs damp around her ankles. Frightened and worried, she stood there as if rooted to the floor. She watched him cross the big central room and turn up the thermostat. The furnace rattled once, then the blower hissed on.

The man bent to the large stone fireplace, opened the flue, then touched a match to the stacked wood and kindling already in the grate. In moments the flames were shooting up, drawing Kari closer to the heat, her hands outstretched.

While he fussed with the fire, she huddled there, wondering what to say and do. She wasn't anxious to reveal her true identity to this stranger. Once he found out who she was, what if he'd keep her here and try to collect ransom from her father? Kari wasn't paranoid, but she'd been warned since her early teens that kidnapping was a very real threat for the family of prominent political figures. Besides, the last thing she wanted was for her father to find out that she'd snuck away from the Secret Service, gone walking alone at night, then crawled into a stranger's truck and gone to sleep. She'd have to think up a believable story—and fast!

Dusting off his hands, Dillon turned to look at her. She was damn near frozen after hours in the back of his truck. The boxes and feed sacks along with the tarp had cut down on the wind, but it was barely thirty out there and dropping. He'd have to get her something dry to change into. But first, a little information would be nice.

"You didn't answer my question. What were you doing in my truck?"

Nervously, Kari swallowed before answering. "There was this dog, a really *big* dog. He frightened me, so I got up and tried to get away from him, but I wasn't very steady so I fell down and hit my head. I kind of passed out for a minute and when I woke up, he was standing over me, drooling. I scrambled up and crawled into your truck.'' All right, so that was embellishing the truth a little. But she'd had to make her tale convincing enough so he'd believe her without revealing her name.

''Uh-huh. I don't suppose it occurred to you to step inside Jack's store to get away from the dog?''

Kari frowned, wondering why she hadn't done that. ''No, it didn't.''

''I see.'' He took a step closer, trying to catch the lingering smell of alcohol. The scent he inhaled was something lightly floral and very feminine, like bath powder, maybe. Still, how could he be sure she hadn't merely slept it off? ''Had you been drinking?''

''No. I'd taken two allergy pills. The flowers play havoc with my allergies. My nose runs, my eyes water. Just awful. The pills made me groggy, so I went for a walk to…to get some fresh air, to clear my head. I felt fine when I set out. I didn't get woozy until I got to that feed store. I don't know if you've ever taken antihistamines, but they make me groggy.'' Why did he have his big fists clamped on his hips like some sort of challenge? She was mostly telling the truth.

''So you took two allergy pills, then decided to go for a walk outside among the growing things that you're allergic to. Is that about it?''

Put like that, her actions sounded worse than ever. ''The pills got rid of my allergy symptoms. I admit it wasn't the brightest thing I've ever done, but you needn't make it sound like a criminal act. I asked you to call me a cab, but you just left me there.''

''You were slurring your words. I couldn't make out

what you were saying. I thought...well, that you were—''

"That I was drunk. I see. So since you thought I was drunk, it was all right in your mind to just leave me there? Not very compassionate, are you?'' Pulling the scarf from around her throat where it had slipped, she shook out her hair as she watched his already moody blue eyes darken and turn hard.

"Not when it comes to drunken women, no.''

Whoa! Apparently she'd touched a nerve there. "Well, I hadn't had anything but tea. I was drowsy and cold and disoriented. I'm sorry if I...inconvenienced you.''

Dillon watched her thick cloud of blond hair settle around her shoulders. Great hair, he thought, then frowned, thinking he'd better concentrate on trying to piece things together, rather than on the woman's looks. "Do you live around the feed store?''

She switched her gaze to the fire, finding it easier to lie when she wasn't looking into those piercing eyes. "I don't think so.''

Dillon found it difficult to keep his irritation from showing. It was the middle of the night, and he was in no mood for games. He still had to settle his stallion and unload his supplies. And he was wasting time with this woman with the frightened doe eyes. "What do you mean, you don't *think* so? Don't you know where you live?''

"I can't remember.'' Kari rubbed her head, hoping she wasn't overdoing it. "I told you I hit my head.'' Amnesia. If she faked amnesia until morning when she could call Norma, he'd never know who she was until the car arrived for her.

"What's your name, then?'' When she just looked blank, Dillon clenched one fist in frustration and took a step closer. She appeared clear-eyed and sober as a judge, and suddenly anxious. Was the medication still confusing her or was she trying to snow him? "Are you telling me you can't remember your name and address? You remembered the dog and me in front of Jack's and crawling in my truck."

"Yes, but nothing much before I took the pills. It's sort of a blank up to then." Kari dared a glance at his face, wondering if she was overplaying her hand.

Exasperated, Dillon ran a hand through his thick black hair. He didn't for a minute think this woman was an empty-headed blonde. There was intelligence in her eyes and shrewd speculation. She wasn't telling him the truth, for whatever reason, at least not all of it. But why was she lying? Had she deliberately chosen his truck to hide in? For what purpose? Was she on the run? He'd caught a hint of fear in her expression when she'd first come in. Was there someone after her and, if so, why?

Kari noticed that he'd left his boots by the door and that there was a hole in one of his gray socks. Somehow that small flaw made him seem less scary, more human. "Where are we, anyhow?" she asked into the lengthy silence.

"DeWitt."

She'd traveled Arizona from one end to the other and never heard of DeWitt. Had they crossed the state line? "Where, exactly, is DeWitt?"

"About twenty miles northwest of Flagstaff. Farming, horse ranches, some cattle. Population about three thousand." Why was he telling her everything and she was telling him nothing? No matter. He'd turn her over to the sheriff and be done with it.

Dillon walked over to the phone and lifted the receiver. No dial tone. He should have guessed. Whenever there was a storm up this way, even a minor one, it seemed the phone lines went out before the first flake hit the ground. Often they'd lose power, too, which was why Dillon had invested in his own generator plus several kerosene lamps. So far the electricity was holding.

Swearing under his breath, he hung up the phone and stared at her. "Phone's out, but that doesn't mean much to you, does it? Since you can't remember your name, I don't suppose you could tell me who to call to come get you."

"I guess not." His tone was making her uncomfortable. She wouldn't be surprised if he unhitched his horse trailer, shoved her back in the truck and drove her to the nearest hotel, motel or whatever, regardless of the weather.

Still, he didn't look like an unreasonable man, despite his impatient manner and irritated expression. He had a raw-boned face, his cheeks almost gaunt, as if he'd missed a few good meals lately. Yet he looked strong, with wide shoulders on a tall, lean frame. He had at least two days' growth of dark beard, but instead of looking unkempt, he appeared mysterious. Especially his eyes— deep blue and assessing. Under the circumstances she couldn't blame him for being annoyed with her. "What's your name?"

"Dillon Tracy."

"Do you have a wife?" she asked hopefully. Another woman around would ease her mind considerably.

"No wife, no children, no one but me and two ranch hands." He wanted her to get the picture, to get worried enough to tell him the truth. Amnesia, my aunt Sadie, Dillon thought.

Rubbing his gloved hands together, he struggled for control. "I don't suppose you're aware that up this way, when a storm hits, it could keep coming down for three or four days. Drifts pile the snow higher than the tops of the windows. The roads become impassable, and we often become marooned. Now, do you remember your name?''

Kari thought a moment, then decided she was stuck with her story unless she wanted to look like a complete fool, which she did not. She was getting in deeper and deeper. She didn't have to fake the unease she felt when she answered him. "No. Look, I don't like this any more than you do. I'm stranded in this place miles from anything familiar, wet and cold after hours rattling around in your freezing truck. And you look at me like I've set out to deliberately mess up your life. I'm sorry. What more do you want me to say, other than I'll try not to be a bother?''

Right. No bother, trapped on a ranch with him and two other weathered ranch hands. Even his dog was male. What in hell would they do with her, even for twenty-four hours? Well, as soon as the phone service came back, he'd call the sheriff's office and let them worry about her.

"I've got to see to my stock and unload the truck. I'll be back when I'm finished. There's a blanket on the back of the couch and the bathroom's the second door." Afterward he'd see if he could find her some dry clothes. The longer he stood there, looking into her big brown eyes, the worse he felt. Securing his hat, Dillon left the cabin.

As soon as the door shut behind him, Kari let out a sigh of relief. Stepping out of her wet shoes, she set them on the hearth to dry. She scooted the padded, maple rocking chair close to the fire, wrapped herself in the big blanket and sat down, pulling her feet up under her and looked around.

The room she was in was large with paneled walls and hardwood floors covered with several colorful area rugs. A big comfortable corduroy couch, which looked as if her reluctant host had spent many an hour stretched out on it, faced the fireplace. A small kitchen to the right held a maple table and two chairs, and there seemed to be a laundry room off that. Three doors on the far wall led, she assumed, to the bath and two bedrooms.

Two bookcases filled to overflowing, flanked the stone walls of the fireplace. There likely wasn't much else to do up here on long winter nights except read, she supposed. A leather easy chair and ottoman alongside a reading lamp was nestled cozily into a small nook by the front window. And there was a large-screen television with VCR tucked into a space on the maple stand. Next to it were two teetering stacks of tapes. It would appear that Dillon Tracy liked to read and watch movies.

Rubbing her chilled feet beneath the blanket, she studied the wooden slanted blinds at the windows, the no-nonsense utilitarian furniture, the lack of pillows or pictures or paintings. Definitely the house of a man, one that hadn't seen a woman's touch in years, if ever. No matter. She'd only be here a short time.

Leaning her head back, Kari sighed. What on earth had she gotten herself into?

Dozing lightly, Kari heard the door open and a gust of cold wind and snow whoosh in, followed by a big brown dog with black ears that pointed straight up. He barked low in his throat and headed straight for her rocking chair at a near gallop.

"Oh!" she yelped, and nearly slipped off the chair in her haste to back away.

"Zeus, sit!" The commanding voice of the dog's master from the doorway stopped him mere inches from Kari. Obediently, he sat down, but his brown eyes watched her carefully, his big tongue hanging out as he breathed.

A magnificent German shepherd, Kari thought, wondering if all strong men were attracted to this breed. Her father had two.

Dillon walked over to stand alongside his dog, but he spoke to her. "He needs to get to know you. Reach out your hand and let him smell you. He won't hurt you with me here."

Hesitantly she did as he asked, noticing that her hand trembled only slightly.

"Okay, Zeus." He watched the big dog move closer, sniffing her hand, her sleeve, the blanket covering her. Apparently satisfied, he strolled over to a large overstuffed pillow near the hearth, climbed on and lay down.

"He's beautiful," Kari said honestly.

"Don't let him hear you say that," Dillon told her, shoving his gloves in the pockets of his jacket, then hanging the jacket on a hook by the door. "He prefers handsome."

Was that a sense of humor sneaking out of that stern mouth? she wondered.

He watched her uncurl her legs, noticing her feet were still red and probably chilled. "Come with me," he said again.

Was that the only way he knew how to ask someone to do something, ordering them about? Kari found herself wondering as she hesitantly followed him. He opened the door to the third room on the right, switching on the bedside lamp. The sight of a big four-poster bed made of rough pine and piled high with what looked like a feather bed and several huge pillows almost had her drooling.

Then a fearsome thought hit her, and her eyes flew to his face. But he was busy opening a large cedar chest at the foot of the bed.

"My aunt Edith was only fifty when she died a while back," Dillon said. "She was about your size, only a little taller. Some of her clothes are stacked in there. They're probably outdated, but they're clean, if you want to change." He nodded toward the door opposite a small closet. "That connects to the bath. Maybe you should get out of those wet things. I'll put on some coffee to warm us up." Rubbing together his chilled hands, he left the room.

Forcing herself to relax, Kari took off the raincoat and hung it on a hook on the back of the bathroom door along with the damp scarf. She noticed beige tile and navy towels, shaving cream, one toothbrush, toothpaste and a bottle of aspirin.

Her reflection in the mirror was pale and tired and slightly bedraggled. Who wouldn't be? Looking like this, her own mother might walk past her. Living in this remote farm country, surely this rancher wouldn't recognize her.

She rinsed her face, then found a comb in the medicine chest and ran it through her hair. That was when she noticed another bathroom door opposite hers. So if this was to be her room, that meant they'd share a bath. Terrific.

In the bedroom she checked out his aunt's clothes, finally choosing a pair of well-worn jeans to change into, then hanging her linen slacks on the shower rod to dry.

The fit wasn't bad if she used the belt she'd found and rolled up the pant legs.

There were no slippers or shoes in the chest or closet, so she settled for a pair of thick white socks. Slipping a gray-and-blue plaid, long-sleeved shirt over her own black top, she was pleased at the warm feel of the well-washed flannel. Taking a deep breath, she went back into the main room, drawn by the tantalizing scent of fresh coffee.

Dillon got up from the table and poured her a hot, steaming mugful, then sat down opposite his uninvited guest and studied her over the rim of his own cup. She was quite attractive, if a little too pale. Funny how a woman wearing too-large clothes somehow managed to look small and vulnerable, even if she wasn't.

Her hair was thick and blond, falling past her shoulders, shiny even after her ordeal. Her eyes were huge, watchful, hesitant, the color of good brandy. She obviously had led a somewhat pampered life, her nails manicured and painted a light pink, her skin like satin. She wore no makeup, didn't need it.

He might be a small-town rancher, but Dillon knew quality goods. Those soaking-wet shoes she'd left on the hearth were Italian leather and likely cost a hundred and a half. She wore a good-size amethyst in a gold setting on her right hand and a gold heart on a delicate chain around her neck. In her ears were diamond stud earrings. Real diamonds, he'd wager. Not cheap items, any one.

She looked like money, like trouble.

When he found himself staring at her mouth, wondering what she'd taste like, he looked away. Perhaps he'd been alone too long. "Are you hungry? I could scramble some eggs." He might not be the world's greatest host, but he was not unkind.

"No, thanks. This coffee's heavenly." She sipped, enjoying the warmth sliding down her throat. Seated across from him at the small table up close, he loomed much larger than before, it seemed to Kari.

All right, she was dry, warm and having coffee, Dillon thought, scrubbing a weary hand over his stubbled face. Time for some answers. "Are you ready to tell me the real reason you got into my truck?" he began.

Squirming under the scrutiny of his fierce blue eyes, she tried to remember the cover story she'd thought up in the bathroom. "I think I'm a secretary to someone important. An executive of some sort." Which flirted with the truth. Her official title was personal assistant to Senator Sinclair. "My name, I believe, is Kari Smith." Smith was her mother's maiden name so this bit of information would explain the *K S* embroidered on the pocket of her black shirt. She reached into that pocket and held out the key to the Bonaventure Hotel. "I think I was staying at this hotel near the feed store, maybe to attend a convention."

To say that his face looked skeptical was to understate the matter greatly. Dillon saw that the key was the modern plastic type, coded with in-house digits, no room number discernible except to the folks at the Bonaventure.

"Smith, eh? Nice name. Has a ring to it." A false ring. When she didn't answer, he went on. "A secretary, you say. You must be well paid." His eyes lingered on her delicate gold chain. But besides the jewelry, there was a polished look about her that spoke of wealth and privilege.

Kari's hand flew to her necklace, her face heating. "I suppose I am." She took another long sip of coffee, knowing she had to end this midnight confession before she got into more hot water. Setting down her mug, she rubbed her head. "Listen, my head is beginning to ache again—from that fall, you know."

Rising quickly, Dillon went to stand behind her chair and look down at her scalp. "Where exactly did you bump it?"

Caught! Kari thought. Gingerly she shifted her fingers around a small area, then deliberately flinched. "There, I believe."

His big hands settled on her head, more gently than she'd have thought possible. Carefully, he parted her hair, looking for a bump or bruise. "Where does it hurt? I can't see a thing." But he could feel, and what he felt was strands of silk sliding through his fingers. The warm scent of her reached out and drew him to lean closer, to inhale that indescribable feminine fragrance.

Shivers raced down Kari's spine, fueled by his fingers moving through her hair, lightly massaging her scalp. Enough of this. With a small sound, she pulled away and stood. "Mostly just a dull headache by now. I think I need sleep more than anything."

"I've got aspirin," he offered, betting himself she'd turn him down. Because she didn't really have a headache. Aware his fingers were still tingling from touching her so personally, he shoved his hands in his jeans pockets.

"No, thanks. I'll be fine by morning." She indicated the room with the cedar chest. "Is that where I'm to sleep?"

"Yeah. I get up pretty early, five or six, depending on the season and weather, to take care of my stock." Which was only a few short hours away. "Just thought I'd let you know, in case the cabin's empty when you wake up."

"I'm a fairly early riser myself."

He cocked his head at her. "How would you know?"

Berating herself for the slip, she nonetheless met his steady gaze. "Some things you just know. Good night, Dillon Tracy."

"Good night, Kari *Smith*." He watched her walk to the spare room and close the door behind her.

Why was she deliberately lying? Was she afraid, even though she didn't really appear to be? Wouldn't a woman far from everything familiar, marooned with a stranger, be more fearful if she couldn't even remember her name?

Tomorrow, he reminded himself. She'll be out of here tomorrow and the mystery will be solved. Turning out the lights, he gave a short whistle, and Zeus followed him into the larger master bedroom. Though he was exhausted and knew he had to get up in a couple of hours, it was some time before Dillon could fall asleep.

Chapter Three

Norma Brice stood at the window of her room at the Bonaventure in Phoenix as she polished her granny glasses and decided that, although the sky was still dark, it was probably going to be another lovely day, warm and sunny. She felt sorry for her folks back in Montana slogging their way through another heavy winter snowfall. The weather had been one of the reasons she'd decided to work for Senator Sinclair since both Washington and Arizona were much warmer. That and because she'd hated living on a sheep ranch.

Putting on her glasses, she checked her watch. Precisely four-thirty. Norma prided herself on being prompt. She'd already ordered the limo for five, and Kari's juice and coffee—all she'd want at this hour—would be arriving from room service momentarily. She'd had to pull a few strings to get early service, but Norma knew just when and how to drop the senator's name here and there.

She would waken Kari, go over the morning schedule again with her while she dressed and have her downstairs on time.

She loved her job, Norma thought, smiling as she knocked once, then opened the connecting door to Kari's room. Flipping on the table lamp, she took a step toward the bed, then stopped. The bed hadn't been turned down or slept in. A glance at the windows told her the drapes hadn't been closed for the night, one window left slightly ajar.

Immediately Norma's mind went on red alert. It couldn't be, could it? Had someone scaled the hotel wall, climbed up to the sixth floor, somehow opened the window and gotten in, then kidnapped Kari Sinclair—all without making a sound? Fighting panic, she checked the bathroom and found it empty. Kari's suitcase was still on the stand, and a peek in the closet revealed the outfit she'd planned to wear today still on its hanger. Heart pounding, Norma went to the hall door.

Hilda and Tony weren't there yet. She went to Hilda's room on the other side of Kari's first and knocked vigorously, then moved to pound on Tony's. In moments both agents came out into the hall, a question in their eyes.

"I...ah...can't find Kari," Norma managed to say.

"What?" Tony abandoned the tie he'd been knotting and rushed into Kari's room.

"What do you mean, you can't find her?" Hilda wanted to know as she followed Tony.

All but wringing her hands, Norma trailed after them. "I mean she's not here."

Having checked the room and bath thoroughly, Tony frowningly zeroed in on Norma. "Tell me when you saw her last."

Shakily Norma went over her conversation with Kari after last evening's dinner, how she'd left her after going over today's schedule. "She was running a bath and talking on the phone to the senator."

"Did you hear any sounds from her room during the evening or later?" Hilda asked.

Struggling to hold back tears as she thought about how the senator would take this news, she shook her head. "No, nothing. I read for a while in bed and turned out the light about ten. I was sure Kari was asleep by then because she'd taken an allergy pill."

"But you didn't go check on her?" Tony's gruff voice carried just a hint of accusation.

Norma squared her thin shoulders. "No. I'm her assistant, not her keeper. I give her the courtesy of privacy when we're not working. Guarding her is *your* job."

Tony's full lips thinned at the reminder as he turned to his partner. "Let's split up and check around the hotel before we bring anyone else in on this."

Hilda looked uncertain. "I think the senator would want to know immediately."

Tony had a spotless record. He wasn't about to tarnish it by calling in the troops only to find Kari Sinclair sitting in the lobby, for whatever reason. "Not yet," he said firmly. "There could be any number of explanations. Maybe a couple of old college friends called and she went to meet them."

"Kari would have left a note," Norma interjected, then flinched as he sent her an icy glare.

"Hilda," Tony said in his best commanding voice since he was senior agent, "you start by checking out this floor and work your way down. I'm going to have a look around the lobby, speak with the people on duty, talk with the manager. Get your phone and contact me if you find out anything.'' He checked his watch. ''I'll meet you at the front desk at oh-five-thirty.'' He stepped to the doorway. ''Norma, you stay here in case Kari calls or returns. If you hear from her, I'll have my phone on channel three.'' He hurried out.

Hilda took a moment to pat Norma's shoulder. ''Try not to worry. We'll find her.''

Norma closed the door after them, every terrible thing she'd learned during half a dozen training sessions before she'd been hired coming back to haunt her. Abductions, kidnappings, ransom. Or someone obsessed with a public figure stalking them. Or some nutcase who disagreed with the senator's policies and who might decide to get his attention by harming his daughter.

''Oh, God!'' Norma whispered as she sank into a chair. Yes, the Secret Service would find Kari Sinclair. But would she be alive or dead?

A scraping sound from outside the window alongside her bed woke Kari. She blinked in the unfamiliar room, orienting herself as she looked around in the semidarkness. She hadn't bothered closing the drapes last night, thinking there'd be no one to invade her privacy in this remote area in the midst of a winter storm. She could see clumps of white snow clinging to the screen framing the window. A sliver of light was visible under her bedroom door, which meant her reluctant host was probably up.

Lazily she stretched and yawned expansively. She had no idea what time it was without her watch or a clock in the room. She squirmed cozily under the comforter, luxuriating in its warmth. Kari honestly couldn't remember when she'd slept so well before. Of course, she'd been tired and the hour had been late. But it was more than that.

There was a peacefulness here so far away from the
hustle and bustle of the city. And she had no schedule
this morning, no assistant prodding her to get going, practice her speech, rehearse the answers to probable questions she'd be asked. That alone was worth the cold,
bumpy ride she'd endured yesterday.

From a distance she heard a dog's deep-throated, sharp
bark. Zeus, undoubtedly outside with his master. And
who exactly was this man who chose to live in this isolated place with only horses and a dog for company,
along with two helpers? He gave the appearance of the
quintessential cowboy, a craggy-faced loner. In direct
contrast, he was well-spoken and appeared educated. Was
he perhaps self-taught, having read all the many books
on his shelves? Or had he walked away from another life
and chosen this solitary one for reasons of his own? If
that was so, they had more in common than she'd orig-
inally thought, except he'd acted on his heart's desire and
she had yet to do the same. Chances were he didn't have
a formidable father such as James Sinclair who he had
to convince that he needed to walk his own path.

Sighing, Kari slipped out from under the covers and
shivered immediately. The furnace was on, but it was still
much warmer in the feather bed. She debated about
crawling under again but knew she rarely fell back asleep
once she awakened.

Kneeling on the bed, she gazed out the window and
saw a far-reaching blanket of white covering everything
as far as she could see. Drifts piled high as Dillon had
predicted, the trees hung heavy with snow, and the wind
was still swirling and tossing. On the horizon she noticed
a faint lightening of the sky, indicating the sun was
slowly rising. There was a sense of isolation, of
cathedrallike quiet, of being marooned.

A huge sneeze shook her and she wondered again if she might be coming down with a cold. She felt chilled, but was it brought about by her situation more than anything? The thought of being marooned in a place where no one she cared about knew where she was should have frightened her. It did make her uneasy, but only in so far as she realized that for the first time in her life, she'd walked away from her obligations. Been driven away without her knowledge actually, but nevertheless, the results were the same.

The appointments she had scheduled for today, the ones Norma had gone over with her last night, would have to be rearranged. Poor Norma would be worried and her father would go ballistic when he found out. She had to call Norma, ask her to see if Dana was available to fill in some of the spots, then cancel the rest. Try as Kari would to consider returning right away, the very thought had her feeling truly ill.

Stretching, she decided that what she needed was some time to regroup, some R and R, a break in her routine. She'd only been campaigning three months so far this year, but ninety days doing something she dreaded was about eighty-nine too many.

A new thought struck her, and she wondered if she would dare follow through on it. What if she didn't go back right away, if she took several days off, maybe even a week? Surely her father wouldn't lose the election because one of his campaigners dropped out for a while. What if she *were* sick? He'd have to do without her then. And she *was* sick—of doing only what she was told to do, of following orders daily, of smiling and being charming and going from city to city until she scarcely knew where she woke up most mornings.

Her father wasn't cruel, wasn't a beast who'd make

her toe the mark if she went to him honestly and said she needed time off. It was just that at home, she'd feel guilty hanging around the house while every other member of her family was out doing their share. Her journey to this place had occurred through an unusual set of circumstances, ones she couldn't have imagined in her wildest dreams. But now that she was here, she could pretend, if only for a little while, that she lived a different life, a more normal life.

But would Dillon Tracy allow her to stay?

Arms propped on the chilly windowsill, Kari peered out. She saw that this bedroom was on the far side of the house, the one opposite the stables. That was probably where Dillon and Zeus were. Kari hadn't the foggiest notion what taking care of his stock meant. Surely with the snow at least two feet high out there and still coming down, he wouldn't take horses out in that to exercise, or whatever it was he did with them in that big fenced area. Did he just go to the barn to feed them, give them fresh water? How many horses did he have in that big stable, anyhow?

Drawing in a deep breath, Kari hoped Dillon would show her around, if he let her stay. But first things first, and she needed a shower. Rummaging through the chest, she found a pair of gray sweatpants with a drawstring waist that she thought might fit better than the jeans. And there was a white T-shirt and a black sweatshirt. They would do. Humming, she went into the bathroom.

Being with his horses always made Dillon feel good. There was something about being in the stables, the familiar smells and sounds, that never failed to cheer him. Maybe because he knew everything inside the building and surrounding acreage was his.

Watering and feeding as he walked the stalls with Zeus at his heels, he stopped first to check on Calypso, his pregnant chestnut. With experienced hands, he patted her down as she watched with her sad brown eyes. "Won't be long now, girl. You're doing fine." He slipped her a sugar cube and went on.

The gentle Appaloosa named Rainbow that he'd inherited from Uncle Quinn was five now, getting up there. She was perfect for a child to own, but he hadn't had the heart to sell her. Rainbow's lineage went back to the Indian ponies that had roamed the Arizona plains many years ago. She nudged him now, looking for her apple. He gave it to her and could have sworn she smiled at him.

The other two chestnut broodmares, Dixie and Holly, were doing well. "Soon, girls, it'll be breeding time and we'll see if you can handle Domino." He streaked a hand down one sleek flank and walked on.

Also on the other side were Henry, the older gelding that had been Quinn's favorite, and Dillon's two colts, Remus and Caesar. The colts weren't twins but looked a lot alike since they had the same sire. Dillon was training both of them for a buyer in California. He noticed that the horses on this side of the divider seemed none too pleased to have the largest stall suddenly occupied by a newcomer.

Finally, he checked on Domino and found him restless. Despite the solid wall dividing the stables down the center, Dillon knew the big stallion had picked up the scent of the mares nearby. "I know how you feel, buddy," he told his newest acquisition. "Having females around makes all of us jumpy."

Which brought Dillon back to thoughts of Kari Smith, who was sleeping in his guest room. Quinn had made the furniture in that room out of rough-hewn pine, and Edith had sewn the feather bed and pillows. All through his short, restless night, Dillon had found himself picturing Kari Smith, or whatever her real name was, lying in that warm, snug bed that had been in his family for years, all that silken hair spread out on Edith's embroidered pillow cases. No other woman had ever slept there, to his knowledge. Funny how that seemed to make her being there more personal.

He wondered if she'd found some of his aunt's night-clothes in the big chest. Probably a long-sleeved, high-necked, floor-length flannel gown in soft pink or yellow and...whoa! What the hell was he doing, daydreaming about a woman he scarcely knew, one he'd met a scant few hours ago? Maybe he needed a vacation. Or his head examined.

Carrying the nearly empty feed bucket back to his supply corner, Dillon frowned. He'd had the devil's own time making his way to the stables from the house. The snow drifts were four to five feet in some places. He'd had to shovel a path, but the wind kept rearranging his work. He didn't think he'd put his horses out today, even though they still had their thick winter coats. Most people didn't realize how easily horses could catch cold. The temperature in the barn was a comfortable fifty, compared to barely twenty-five outside. The colts loved to run in the snow, but tomorrow would be soon enough when the wind died down.

Dillon washed his hands in the corner sink, then grabbed the towel. Zeus was burrowing in the haystack in the last empty stall. He'd probably cornered a field mouse or two that had come in out of the cold.

Yet again his thoughts drifted back to his current problem, the approximately hundred-and-ten-pound blonde inside his home. What was her real name, and why wouldn't she tell him? With the weather as bad as it was, the phone might not be working yet. Even so, who would he call? The sheriff's crew likely wouldn't plow through three or four feet of drifted snow to pick up someone today, provided they could even get through. The storm also meant Dillon couldn't do much outdoor work today, so he'd be hanging around inside the house. There were just so many things he could keep himself busy with in the stables and barn.

He had some paperwork to do, of course. But first and foremost, he needed to get some information out of *Ms. Smith*. He hoped that after a good night's sleep, she'd tell him the real story. She couldn't know, of course, but Dillon hated liars more than anything on God's green earth. He'd been lied to by his mother when she'd been alive and by the woman he'd almost married. Lying, cheating, deception—all of it amounted to exactly the kind of person he wanted nothing to do with. Maybe if he made that perfectly clear to Kari, she'd stop insulting his intelligence with her cockamamy story about hitting her head and winding up with amnesia.

Hearing a sound, he turned to the big double doors and saw Mac Potts hobble in. About sixty, the crusty old ranch hand had spindly legs on a slightly stooped frame. But that didn't mean he wasn't strong. Mac could put in a ten-hour day without a complaint, something few men his age could match. And he was one of the few people Dillon trusted completely. Dillon also respected the fact that despite quite a few aches and pains, Mac wouldn't move in with his son and his family in town, but preferred living in his trailer. Independence was very important to him, as it was to Dillon. As long as he kept this ranch going, Mac would have a place here.

"G'mornin'," Mac said, stomping snow from his boots. "Told you we weren't finished with winter yet, didn't I?"

"You called it, all right." He wasn't sure what Mac's relationship with his wife had been, whether they'd been divorced or separated or if she was still alive, since he never spoke of her except to say he'd been married once. Dillon only knew that the old man wasn't very keen on the female of the species.

Adjusting his black hat, he decided he'd tell Mac about their unexpected guest before they ran into each another. "Listen, I—"

"Got yourself a woman, eh?" Mac said, rubbing his gloved hands together.

Dillon raised a brow. "How'd you know?"

"Saw her in the window just now. She smiled and waved at me. Friendly little thing. She staying on?" Mac reached into his pocket for his chewing tobacco.

"No." While Dillon pondered how to explain the events of last evening, Mac went right on.

"None of my business, you want to move in a woman." He stuck a chunk in his mouth, then wrapped up the rest.

"It's not like that. I—"

"Don't have to explain nothing to me. I was young once. A man has his needs."

"Mac, she's here by accident. She was woozy from allergy medication, climbed in my truck without me knowing it and fell asleep right before I started home. I was shocked to find her there when I drove in."

Closing one eye, Mac looked up at Dillon, squinting. "Good story, son. You stick to it." He walked over to Maisy, the big sorrel. "How you doing, lady?"

Annoyed, Dillon shook his head and adjusted his hat.

The more he tried to explain, the more convinced Mac would be that he'd moved in a playmate. Well, the old man would find out, just as Kari Smith would, when he sent her on her way real soon. The last thing he needed was a soft woman in his house muddling his mind.

Strolling down the cement walk, he went back to examine his pregnant mare.

Her hair still damp from her shower, Kari left the bedroom and gazed about the big room. Sure enough, she was alone. The sky was a pale gray now, with a weak sun trying to push through. The first order of business was to check the phone. It was nearly seven and she knew Norma would have her nails chewed down to the quick. Praying service had been restored, Kari picked up the receiver and nearly cheered out loud when she heard the dial tone. After a quick peek toward the stables to make sure Dillon wasn't on his way in, she dialed the Bonaventure Hotel in Phoenix and asked for her own room.

"Hello?" Norma's voice trembled with anxiety.

"Norma, it's me," Kari told her.

"Oh, God, Kari! Where are you? Have you been abducted?"

Kari was surprised that her normally unflappable assistant was considering the worst possibility first. In a way, she had been abducted, but she didn't think it wise to mention that. "No, of course not. I'm fine. I'm calling to tell you that I'm going to take a few days off." At least she hoped Dillon Tracy would allow her to stay a few days. "I'm really tired and I need some time away from campaigning. Would you please locate Dana and ask her to sub for me as much as her schedule allows? She adores making speeches. And just cancel the rest. I can't face returning just now."

"Are you ill?" Norma sounded genuinely concerned.

In a way she was, or would be if she were pushed into doing more campaigning just now. "Not ill, just not feeling well enough to make public appearances for a while. I need to get my head on straight. Can you understand that, Norma?"

"I suppose so. I know how you hate going on the road. But where are you, Kari? Hilda and Tony have been looking for you for nearly two hours. They're so worried, and so am I. Your father…"

"You haven't called Dad, have you?" James Sinclair was like a steamroller. He'd go charging after her for sure if he thought something had happened to her.

"Not yet, but I know Hilda's going to any minute now. Tony's talked with the senator's advisors already. They're downstairs with the hotel manager and…"

"I want you to listen carefully, Norma." Kari had to calm down the distraught woman and take control before it was too late. "I'm fine. I'm in a safe place with…with nice people. Please just tell everyone I'm not feeling well and have to cancel all appointments for a while. I don't mean to worry everyone, but I need to be away for now."

"But when are you coming back? Your schedule's already screwed up and…and—"

"I don't know exactly when I'm returning." Maybe sooner than she hoped, if Dillon chose to adopt a hard attitude. "I want you to call Dad yourself and give him this message—Pinnochio's just fine. Can you do that?"

"Yes, of course. But I don't know how he'll take this."

"He'll have to understand. I need this time." From the window she saw the stable door push slowly open against the blowing wind and snow. "I've got to go now. I'll call again later."

"But where do I tell the senator you are, Kari?" Norma whined on.

Kari hung up the phone and hurried into the kitchen. A pang of guilt swept over her as she thought about the uncomfortable position she'd put Norma in. But she knew that her father was a fair man and would ultimately put the blame where it belonged: on Kari's shoulders.

While she'd been showering, she'd gone over in her mind the argument she would present to Dillon when he returned. Maybe, if she worded her request just right, he'd let her stay on and help him around the ranch for one tiny week or so. Of course, she didn't know the first thing about horses or ranching, but she was a quick study. Or she could help out in the house.

Gazing about the small kitchen, she had to admit she wasn't exactly Julia Child, either. As far back as she could remember, her family had always had a cook—a wonderful, grandmotherly woman named Clara who'd ruled the Sinclair kitchen with an iron hand. Kari and Dana had been allowed to watch, but not touch, most of the time. Except for making Christmas cookies, where Mom took over.

Still, how complicated could cooking be? Kari asked herself. She spotted the coffeepot in the sink. It took her a few minutes to figure out the drip directions on the side of the free-standing machine and then to locate the coffee grounds, but she soon had a pot going and felt very accomplished. If you could read, you could cook, she told herself. Maybe she could surprise Dillon and make breakfast. Judging by her father, who was every bit as big as Dillon, men loved to eat and were usually in better moods after a meal. She'd scrounge around the refrigerator and cupboards and see what she could find.

She was taking down two mugs when Dillon stomped

inside, shaking snow from his jacket. "I'll bet you could use some fresh hot coffee," she said, trying to sound cheerful without being maddeningly so.

Hanging up his coat, Dillon eyed her. She looked freshly showered and very young, possibly even under twenty. Good Lord, she surely couldn't be underage, could she? That would just tear it, on top of everything else, that she'd be jailbait. Walking to the table, he scowled in her direction. "How old are you?"

"Twenty-six," Kari answered automatically. She set both mugs on the table. "Would you like me to fix some breakfast?"

"What I'd like are some straight answers." Despite his anxiety over her identity, he couldn't resist drinking some coffee first, since the walk in from the stables had been cold and windy. The coffee was hot and strong, just as he preferred it.

Taking her time, Kari sat down, studying him surreptitiously. He wore a black turtleneck sweater and black jeans, his unshaven face giving him a dangerous look. She sipped from her mug, swallowed hard, going over her story in her mind, finally ready. "All right, I'll tell you the truth."

"Good, because I'm fresh out of patience." He watched her carefully, wishing that just-scrubbed look didn't appeal to him so much. Why couldn't some woman with scraggly hair instead of sunshine yellow, and with warts on her face instead of satin skin, have hidden in his truck instead?

"My name is Kari Smith and I live in the Phoenix area. I was staying at the Bonaventure with a friend, attending some political speeches, taking notes for another friend who's a political science major at ASU. I really did take two allergy pills and get disoriented when I went

for a walk. The…the rest is kind of hard to explain."
She dropped her gaze, studied the liquid in her mug.

"Try me," he said, his voice sounding noncommittal.

She swallowed with difficulty, hoping he'd believe the
rest. "My father is very domineering." Which was certainly the truth. "He wants me to live my life his way,
to work for him, to travel where he sends me. I'm tired
of doing that. He wants to approve my friends, even pick
out a husband for me." This, too, wasn't so far-fetched,
for James had suggested that very thing, constantly introducing her to men he thought suitable as a son-in-law.

Kari looked up, found he was listening intently and
that his expression had softened slightly. "I want you to
know I love my father very much. But I want to lead my
own life. I need some time to sort things out, to decide
just what I want to do, before I go back and confront
him with the changes I'd like to make. My landing here
was an accident, but now that I'm here, please, Dillon,
let me stay for just a little while. I promise I'll keep out
of your way and I'll help you in any way I can—cooking,
mending your socks, things like that."

Either she was one hell of an actress or she was close
to the truth with this story. "What does your father do?"

"He works for a big outfit that has him traveling a
good deal of the time, and I'm his assistant, always at
his beck and call. He worries about me, I know, but he's
smothering and very demanding." She hoped her words
had the ring of truth, for every word was so.

Dillon let out a frustrated breath. He could relate to
her dilemma all too well. His own father cared for him,
too, but he was very demanding and domineering. He'd
handled it well enough when he was young, but at age
thirty, his father pushing his own agenda on him rankled
more than a little.

Studying her eyes, he wondered if she was telling him the whole truth. Of course, there was one thing in her favor—his best educated guess from what he could see was that the roads were still impassable and probably would be for days, at least those off the major highways. The sheriff and his deputies were undoubtedly very busy right now and not likely to come unless someone reported her as a missing person, which might be another problem. "What if your father reports you missing and the police come looking for you?"

She shook her head. "I already called one of his assistants. The phone's working again. I told her I was fine, taking some time off and that there's no point in Dad coming to look for me."

"And you think he'll listen, this domineering man?"

Her smile was bittersweet. "He has no choice. He hasn't a clue where I am. *I* didn't even know where I was until you told me."

Dillon sat, reflecting. He supposed he could plow his long drive out to the road and take her to the nearest town and be done with her. He was, after all, a man who lived alone by choice, unused to sharing his bath, his private space. But there was something about her expression. Not exactly pleading, yet asking for just a little time. It reminded him of when he'd asked his father for a little time to find out if he could cut it as a rancher. He supposed he could give her a couple of days.

"I don't like liars. Are you sure what you've told me is the truth?"

As far as it went, it was. "Yes."

"*If* I let you stay, we need to establish a few ground rules," Dillon said, his eyes on hers.

He was going for it, Kari thought, careful to keep her face expressionless. It wouldn't do to flash him a triumphant grin. "Like what?" Kari held her breath, hoping he wasn't going to be unreasonable.

Dillon thought he might as well get something out of the arrangement, even one that would last only a few days. "I hate to cook for myself after a long day. Can you cook?"

Her first real bona fide trial by fire, Kari thought. "Some. I noticed a couple of cookbooks above the stove. I can manage. What else?"

"About my two ranch hands. Mac lives in a trailer behind the house, keeps to himself pretty much."

"I think I saw him on his way to the stables. An older man, has trouble walking?"

"Right. He said you waved to him. Then there's Rich, but he just comes over when I need him. Mac doesn't get along real well with women. Rich gets along all too well, if you know what I mean. Stay away from both of them." Dillon hadn't meant to sound so restrictive, but she had to know where things stood. Rich, he knew, thought of himself as irresistible to women. He'd have to warn the guy to steer clear of Kari.

"No problem. Anything else?"

Dillon rubbed along his jawline, suddenly aware of how scruffy he must look. He hadn't shaved in three days, hadn't showered yet this morning. Funny how the presence of a woman made a guy think about things like that. His horses certainly didn't mind if he never shaved. Some winters he'd grown a beard. Warmer that way. Maybe he'd shave later.

"Can't think of anything else right now. Maybe later." He drained his mug. "Coffee's good. I like it strong." He saw the slow smile coming and was surprised how such a minor compliment pleased her. "I don't know what you plan to do all day, how staying here away from everything familiar will help you sort things out." He still had some lingering doubts.

She leaned forward, her look sincere. "I'll have some freedom to think things through without someone trying to push me into decisions they think are best for me. I think I'm old enough to decide that for myself. I'm generally leery of people who bully you into doing this 'for your own good.'"

"Yeah, me, too. All right, you can stay. For a few days, until the weather breaks."

Kari let out a relieved sigh. "Thank you."

Dillon hoped he wouldn't regret his decision. "Listen, there's bacon, eggs and bread in the refrigerator. You want to make breakfast while I take a shower?"

"Sure." Kari got up and headed for the fridge. That had been easier than she'd dared to hope. Now if only she could put together a decent meal.

In the bathroom that he was now sharing with a woman, Dillon stood looking at several pricey feminine garments strung on hangers on the shower curtain rod. Pale blue silk, undoubtedly from some boutique. It had been well over two years since Lisa Morgan, who'd lived with him briefly, had hung up a few hand washables. Was he nuts, letting another woman into his life, one he had a feeling wasn't being a hundred percent up-front with him? He'd trusted once before and been badly burned. He hoped history wasn't repeating itself.

Stripping down to his briefs, Dillon turned on his electric razor, determined not to spoil the day by dwelling on the past. He took extra care shaving, telling himself it was because his beard was heavy.

Moving Kari's clothes aside, Dillon turned on the taps, adjusting them to hot, and stepped into the shower. Lathering up, he decided to wash away any bitter recollections. He dredged them up occasionally to remind himself never to be taken in like that again. A relationship based on lies and subterfuge was doomed. He was definitely better off without a woman who couldn't be honest.

Rubbing shampoo into his hair, he thought maybe it was time to get a haircut, too. Then the thought had him frowning. Not even twenty-four hours with a woman in the house, and he was making changes. What was wrong with him?

After Lisa, he'd decided that women and marriage would have to wait. Besides, he wasn't sure that the sort of woman he'd want in his life permanently—the kind who would love the land and horses and ranching, the peaceful country life, as much as he did—even existed. Most women were too spoiled and pampered, afraid to get dirty, needing their nails done weekly, wanting to party. The simple life of a rancher wasn't for everyone, he knew that. But it was the life Dillon had decided he wanted, and he was willing to work long and hard for it.

The rewards were plenty. If he couldn't find a woman who'd be happy at the end of a tiring day to simply sit quietly together and gaze at a blazing fire on a cold winter evening, or one who'd love jumping into the spring-fed pond and skinny-dipping on a summer evening, then he'd stay single. That would be a difficult thing to accept, for he would love to have sons to teach about ranching—tall, strapping boys who'd work alongside him and one day take over the ranch. And girls who would love hayrides and county fairs and riding their own horse. A family unit, happy to be with one another, like his friend, Ted Maynard, had with his wife and three sons.

Dillon had witnessed firsthand his parents' unhappy marriage, which had been spoiled by a self-indulgent woman whose main concern had been herself and her needs. He knew he'd rather live alone the rest of his days than live like that again.

It wasn't often he let himself think about the past. But with a woman once again in his house in close quarters, it was important to remind himself not to let her feminine presence start to get under his skin. He surely didn't want to be pawing the ground like Domino just because a female was nearby. He was merely Kari Smith's host for a couple of days and no more. It was only human to notice how well put together she was, but a man with a goal wouldn't allow a distraction, no matter how appealing, to veer him off the path he'd set for himself.

Pleased with that assessment, Dillon turned off the water.

Ten minutes later, dressed in clean jeans and denim shirt, Dillon walked out of his bedroom and could scarcely believe his eyes. The whole main room was filled with gray smoke. "Whoa, there," he called out. "What's happening?"

Fanning at the smoke with a magazine she'd found, Kari stood by the stove, her eyes tearing. "I'm not sure."

He rushed over, turned off the burner and placed the iron skillet onto a trivet. Through the smoke he could see shriveled-up pieces of bacon floating around in the hot fat.

"I turned the burner down, but it stayed hot and wouldn't cool off." Stepping back, she swiped at her wet eyes. "We cook with gas. I'm not used to electric stoves, I guess."

Dillon shoved open the window above the sink so the smoke would draw out. "No, I guess not." He turned and saw her stricken look. "Gas flames turn down instantly, but electric coils take a while to cool off. You're better off not starting on high. Try medium next time.''

"Thanks, I will.'' She glared at the pan. "I'm sorry I ruined your breakfast.'' She'd wanted so badly to impress him.

"No harm done.'' He watched the smoke swirl out the window. "You want to try the eggs, or you want me to do it?''

"No, I'll do it.'' She bent to the cupboard for another pan. "How many would you want?''

"Four, probably. And two or three slices of toast.''

Good grief, Kari thought, reaching into the refrigerator for the eggs. Did he eat like that all the time?

Dillon fiddled with the radio, trying to get the old set, which dated back to Quinn's early days, to come on. From under lowered lashes, he watched Kari concentrate on breaking the eggs into the pan just so, unaware her tongue was caught between her teeth. He'd wager she hadn't cooked an egg in a long while, if ever. His lips twitched when he saw her flash a smile at the pan as all four eggs landed upright without breaking.

Maybe it wouldn't be so bad, having someone around. There was no getting around the fact that he got lonely at times, especially during the long winter, when even trips into town were few and far between. Mac was no company, seldom stepping into the cabin unless he needed something, not much of a talker when he did. His father worked long hours, six days a week at his store and rarely drove over. Terry's hours at his office and the hospital kept him busy, plus he had a wife and a new baby to occupy him.

Most of the time, Dillon thought as he twirled the radio's knobs, he enjoyed the solitude. But occasionally, like now when someone was in his home, he was reminded that it would be nice to interact with another human being. Man wasn't meant to live alone, his uncle used to tell him. Certainly Quinn had gone downhill after his wife had died. Yet Dillon's father had lived alone for years and Mac had too. Different strokes for different folks, he supposed.

"Oh, no!" Kari cried out.

Amused instead of angry, Dillon walked over and saw that the egg she'd tried to flip had landed on top of another, and the spatula's edge had caught and shifted a third one onto the pile. "That's all right. I prefer scrambled, anyway."

"You do?" Looking enormously relieved, she dragged the spatula through the gooey eggs. "Scrambled it is."

As Dillon sat down at the table, the radio squawked on. "Worst storm of the season…eighteen hours and still coming down…highway accidents reported from Prescott all the way up to the Grand Canyon. Weather man predicts another five or six inches before it stops." The announcer chuckled. "So grab your sweetie, settle down in front of the fire and forget going outside. Those of us in the Flagstaff area and surrounding vicinity are officially marooned!"

"Too bad," Kari said, dishing up the eggs. "I'd hoped to go out and build a snowman later."

"Tomorrow, maybe," Dillon said, picking up his fork.

"Mark my words, boys and girls," the announcer added, "it happens every time we get a big one like this—people hereabouts hole up in their feather beds, and nine months from now we'll have a lot of squealing babies in northern Arizona to remind us of this winter storm."

Kari's face flushed as Dillon dropped his fork with a clatter.

Chapter Four

Kari stood in the mud room by the side door of the cabin intently studying the knobs on the washing machine and dryer. For years she'd seen the Sinclairs' housekeeper, Clara, do the laundry and, much to her regret now, had never paid the slightest bit of attention.

Of course, their home had had a much newer model, probably state-of-the-art, since her father always demanded the top of the line. Squinting at the markings circling the knob, the black print nearly worn off by time and the touch of many hands, she decided this washer was an old relic that should have been discarded long ago. However, it was the only thing she had to work with, and she was determined to earn her keep.

Not that one egg and a piece of toast along with two cups of black coffee indebted her too much. Still, she'd promised Dillon she'd help out, so when she'd asked if he had anything he wanted her to do, he'd brought her an overflowing basket of dirty clothes. She could have sworn he'd smirked as he set the basket down. Which only made her more determined than ever to get the job done.

First she sorted the clothes into piles as she'd remembered Clara doing. Whites, colored and dark things. The dark things made two large piles since Dillon's blue jeans and work shirts were mostly navy or black, it seemed. She came across a red shirt that seemed almost frivolous compared to the rest of the somber lot. The sorting done, she opened the cupboards and found soap, bleach, even something called fabric softener. Did that go into all loads? Surely he wanted all his clothes to be soft, didn't he? Studiously, she read the labels.

Glancing through the arch, she saw Dillon seated at the scarred wooden desk across the room, watching her instead of doing his bills, which was what he'd told her he planned to do. When she met his eyes, he quickly looked down. Was he worried she'd wreck his clothes? To tell the truth, she had a few qualms herself. But she wasn't about to admit that she'd never done a load of laundry in her life, except for hand washables.

The only thing left in the cupboard was a bottle of prewash spray for hard-to-remove spots. Why couldn't she just pour some in the washer along with the soap rather than go through each item, searching for spots and spraying individually? That seemed a more efficient way to do things.

Kari decided to tackle the white load first, which consisted mostly of underwear, some socks and a couple of towels. She sprinkled a half cup of soap on top of it all, according to the directions on the box of detergent. Frowning, she decided that little bit of soap would never clean that big pile of clothes, so she tossed in another full cup for good measure. Next she poured some bleach into the triangular receptacle in one corner, then the fabric softener in its special container. A dash of spot remover and she was ready to roll. Who'd have thought you needed so many products to get your clothes clean? she wondered.

Finally she closed the lid and set the wash on the longest cycle. Everything was pretty dirty so she was sure it would take some time to get it all clean. Briefly, she read the instructions on the lid of the dryer, then left the wash area, pleased to have begun another chore.

The kitchen clock hadn't yet reached nine. Stifling a yawn, Kari had been certain it was closer to noon, since she felt as if she'd been up for days. Her gaze drifted over the bookcase with longing. It was a perfect day for curling up with a good book. The snow was still coming down outside, but not as heavily as before. The fire crackled and popped in the grate, a sound and smell Kari loved. She would also love to peruse Dillon's shelves and see what kind of reading material he preferred.

But she had the kitchen to clean up from breakfast. Like a magnanimous fool, she'd offered to do it herself, freeing Dillon to do whatever he would. Shoving up the sleeves of her sweatshirt, Kari dribbled liquid soap into the sink and turned on the hot water.

The radio sputtered and paused, annoying her, so she turned it off. The clean, soapy scent of the suds pleased her, as did the pale sunshine coming in through the window over the sink. This wasn't so bad, she decided. Certainly it was as different from her regular daily routine, whether on tour or at home, as night was from day. Despite the age of the cabin, Kari noticed that Dillon kept it spotlessly clean. The laundry facilities might be ancient, but the kitchen, small as it was, had been updated with a new stove and refrigerator, modern cupboards and counters and what appeared to be a recently tiled floor. Smiling at the rather bedraggled solitary African violet on the window sill struggling to stay alive, she began to hum an old Beatles tune, "Yesterday."

Dillon looked up from his ledger and watched through the arch as Kari worked. She'd tied her hair back with a piece of yarn she'd probably found in the spare room. He remembered his aunt Edith had done lots of knitting and crocheting. He recognized the tune Kari had begun, heard her sing snatches of lyrics almost under her breath, humming the rest. It felt odd, seeing a woman in his kitchen looking for all the world as if she were enjoying the simple act of washing dishes.

She'd soon grow tired of it, he knew, as Lisa had in short order. He had let Kari attempt to cook, accepted her offer to clean up, even let her do the laundry, when it was perfectly clear to him she'd never done those chores before. Maybe he wanted to see how long she would last. His first appraisal of her expensive jewelry, her obviously professional haircut, the few clothes she had, had been right. She came from money, had been pampered by the father she thought too domineering, had lived a soft, cushy life, despite her complaints.

She was probably like a lot of people who had romantic notions of ranch life, garnered undoubtedly from the movies, and wanted to have a fling at it. Sprawling white ranch houses, rustic barns, gorgeous thoroughbreds who pranced in a green pasture under cloudless blue skies. Rarely did they depict the eighteen-hour days it took most ranchers just to keep up with necessary chores, their stock and the planting and harvesting. They didn't show anyone mucking out a stall or tending to a sick horse or the devastation of a drought on crops that the owner was counting on to feed his family or sell to pay for necessities. They certainly didn't picture the blood, sweat and tears it took, even with modern technology, to be a rancher today.

So "Ms. Smith" wanted to rough it a few days before she ran home to wash the animal smells off her and resume her former life. Dillon had seen the type before. Sure, he would give her her little interlude. He'd play along, teach her about life in the country, so she could regale the folks back home with stories of her ranch respite.

Narrowing his eyes, he watched her poke and prod at the soil in his African violet pot. She was actually talking to the plant, snipping off a dead leaf, giving it a drop or two of water. He still wasn't certain why she wanted to stay here. She was a puzzle, and he'd always been fascinated by puzzles. But he mustn't be taken in by her easy acceptance of a few minor chores, by her gritty determination to do things herself. She was a visitor here, one who'd soon tire of this game and move on.

Even as his hands literally itched to touch her incredibly silky hair, to run a finger along that long, satin throat, Dillon pulled his gaze from her. His sensual thoughts and interest in her was only the normal reaction of a man who lived alone without female companionship, that was all, he reminded himself. He was a responsible adult, one who was in control of his body and emotions. Like his father. *Un*like his mother.

Dillon bent to his paperwork and didn't look up again until he heard a clumping sound coming from the direction of the washing machine. He jumped to his feet, his eyes widening as he watched mounds of soap suds spiraling out from under the washer lid, cascading down and

onto the floor, and the washer literally bouncing in place.
"Damn," he muttered, hurrying over.

Kari rushed after him, a look of horror on her face.
"Oh, no!"

Dillon shoved in the knob, turning off the machine,
but the suds kept on coming as the agitator slowed. Putting his hip to it, he moved the washer back into place.
Opening the lid, he stared inside, then unbuttoned his
cuffs and rolled up his sleeves. "You put too many
clothes on one side and not enough on the other. Causes
a lopsided load."

"Oh," she said, subdued.

He reached in and evened out the distribution before
wiping his hands on a towel hanging on a peg. He bent
to a cardboard box alongside the dryer where he kept a
pile of old terry cloth towels now used as rags. Quickly
he began to mop up the suds, noticing that Kari was
pitching in, wiping down the machine while he cleaned
the floor.

"I'm so sorry," she murmured. "I thought I followed
all the directions."

Wringing his rag out into a bucket, Dillon sent her an
inquiring look. "Do you think you might have put in too
much soap?"

That had to be it, Kari knew. "Half a cup just didn't
seem enough to clean a whole load, so I—"

"Doubled it?"

"More like tripled it. I added another whole cup."

Down on all fours as he finished up near the side door,
Dillon had to smile. She sounded so woebegone. "Hey,
don't sweat the small stuff. The floor needed a washing
anyhow."

Straightening and tossing her wet rags into the bucket,
Kari stopped to study him as he rose. "Are you always

this easygoing?'' James Sinclair was really the only man she'd ever observed on a regular basis and he had a habit of making mountains out of molehills, in his personal and business life.

"Not really. I've got a temper, one I'm not proud of. But I save it for the really rough things. This…this is minor." She was looking up at him as if trying to see into his mind, her forehead scrunched into a puzzled frown. "What?"

"Nothing. I…"

He tossed the rags into the bucket and touched her arm. "Yeah, something. You're looking at me like a buyer at a horse auction, trying to figure out if I'm a cayuse or prime stock." His mouth held a hint of amusement, but his eyes were more serious.

"What's a cayuse?"

"A scrawny horse."

Her gaze took in his wide shoulders, his deep chest, his long, muscular legs, his big hands. "I wouldn't say you're a cayuse."

"But you're not sure I'm prime, either?"

Kari thought it best to keep it light. "Too soon to tell." She started to turn away, but his hand on her arm turned her back.

"You've got some suds on your face." Dillon touched two fingers to her cheek, felt his throat clog as he found the skin as soft as he'd imagined. Drawing his fingers down, he scooped off the suds, held it out for her to inspect. "See?"

But Kari could only see his blue eyes turning suddenly dark, could only feel the heat rise in her face. Surprisingly shaky, she stepped back. "Thanks." Quickly she walked to the kitchen, hurriedly washed her hands, needing a distraction. How could she feel so much from the merest of touches? Silly. She was being really silly.

Dillon scooped excess suds from the washer, tossed it all into the utility sink, then turned the controls back on before following Kari to the kitchen. She was flushed, he couldn't help noticing. He wasn't sure if that pleased him or not. This wasn't working, spending so much time inside these four walls in close proximity to her. "There's some stew meat in the freezer if you want to try your hand at that for dinner." Walking to the door, he grabbed his jacket. "I'm going to check on Calypso. She's due anytime now."

Kari heard the door close and let out her breath in a whoosh, her hands moving up to her warm cheeks. It was good that he left before she made a complete fool of herself. Things had shifted into a direction she hadn't considered. Suddenly she didn't look on Dillon Tracy as the rancher who'd driven her up here and was giving her an opportunity to take a break and sort things out.

Suddenly, she was looking at him as a man.

A very attractive man, at that. Be that as it may, she had to set any attraction she felt aside. It was all right for her to stay here with him as long as the arrangement was strictly platonic. Having her busy little mind explore possibilities about what it would feel like to have him touch her again, more thoroughly this time, or how it would feel to have that generous mouth kiss her—well, that changed things.

No, she couldn't let that happen, because that would mean she'd have to leave. She couldn't have this man who'd opened his home to her think she would come looking for a seduction. Was he already thinking that, after that hot look they'd shared? She sincerely hoped not.

For she was as far from a seductress as anyone could imagine. Perhaps, because he thought she had a job as an assistant to a high-powered executive—which was the truth, after all—he might also think she was experienced and worldly wise. *That* was definitely not the truth. She had dates, but nothing serious, and had had only one brief but exciting affair with a college senior when she'd been a freshman, away for the first time from Daddy's watchful gaze. Her sister, Dana, was the experimenter in their family, an admitted bed hopper who'd repeatedly advised Kari that she would have to kiss a lot of frogs before she'd find her prince. Kari hadn't found too many frogs worth considering.

She could inevitably tell, when she was around a man, whether she'd like him to kiss her. And the nays far outnumbered the yeas. At political gatherings and the many cocktail parties and dinners and luncheons she'd attended over the years working with her father, she'd quickly become aware that most men, especially older men, weren't satisfied with just shaking a woman's hand. They'd take her hand, then use it to urge her closer for a kiss. Except Kari had learned the value of a turned cheek. She rarely had a kiss hit the mark unless she herself wondered what the man would be like. And that didn't happen often.

But she wondered what Dillon Tracy would taste like.

Staring out the window at the stables, she allowed herself a moment to dream. He was so different from men she'd known. In Arizona and in Washington, the men she knew wore beautifully tailored suits, sparkling white shirts—rarely colored ones—and just the proper tie. Their shoes were polished to such a shine you could put your makeup on in them, and they all wore cologne, something expensive and all too often applied with a heavy hand.

Their nails were buffed, their hair cut weekly, their manners impeccable as they flashed their platinum credit cards.

They were assorted clones of her father, in a variety of ages, most of them intense and intelligent, quite a few who took themselves too seriously and many who lacked a genuine sense of humor. She'd bet that very few had ever been on a horse, much less chose to live among them. For a long while now, Kari had known that though she loved her father, she couldn't possibly settle for an antiseptic man like that.

Which made Dillon stand out all the more. He was far from perfect, which held an odd appeal. His hair needed trimming, he had one slightly crooked eyetooth and a small nick on his chin where he'd cut himself shaving. Frankly, she rather liked him unshaven. His hands had never known a manicurist, she was certain. They were large, with scrapes and bruises like proud badges of hard, physical work. She doubted he owned a suit and wondered at the size that would fit those powerful shoulders. He exuded strength, yet his touch on her scalp had been as tender as a child's. She had a feeling he was also cash-and-carry, a man who lived within his means as a way of life.

In high school and later, Kari had never had a particular type of man in mind as the ultimate one. Her movie star crushes had been varied, and changed frequently. The guys she'd dated also bore little resemblance to one another, for she was drawn to all sorts of people. Only the men her father fixed her up with were basically the same: upwardly mobile, politically correct—at least in her father's eyes—clean cut, clean shaven, clean living. Marrying one of them, Kari was certain, would put her smack dab into the same situation she was now trying to escape.

Small wonder she was attracted to the first man who was as different from her father as oatmeal was from salsa. The one fling she'd had, had been with a man she knew her father wouldn't approve of. Something to think about, she decided, moving to the freezer. Not that she planned to act on this newfound knowledge about herself. But it was nice to know there were men on the planet who could excite her. She'd been beginning to wonder if maybe she wasn't just a shade too picky, especially since Dana was so easily able to enjoy one man after another. Nothing wrong with being a bit choosy.

Kari opened the freezer and found it crammed full of packages wrapped in white and marked with the cut of meat and the date. An organized man was Dillon Tracy, she decided. She found the stewing beef, unwrapped it and picked up one of the cookbooks on the shelf above the stove. Settling at the kitchen table, she searched for the best recipe.

The arena he was building onto the stables wasn't finished and wasn't nearly large enough yet. Nevertheless Dillon had exercised both Remus and Caesar, one after the other, knowing the frisky colts had too much energy to stand around their stalls all day and wait out the storm. Patiently, he'd taken them through their paces, just some mild stuff, walking on the rope, some familiar drills. Tomorrow he'd start up the old tractor and plow the heaviest snow from the paddock so he could let the others out awhile, except Calypso. Walking in snow would be a strain on the mare's pregnancy.

The weather up this way was the reason he was building the arena. In the worst of it, when the snow piled up, the wind sang through the trees and the temperature turned frigid, the horses got restless. If too many days elapsed in their training schedule because they couldn't go through the drill outside, Dillon had to almost start from the beginning again to refresh memories. Rain was even worse than snow. This spring he'd finish the arena so that by next winter it would be fully operational.

The exercise had helped him, too. A man used to working physically, he felt penned up when he couldn't get out. That's probably how he would feel all the time if he had to go back to the law. It had been that way in school, having to *make* himself go to classes and study afterward. A means to an end, his father had said, but now Dillon thought of it as so much wasted time. He could have been here at the ranch, working with Quinn, learning even more, keeping the place up when the old man got sick. They wouldn't have lost most of the herd nor would the buildings have deteriorated so badly.

Water over the dam, Dillon thought as he led Remus back to his stall after cooling him down. He'd go forward, plan for the future, think about tomorrow, not yesterday. Slapping the auburn flank affectionately, he locked the colt's gate and went to check on Calypso one last time. He found her clear-eyed and looking for a treat, which he gave her before walking to the big double doors where Zeus was waiting for him. The dog often stayed in the barn, but Dillon could see he was anxious to go to the house by the way he sat, ears up and sharp, looking at him.

"Okay, boy, I guess we'll go in. I've tired myself out a little and stayed clear of our visitor for a couple of hours." Maybe Kari, too, was tired and napping on the couch, which was what Dillon felt like doing. Last night had been too short. He locked up and followed his dog to the porch, walking with head bent against the blowing snow. Hard to tell how heavy the snowfall was with the wind still whirling everywhere.

Dillon heard the music before he had the door all the way open. Holding Zeus at bay, he peeked inside the house. The kitchen window was steamed up from the big pot on the stove. Wonderful smells filled the room. Apparently Kari had become warm as she worked, for she'd tossed aside the black sweatshirt. The sweatpants hung on her somewhat crazily, the drawstring ties flopping around her knees. The white T-shirt was loose, yet nearly transparent, and what he could see had him tightening in response.

But it was her motions that held him mesmerized. The song blared out as she sang along, dancing in step with the music, wielding a wooden spoon as she spun.

"'You make me feel like a natural woman,'" she crooned, then repeated again, emphasizing each word more slowly. Scooting on stocking feet on the tile, her cheeks flushed, she waved the spoon as if it were a musical wand, eyes closed as she held the last note.

Dillon found himself smiling in appreciation. A woman who thought herself alone, enjoying a little impromptu sing-along. Quietly he pulled the door closed, guessing she'd hate to be caught like that.

Stomping his feet on the wooden porch, he made lots of noise before shoving open the door a second time. She was just pulling the sweatshirt over her head as Dillon walked in, preceded by a sniffing Zeus, whose mouth was watering from the great smells. Taking off his hat, Dillon glanced at her and saw she was busying herself at the oven, once more sober-faced. The radio was off.

Removing his jacket and boots, he wondered what she was baking. "Smells awfully good in here," he said, slipping his feet into his scruffy old moccasins. Quietly he came up behind her. "What is it?" he asked, bending to peek over her shoulder.

"Biscuits. From a mix I found in the cupboard." She closed the oven door, straightened too quickly and found herself closer to him than she'd realized. His eyes weren't just blue, she noticed, but flecked with silver. He smelled very male, of the outdoors, oiled leather and animals. Awareness crackled in the warm air of the kitchen.

Dillon felt it, too, and stepped aside, needing a little distance. The homey scene was rattling him. Leaning to the stove, he peeked inside the pot, saw the rich stew burbling away. "You've been busy."

She hung up the dish towel with unsteady hands. "I never realized how much fun cooking can be, if you have the time." She pointed to the last cupboard. "Did you know your aunt collected spices? Must be seventy or eighty in there, some I've never even heard of."

"I remember looking in there once, but since I didn't know what to do with them, I just let them be. Salt and pepper's all I ever use."

"Not tonight."

Anything would beat his bland stew. "Which ones did you use?"

She sent him a mysterious smile. "You'll see."

He'd just finished washing up in the bathroom and was walking past the laundry area when he heard a muffled, "Oh, no!"

"Got a problem?" he asked, joining her at the washer.

"You could say that." Kari offered him a sickly smile. "I don't know how this happened."

She was holding something behind her back. "What is it?" he asked, trying to sound interested and not stern.

She had a "little girl caught with her hand in the cookie jar" look about her that had him struggling not to smile.

Her hands came forward, one holding his red shirt, the other hanging on to several pair of briefs that had once been white and were now bright pink. "I thought I'd put this shirt into the colored pile. I'm sorry." If ever there was a man who wouldn't choose pink underwear, she was looking at him.

Gingerly he took the briefs from her, then gazed into the washer where everything else was also pink. "Interesting color."

"I could maybe run them through again, without the shirt, with lots of bleach. What do you think?" She wished he'd frown or smile or something instead of just staring at his ruined clothes.

"Nah, just toss them into the dryer. The horses don't much care what color I wear. Nobody else sees them." Opening the dryer, he threw the clothes he held in, then helped her with the rest.

Nobody else sees them. Did that mean he didn't date anyone, had no love interest? None of her business, Kari thought, taking firm control of her thoughts. What was she doing, speculating about his love life? "Anything else in these piles that might run?" she asked him.

He bent down, gave his clothes a perfunctory check. "Not that I can see." He'd better make sure Mac didn't see him using a pink handkerchief. He'd never hear the end of it.

Watching her prepare the next load, he crossed his arms over his chest and leaned against the arch. "I take it you don't do a lot of laundry, right?"

There was no use pretending, Kari decided as she piled clothes into the washer, evenly distributing them this time. "I live with my folks and they have live-in help."

Just as he'd thought, rich and pampered. "Nice arrangement."

"Actually, it isn't." Kari tossed exactly half a cup of
detergent in and shut the lid. "It's just another way my
father controls things. I plan to get a place of my own
after—" she almost blurted out *after the election*
"—sometime this fall."

"So while you're here, you're trying to get up the
courage to tell him you want to move out?"

She leaned against the washer, mimicking his crossed-
arms position. "I know that must sound pretty cowardly
to someone like you, living alone here, doing exactly as
you please, your own boss."

"You might be surprised."

"It's just that I love my father, and I don't want to
hurt him. It's hard for him to let go, but he means well."

Dillon's thoughts were on his own father. "They all
do."

She raised her eyes to his as his words registered.
"You've had a similar situation?"

But before Dillon could answer, the bell on the stove
went off, and they both looked to the kitchen. "The biscuits," Kari said, hurrying to check. "I hope you're hungry," she added over her shoulder.

"Starved."

The biscuits were plump and hot, the salad crisp, and
the stew had a bite to it that he couldn't quite define.
"What's in this?" he asked, studying a hearty spoonful.
"Curry?"

"No, paprika. It's more goulash than stew, a Hungarian dish. When I found all those spices, I just had to try
this recipe. My maternal grandmother's from Hungary. I

remember eating this as a child." His expression was hard to read. "You don't like it?"

"It's great." Dillon smiled before popping the spoonful in his mouth.

He had a nice smile, Kari thought, watching him eat. It changed his face, made him look less threatening. Suddenly she wanted to know more about him. "With a name like Tracy, I imagine you're Irish, eh?"

"Through and through. My father and my uncle Quinn were born in County Cork, came over as young men to seek their fortune."

"And did they find it?"

Shrugging, Dillon broke apart a steaming roll. "In a way, I suppose. Dad owns a grocery story in Prescott, and Quinn had this ranch and a dream of raising Irish thoroughbreds on it. They didn't exactly wind up with a fortune, but they did all right."

"Does your mother work in the store with your dad?"

Dillon's eyes turned cool, and his face tightened as he concentrated on his plate. "She died when I was ten."

"I'm sorry." Kari let her gaze linger on his features as they slowly relaxed. She'd certainly hate to be on the wrong side of one of those frosty looks, she decided. "And your aunt and uncle are gone, too. What a shame. That leaves only you and your dad, then?"

He drained the last of his milk before answering. "I have a brother, Terry. He's a doctor." How was it she'd managed to get him to tell her about his family without revealing a thing about hers? "How about you? Any siblings?"

"One sister. Unmarried. Also works for Dad, but Dana loves all the traveling and whatnot. We're not much alike." Finishing, she rose to turn on the coffeepot.

"Is she as beautiful as you?"

Kari opened her mouth to answer, then closed it again. Beautiful was not how she regarded herself. "Dana's a beauty. She sometimes has two dates in one day." Wondering if he was teasing her, she held out both hands, indicating her outfit, her lack of makeup, the overall picture. "*This* is hardly beautiful."

Swallowing the last bite of his second helping, Dillon carried his plate to the counter before turning to her. "Are you fishing?"

Her frown was instantaneous. "No, not at all. I'm aware of my looks, which usually are a little better than right now. But Dana stops traffic, literally."

"Are you living in her shadow, then?"

Was she? No, absolutely not. "We're just very different, that's all."

Dillon backed off, just a little. "I'm very different from my brother, too. He did exactly as Dad wanted, without a single argument—set up practice near the family grocery store, married a girl who's the daughter of Dad's best friend and they just had a bouncing baby boy."

Kari read between the lines. "But even though you love your father, you don't fall in line that easily, do you? Who'd have thought to look at us that we have a similar problem?"

It certainly hadn't occurred to him, either, until just now. "I'll bet Dana never would have crawled into my truck that night, would she?"

"Oh, she might have, but it would have been deliberate because…well, because you're an attractive man and she definitely likes attractive men."

"And once she found herself up here in this remote cabin with not many of the amenities she's used to, what would she have done, do you suppose?" He was watching her, wondering if she knew that her expressive face revealed more than her words.

Kari supposed that Dana would have jumped his bones, most likely, then called for a limo the morning after to get her out of this godforsaken place. Or a helicopter. "She wouldn't have decided to stay," Kari answered, putting a kinder spin on things.

Pushing back from the counter, he moved closer to her. "Would she have found me attractive, though?"

Kari's heart did a little trip hammer dance. "Definitely."

"Do you?"

She cocked her head, tried a lazy smile. "Are you hitting on me, Dillon?"

He thought about that long and hard for about ten seconds, then he grinned before stepping back. "No, ma'am. I assure you, when I hit on you, you'll know it." Turning to the cupboard, he took down two mugs. "Why don't we let the dishes go for now and have our coffee in front of the fire?"

Just what she needed, the heat of the fire, when her face felt warm and flushed already. *When* I hit on you, not *if*. She wandered over to the big couch, settled on one side with her legs pulled up, leaving plenty of room for him.

Dillon took a minute to pour dog food into Zeus's dish, then mix in the remaining stew. "We'll see if he likes Hungarian cooking," he told Kari as he set the dish down for the salivating dog. "If he has a paprika bellyache tonight, he sleeps with you."

"I think I can handle that."

He carried the mugs over and placed them on the oak coffee table. He tossed another log on the fire to stir things up a bit, then sat down in the center of the couch, not the far end. The flames caught the dry wood easily and smoke raced up the chimney.

Kari sipped the coffee and studied him. "Can I ask you something?"

Stretching his long legs toward the fire, Dillon decided he was enjoying himself. "Shoot."

"Earlier, I mentioned our situations with our fathers were similar, and you agreed. What is it your father wanted you to do that you didn't want to do?"

"Set up a law practice after I graduated from law school and passed the bar. In Prescott near his store, then settle down like Terry has—live up to my potential."

She heard the faint edge to his voice. So he was educated, as she'd guessed, but had turned his back on the law. Interesting. "But you prefer ranching." It wasn't a question.

"By far." Dillon leaned forward for a swallow of coffee, then flopped back. "I understand that there's more security in the law than in ranching, and Dad wanted both his sons to have that. But what good is security if you hate what you're doing?"

That was it, exactly. "I couldn't have said it better myself."

He turned to look at her, to watch the firelight dance in her hair, turning it from pale yellow to a deep gold. He swallowed around a dry throat, suddenly painfully aware that he never should have let her stay. She was messing up his mind and other parts of his anatomy. Too late, and he was getting in deeper and deeper. "Did your father handpick a man for you to marry, too?"

Kari let out a mirthless chuckle. "Oh, yes. Edmund Pickman Ford. His father's a stockbroker, his mother's an heiress, and one of his ancestors came over on the

Mayflower. At least that's how they tell it. Edmund's not so much stuffy as boring.''

Angling his body toward her, Dillon stretched an arm along the couch back, his fingers inches from her shoulder. "And what does Edmund do?"

She turned her head toward him, a smile playing on her lips. "He's a lawyer." They laughed together, and Kari found herself relaxing even more. "What about you? Who did Daddy pick out for you?"

"The tomato princess."

Kari raised a brow. "The who?"

"Ellen's family owns a tomato processing plant. Big business. Only child, so one day she'll inherit. I had a close call with Ellen. Now I break out in a rash if I even eat a tomato."

"You're making that up."

"Scout's honor. She was on the wrestling team at college and rides a Harley to this day. Actually, Ellen's kind of cute, if you don't mind mustaches on women."

She laughed out loud. "That's mean. Stop."

He shifted fractionally closer. "All right, I made most of it up. But not the mustache." He liked her laugh, the way the corners of her eyes crinkled. Taking a chance, he reached to touch the ends of her hair as the thick strands lay spread on the pillow back, and saw her smile slip. "No, I'm not hitting on you, if that's what you're thinking."

Felt like it. She wished she could let him continue, to see where this might go. Definitely not wise. "It's good of you to keep me informed." Easing upright, she got to her feet. "I'm pretty bushed. Not much sleep last night. I'll just do the dishes and—"

"No, leave them. You go ahead. My turn. One cooks, the other cleans up. House rules."

She looked down at him and saw the merest trace of disappointment. She felt it, too. "If you're sure…"

"I am. Sleep well."

Why did she have the feeling she'd hurt his feelings? Maybe she was just oversensitive from lack of sleep. Leaving him, she walked to her room, feeling vaguely unsettled.

Dillon stayed where he was, staring into the fire. He had no business feeling disappointed because every time he touched her, she pulled back, both physically and mentally. They'd met less than twenty-four hours ago, hardly knew each other. He had the host part of this awkward situation down pretty pat, but all the talking he'd done to himself about ignoring her and sending her on her way quickly wasn't working.

He wanted her.

Ah, but then, the sixty-four-thousand-dollar question: did he want her for herself or because he'd been without the softness of a woman for too many months?

Chapter Five

He hadn't expected her to be up, not at 5:00 a.m. But the moment Dillon opened his bedroom door, he smelled the wonderful aroma of coffee. He found her at the kitchen window gazing out at the quiet, snow-covered yard.

"Have trouble sleeping?" Dillon asked as he carried his boots to a kitchen chair and sat down to pull them on.

"All slept out, I guess." Kari poured coffee into a mug for him, one for herself and carried them over. Actually, she'd slept very well, waking early, rested and eager to start the day, something she rarely was in her other life, as she'd begun to think of it.

Watching his strong, lean hands pull on his boots, she wondered if Dillon had slept well. "Tell me, what do you do in the barn so early in the morning?"

Dillon tugged on his second boot. "Tend to the horses.

Put out fresh feed and water. Make sure the temperature in the stable isn't too hot or too cold, that no one's coming down with a cold. Clean out the stalls, put in fresh hay. Check on Calypso to see how long before she'll deliver.''

"How many horses do you have?''

"Five mares, a gelding, an Appaloosa, the new stallion and two colts." He picked up his coffee mug, drank gratefully. Usually he didn't take the time to make coffee before his first visit to the stables when he was alone. He had to admit this was nice, having it ready and waiting for him.

Don't get used to it, buddy. Don't get spoiled, he warned himself as he studied her over the rim of his cup. She was wearing jeans and a heavy plaid shirt she must have found in Edith's trunk. He would wager that Edith never looked half so good in them, even though Kari had to turn up the cuffs of both. Her hair hung loose and soft and shiny to her shoulders, like last night.

Dillon shifted his gaze to the tabletop.

"Could you use some help?'' Kari asked, somewhat timidly. Since she'd awakened, she'd been thinking about how best to persuade him to let her go out and had decided on the direct approach.

He frowned. "Mac helps me when I need it.'' He got up to pour more coffee.

"I won't get in your way. I…I'd just like to visit the horses.''

Hand braced on the counter, he regarded her. "Have you ever been in a stable? Do you know anything about horses?''

Her gaze was steady. He'd soon find out if she lied. Besides, he'd said he hated liars, and she was feeling guilty enough deceiving him about her real name, her family background. "No."

A flash of annoyance drifted across his already-stern features. "I don't have time to give you a crash course. Besides, you don't have any warm clothing and—"

"Yes, I do." She pointed to a heavy coat with attached hood on the arm of the couch and a pair of boots alongside. "Your aunt's, I imagine."

It would seem she'd thought this out.

"I'm not asking you to teach me anything," Kari rushed on. "I'd like to just watch. If...if I bother you, I'll come back, I promise."

Damned if he could see a way out of this without looking like a real hardnose. "All right, but you have to do as I say out there. I don't want anyone getting hurt."

Her smile was radiant. "Thanks." Kari drained her cup and went to get the boots.

Chances were she'd hate it. The earthy smells, the sounds, the sheer physical power of penned-up large animals pawing the ground. She'd beg to return to the house soon enough. He'd give her fifteen minutes, tops.

She didn't look like she hated it. She looked fascinated, eager to learn, interested.

"Rainbow is four, probably the gentlest horse in here," Dillon said affectionately stroking the Appaloosa's muzzle.

Kari studied the cream-colored horse with the fanciful black, brown and auburn spots scattered about her thick coat while Rainbow's large brown eyes examined her as well. "Is she friendly, then?"

"Pretty much. Here, put your hand on mine. Don't make sudden movements. That scares horses. Just touch her like I'm doing, let her get used to your scent." After a minute, he shifted positions and put his hand over Kari's, stroking slowly, then moved both their hands under Rainbow's nose so the horse could get familiar with the newcomer. Kari looked awestruck.

"If you want to know how a horse is reacting, check their ears. See how Rainbow's ears are forward, how she's paying attention to you? She's interested in someone new, willing to get to know you."

Kari found herself smiling and hoping the horse liked her. Carefully she reached to touch the thick mane, then jumped back when Rainbow's big head bobbed. "Did I scare her?"

"No, she's just acknowledging you. Nodding, sort of."

Stepping away from the Appaloosa, he picked up the feed bucket and moved along to the next stall. "This is Maisy," he told her, leaning over the big sorrel's stall to fill her feeder.

"My, she's really large," Kari commented, hesitantly standing back from the reddish horse sporting what looked like a white star marking on her face.

"She's a beauty, aren't you, doll?" But Dillon's voice held a note of regret. "I'm beginning to think she's barren, though. I've had her mounted twice and nothing happened."

Breeder talk, Kari decided. She'd known a girl at college who'd lived on a farm and spoke about reproduction in dispassionate animal terms. Being exposed to the mating of horses and cattle growing up, she'd had a decidedly casual attitude about sex that Kari had envied.

"So mostly you have these horses, the mares, so you can breed them and sell their offspring?" She was curious as to why he had so many and varied horses.

"I breed and train. I've built a reputation around these

parts for good stock. Some buyers are looking for gentle riding horses, well trained to follow commands. Others want work horses for cattle ranches. Still another might want a gelding for a child's first horse."

"A gelding is what, a young male horse?"

"A male horse that's been castrated." Dillon gave Maisy a pat, then moved along.

"Oh, my. Why would they do that?" she asked, following.

He hid a smile at her worried frown. "Take away the testosterone and you've got a male as gentle as a mare. Quieter, actually, because they've got nothing else on their minds. They're good work horses and no threat to the mares."

"I thought there was, like, a mating season for animals."

"There is. Mares come into heat usually in the spring."

"Couldn't you just keep the males apart from the females during that time without doing surgery on them?"

He paused at the next stall, shaking his head. "Not good enough. A stallion is no different from a man, always aware of a female nearby, only more so. They turn mean and get temperamental if they're kept from mating. I'll introduce you to Domino, my new stallion, and you'll know what I mean. He's clear in the far corner with a solid wall between him and the mares, and he's still restless."

Maybe it would be best to drop this whole conversation, Kari decided as she let Dillon introduce her to Dixie and Holly, two chestnut mares she was certain she'd never be able to tell apart they looked so much alike. Then they came to Calypso's stall and she stared with wide-eyed wonder at the big chestnut's swollen belly.

"How you doing, girl?" Dillon asked, his voice gentle, soothing. He entered her stall, his experienced hands roaming over her. "You getting ready?"

"I would think so. She's huge." Why didn't the poor thing lie down? Kari wondered.

"Won't be long now," Dillon said, thinking he'd better set up his electronic equipment that connected to his bedroom. Inevitably mares went into labor at night.

"Do you have a vet on call to come over and help?"

"Not unless the mare's in trouble, like a breech birth, which you can usually tell ahead. I've delivered quite a few all alone or with Mac's help."

Growing bolder, Kari reached up to stroke along the white stripe running down Calypso's nose. "You're a beautiful lady. I know you're anxious to get this over with."

To Dillon's surprise, Calypso responded to her soft voice, turning her nose into Kari's hand, her ears relaxed and trusting. "Look at those ears. She likes you. Are you sure you've never been with horses?"

"Never, but I like them, and maybe they can tell."

Finished with the mares, Dillon restocked his feed bucket and strolled to the other side. He'd told her he didn't have time to teach her, but he didn't mind talking about his horses, and she seemed avidly interested.

All the while he fed Henry, his gelding, and the two colts, Dillon could hear Domino snuffling and pawing and snorting at the far end. Caesar was subdued this morning, but Remus pranced in place in his stall, showing off for Kari and making her smile. "This one's almost trained. I've got a buyer in California waiting for him."

"He's certainly lively." Just then she heard an impatient whinny and glanced down the cement walk. The big stallion's ears were twitching. "What does that mean?" she asked Dillon. "Is he angry?"

"Probably, but not too much or his ears would be pointing back, and he'd be knocking around inside his stall." They started toward the stallion. "He's just not crazy about being penned up so long and in an unfamiliar place. Plus he's picked up the mares' scents."

"But they're not in heat yet, are they?"

"They don't have to be to make him restless." After refilling his bucket, he stopped by Domino's stall. "Hey, boy, let's calm down. You'll get your chance. All in good time."

The size of the animal and his restive movements kept Kari from moving too close as Dillon gave him fresh feed. "His stall's bigger, so he can move around a little?"

"Yeah, he gets the deluxe suite. Can't make them too roomy or he's liable to bang around and hurt himself." Dillon stroked a hand along Domino's mane, staying clear of his mouth and teeth. He didn't know the horse well yet and wasn't taking a chance on getting bitten out of frustration.

The side door opened with a whoosh of cold air and two men shoved in, stomping snow from their boots. Kari saw that one was the stooped older ranch hand Dillon had told her was named Mac, the one she'd seen yesterday. The other one was tall and lean, his skin leathery, somewhere in his mid-thirties.

"'Lo," Mac muttered as he unbuttoned his jacket, his small eyes flicking from Dillon to the blond woman he'd seen in the window. Taking out a red kerchief, he honked his nose into it. "Catching a damn cold," he complained.

Dillon casually introduced Kari to both of them, then gave the men his instructions. "Mac, I'd like you to stay inside here and clean out the stalls, pass out fresh water. I checked Calypso and I don't think she's got long to go. I'd appreciate your opinion.'' The old hand had been around long enough to be able to call a birthing almost from across the room, having attended hundreds.

With a wordless nod, Mac went to the sink.

Turning, Dillon noticed that Rich had taken off his hat and was running his hand through his sandy hair, his dark eyes lingering on Kari.

''Are you staying long?'' Rich asked her.

''No, not very,'' she answered, not liking his bold gaze roaming up and down her. Moving to the mares' side of the barn, she started walking back.

Dillon's eyes narrowed as he waited for Rich to look at him. Silently he studied his part-time employee. He hoped the cow hand wouldn't make trouble.

Rich was the first to speak. ''Nice package,'' he said nodding in Kari's direction, his smile revealing small white teeth.

Dillon stepped closer, lowering his voice but keeping in that steely edge. ''She's off-limits, Rich.''

The smile switched gears, turned friendly, conciliatory. ''I gotcha. She's yours. What do you want me to do?''

Dillon decided to let it go, for now. ''Use the tractor and make a path to the paddock, clear out the heavier snow. The horses need exercise, so let the stallion and Henry out first, then the colts. The mares can go later.'' He leaned down to put away the feed bucket. ''Before you leave, plow the walks and driveway. I think the snow's stopped for now.''

''Right.'' Replacing his tan hat, Rich couldn't resist a glance in Kari's direction before heading for the garage.

Dillon stood staring after him for long minutes, unaware that Mac had come up behind him.

"Rich's okay, long as there's no women around. Thought you knew that." Mac reached for his chewing tobacco.

Dillon had never had a woman to the ranch in the year Rich had worked for him to test that rumor. The man would bear watching. "Let me know if you see him step out of line, okay, Mac?"

"Yup." Mac walked off in his limping gait.

Dillon found Kari by Calypso's stall, talking gently to the very pregnant mare. "You ready to go back to the cabin?"

Turning to him, she sighed. "This is quite a place." She gazed up at the loft with its haystacks, the ladder leading up, then toward the tack room that Dillon had shown her on the way in with its oddly appealing leather smells. "I had no idea there was so much to raising horses." She looked at him with new respect. "How'd you learn all this and still make it through law school?"

"I spent every vacation and every summer here with my uncle for as far back as I can remember." He inhaled the familiar scents that he'd loved as man and boy. "It's all I've ever wanted to do."

She wasn't ready to go back. "Can't we stay out awhile longer? Why don't we play for a while? All work and no play makes Dillon a dull boy. Let's build a snowman. Come on, bend a little."

Not with Rich out there on the tractor, his greedy eyes following Kari. A protective instinct he didn't know he possessed had Dillon shaking his head. "Not until the men finish. Maybe this afternoon, okay?" What was he agreeing to? He hadn't built a snowman since he was ten years old.

She smiled up at him. It was better than an outright

refusal. "Thanks for introducing me to your horses. I enjoyed it."

Dillon found himself smiling back and wondering when pleasing her had become such a pleasure.

Norma had the habit of wringing her hands and would have done so now if she weren't clutching the phone in a steely grip, listening to Senator James Sinclair on the other end.

"All I want to know, Norma, is how this could have happened. How my daughter, being watched by you *and* two Secret Service men, could disappear without a trace?" Sinclair took in several deep breaths, mindful that his blood pressure was probably going through the roof.

"I don't know, sir," Norma said, her voice nearly a sob. Lowering herself to the wing chair in Kari's suite which the overwrought assistant had scarcely left since that fateful morning, she braced herself for her employer's next tirade. He'd called every few hours for two days now, clear up until midnight last night, wanting news on his daughter. Norma had nothing new to report.

"You're sure she hasn't called again since that one phone conversation you had with her that morning?" He'd had the phone company run a check, but he'd been told it was nearly impossible to run a trace through a switchboard unless they were told in advance.

"Yes, sir. I mean, no, she hasn't phoned again." Why had Kari pulled this stunt—to make Norma's life miserable? Why did a beautiful young woman like Kari Sinclair need time to get away and think, when she had the best life on the planet? Had she cracked under the strain of campaigning, which she hated doing?

James deliberately loosened his grip on the phone, forcing himself to relax. "I've got a tracer on that line,

Norma. If she calls again, keep her talking as long as possible. And patch her through to my cell phone. I'll have it with me day and night. Do you understand?''

"Yes, sir. I will, sir. Thank you, sir.''

"And stop saying *sir!*'' James slammed the receiver down and reached for the crystal decanter on the table, splashing water into a glass. Slowly, he drank, trying to calm his racing heart.

"You're doing it again, darling,'' Dusty Sinclair said, entering their suite, trailing the scent of Joy as she walked. "You're getting yourself all worked up.'' She took his arm, walked him over to the bed. "Lie down, dear. You're going to make yourself ill.'' As he lay back, she tugged off his shoes.

"Aren't you concerned, Dusty? Kari could have been abducted, could have been forced to make that ridiculous phone call to that inept assistant.''

Looking down at her husband of thirty years, she smiled indulgently. "Of course I'm concerned. But I think it's highly unlikely that a kidnapper's going to wait three days before contacting us. Besides, I believe Kari's message. I've seen the signs of restlessness in her for months. And you know how she hates to travel the circuit, yet you insisted she set out.''

He raised his white head. "So this is *my* fault?''

Exasperated, she shook her head. "It's no one's fault. Whether you admit it or not, James, your youngest daughter is *not* going to follow in your footsteps, is not interested in the political life nor in any of the handsome politicians and charming men you've introduced to her. Why can't you let her do her own thing?'' Patting her short, auburn hair, she reached 'for her leather bag to search for a nail file.

"You sound like some women's magazine article," he grumbled. But in a moment he touched her sleeve. "You really think she's all right, just rebelling again, like she did that time in college when she spent spring break with that banjo player?"

"Guitarist. And yes, I do think she's rebelling." Finished with her nail repair, she met his worried eyes. "If you put too many restrictions on someone, they eventually mutiny. You know that, and yet you do it regularly."

James frowned uneasily, wondering if she were right. "But Dana never rebels."

Dusty's robust laugh rang out. "Dana's whole life is a series of rebellions, and she's enjoying herself immensely. When was the last time you saw Kari laughing and having a good time?"

His frown deepened. "A good time? There's more to life than a good time."

"You say that because to you a good time is work." She leaned down to him, her manicured nails trailing along his silk tie. "And when Kari does call, you'd better not storm at her, or Lord only knows when she'll come back to us."

His mouth moved into a pout. "I *don't* storm."

She laughed again. "Yes, you do, and I love you anyhow." Stretching, she kissed him and prayed her assessment of their youngest daughter was right.

The thought of watching a movie in the daytime seemed almost sinful to Dillon. Yet here he was, thumbing through his large collection of videotapes because Kari had asked to see what he had on film.

"*Casablanca*. Ah, I see you have a romantic soul."

"I wouldn't say that," he protested. "Everyone likes

the classics and that certainly qualifies. Besides, I like Bogie.''

"Me, too. Have you got *The Big Sleep?*''

"I'm not sure." He turned to his other even taller stack, wondering how Mac and Rich were coming along. Normally he'd be out with them, shoveling, mucking stalls. But he'd worked alone yesterday and decided to let Rich earn his pay today. As for Mac, he pretty much worked every day, a proud man who needed to feel he was earning his keep. That being so and due to the weather, there wasn't much more he could do out there today.

He still felt like a kid playing hooky.

"Oh, here's *Laura.* I love that movie. Imagine falling in love with someone's portrait, then having them show up." Even her voice was dreamy.

"I sort of like old Waldo. He's got the best lines in the movie." Dillon picked up another old favorite. "How about this one, *To Have and Have Not?*''

Moving closer to look over his shoulder, Kari frowned. "I don't think I've seen that one."

"Sure you have. It's the one where Bogie teaches Bacall to kiss." He turned his head, realized he was almost nose to nose with her, and felt the heat move inside him.

She felt it, too, and drew back. "No, I'm sure I would have remembered that." Seated safely several feet away on the floor, she wrinkled her brow. "Is that where she says something like 'You know how to whistle, don't you? You put your lips together and blow.'?''

"No, that's when she teases him about whistling. Kissing is something else entirely."

"Close enough." She went back to checking out titles.

He scooted nearer, enjoying her more than any movie

she could choose. "Let me ask you then, would you rather I teach you to whistle or to kiss?"

She took her time turning to meet his amused gaze. "I don't believe I need lessons in either, thank you all the same."

"I see. Interesting." He flopped onto his back, raising his arms and placing his hands under his head, watching her. "Who taught you to whistle?"

"My sister. She could outwhistle most of the boys in grade school."

Rolling to his side, he bent his elbow and propped his head in one hand. "And who taught you to kiss?"

She smiled, remembering. "Billy Fisher in the fifth grade on the playground one recess tried to teach me. I thought it was all very wet and sloppy. He turned me off kissing for several years."

"A case of arrested development. Who coaxed you into trying again?"

She picked up a tape of the "X-Files," set it down. "I don't remember his name. I went to a friend's birthday party. All the boys had on dress pants and shirts with ties, the girls were in party clothes. Then there was this tall boy, someone's cousin. He had on jeans and a red-striped rugby shirt, and he had all this dark hair and green eyes. He caught me on the stairs. He was some kisser." Laughing at the memory, she turned to see him smiling at her. "All right, what about you?"

"I was fairly precocious. I'm pretty sure I reached over and kissed the little girl in the pink knit cap in the bassinette next to mine in the hospital." He gave her a cocky grin. "Kissing's fun. Wanna try?"

Looking down at his sky blue eyes and his full, smiling mouth, she most certainly did, which was exactly why she changed the subject. "I think we need to put on a movie.'' She reached to grab the closest one. ''Here's *Rear Window*. Hitchcock.'' Scrambling to her feet, she held it out to him.

With a regretful sigh, Dillon put on the movie.

Kari leaned over the bubbling pot and sipped from the wooden spoon. Not bad, if she did say so herself.

Chicken and dumplings was Dillon's favorite dish, he'd told her, so she'd decided to try making it. She'd found the recipe, the cut-up chicken pieces in freezer wrap and all the other ingredients in his cupboards and refrigerator. Who said that cooking was so difficult?

Setting out the ingredients for the dumplings she would drop in later, she thought about the hour and a half they'd spent watching the Hitchcock movie. Dillon had insisted on making popcorn, which had turned out to be lunch, along with the lemonade she'd made from a mix. They'd sat on the couch with the huge bowl between them and discussed the merits of *Rear Window,* which they'd both seen before. Kari was grateful there was nothing suggestive in the movie, since Dillon had a way of angling most everything around to the male-female thing.

It had started in the stables with all that talk of geldings and castration and Calypso's delivery, which she knew was natural and familiar talk on a ranch. But then he'd asked about her first kiss, and somehow that conversation had started her wondering what kissing Dillon would be like.

When she'd first arrived, she'd decided that in order to stay here, they'd have to keep things platonic. As wary as Dillon had been of her motives for being here at all, she hadn't thought that would be a problem. Until last night when he'd mentioned hitting on her.

Rinsing the wooden spoon in the sink, Kari noticed

that her hands were trembling. It was so rare for her to think about a man physically that the knowledge threw her off balance. Over the last couple of years, she'd seemed to shut that part of herself down, perhaps because she knew she didn't want to get involved with the men she met working for her father. They not only didn't turn her on, they'd utterly turned her off.

That had worried her vaguely, until the night she'd met Dillon Tracy.

Still, giving in to her curiosity would be a mistake. Two people stranded by a snowstorm on an isolated ranch, sharing a bathroom, eating together, mingling their clothes in the washer—the intimacy had already begun. But where would the next step take them?

As grateful as she was for this interlude, she knew that eventually she'd have to go back to the life she'd walked away from. Just as she knew that Dillon would stay on the ranch he loved. They were ill-matched and ill-suited, two opposites thrown together by fate.

But that didn't stop her from thinking, from wanting.

Squaring her shoulders, Kari mentally shook herself. She would enjoy the time she had left here, enjoy sparring with a rugged, attractive, intelligent man, and take pleasure in the fact that he seemed to want her, and let that be enough. They had separate lives, different goals. After all, adults couldn't always have what they wanted, not in the real world.

Reaching for the large thermos on the counter, she filled it with fresh hot coffee. She would take some out to Dillon in the barn where it was certainly colder than in the house. Then she'd come back in and read a book until it was time to make the dumplings.

And she'd stop mooning around like a besotted teenager.

* * *

Surprise evident on his face, Dillon stood in the hayloft looking down at her. "You brought me coffee?" he asked.

He looked like those ads for the Marlboro man, was Kari's first thought. Feeling suddenly shy, Kari nodded. "I thought you might need a break." Behind her, she heard one of the chestnuts, Dixie or Holly, snort loudly. Maybe she shouldn't have come. "If you don't want to stop..."

"Hey, no. I could sure use a cup." Turning, he backed down the ladder, then pulled off his leather gloves, shoving them in his back pockets. He'd gotten warm working with the hay and had removed his jacket.

Relieved he wasn't annoyed at her, Kari unscrewed the top of the thermos and poured coffee, then held it out to him. She watched him drink, his Adam's apple moving in his strong throat as he swallowed, the corners of his eyes crinkling as he kept his gaze on her. The warm leathery scents in the barn wrapped around her and she stepped back, suddenly feeling uncertain.

"This is really great," Dillon said, holding out his cup for a refill. He noticed that some powdery snow had blown into her hair on the way to the barn, making the golden strands sparkle. He could really get used to this, a coffee break with a beautiful woman. "So, did you find something you want to read?" He'd left her checking out the titles on his bookshelves.

"Not yet. I got started on dinner." She glanced toward the double doors. "I thought I might coax you out into the snow for a while. A little R and R. But maybe you're still busy."

In his mind's eye, he pictured making a snowman with her, maybe having a snowball fight, dropping snow down her collar, helping her out of her wet things in front of the fire and—Dillon cleared his throat. "I've got to finish up there." Taking a sip of coffee, he averted his eyes, sure she could read his thoughts.

"I understand." She'd promised to stay out of his way. She looked around for a place to set the thermos. "I'll just leave this here with you then and go build my own snowman." There was disappointment in her tone.

He took the thermos from her, aware of her regret. "Maybe if I finish in time, I'll join you."

"Fine." Turning, she saw Rich enter, stomping snow, followed by Zeus. There was no avoiding the man as she headed for the doors.

Taking in the thermos and Dillon draining his cup, Rich shoved back his hat and gave her a lazy smile. "Did you bring me some, too?"

There was an oiliness about him that made Kari nervous. "There's enough for two," she told him, then walked outside into the sunshine, not bothering to glance back.

Already the afternoon sun was beginning to melt the accumulated snow, causing slush in some spots. She circumvented the tractor Rich had used and bent to scoop up a mound of snow with her gloved hands. Strolling to the front of the cabin where a path had been cleared, she tossed the snowball at a tree and smiled when she hit her mark.

The jacket she wore was so warm she shoved off the hood as she bent to roll a mound of snow and shape it into a snowman's lower body. She'd seen kids building snow figures in the movies and on television, but as a native Phoenician, she'd never actually made one herself. Naturally, it never snowed in Phoenix, and the times she'd traveled to the high country in winter she'd been on speaking jaunts for her father. It wouldn't have met with his approval or Norma's if she'd have stopped to play.

But play she did now, finishing the two parts of the body, then rolling a smaller head. Fixing it in place, she cocked her head and studied her work in progress. She didn't want to track up the house by going inside to look for a hat and scarf, so she'd have to improvise.

A nearby tree devoid of leaves offered small bare branches. Kari snapped off several, formed a curved mouth on her figure's face, a pointed nose and triangular eyes. Not perfect, but certainly original. Finishing up by adding a couple of stones from the dormant flower bed as buttons, she smiled at her first snow creation.

Glancing at the barn, she saw that one door was ajar and that the tractor had been moved. Apparently Rich had finished his work for the day, but Dillon hadn't. Or maybe he had and was just avoiding her. She'd guessed from the start that he wasn't the type to frolic. Truth be known, she usually wasn't, either. But up here, away from her normal environment, she felt free to experiment, to do things she hadn't done before, to be free.

Dusting the snow from her gloves, Kari stood looking about, not yet ready to go inside. It wasn't even four in the afternoon and the long evening stretched before her. It would be dark in another hour or so, and by then Dillon would be finished and inside. Dinner they could manage nicely, but then what would they do to avoid being in too close contact? Another movie? A card game?

No, she'd better choose a book so she could be absorbed in that. Another cold evening spent in front of a hot fire with him close beside her and she wasn't sure if she could hang on to her nebulous control.

But first she'd take a walk. The wind had shifted the snow so that it wasn't very deep along the edge of the fir trees. Squinting through the glare of the sun on the snow, Kari thought she saw a couple of squirrels dashing up the bark of one bare tree. She'd never seen a squirrel up close. Stepping gingerly, she headed that way.

It was good exercise walking in foot-deep snow. The boots she'd found were at least two sizes larger than she needed, so she'd pulled on two pairs of thick socks to fill up the space. They were quite high, reaching to mid-calf. Marching along, she hoped to catch sight of the little furry creatures.

Later, Kari wasn't sure how long she'd been walking when it happened. She spotted the squirrel halfway out on a precarious branch and was creeping closer when she felt something sharp grab her ankle. "Oh!" she cried out.

The sound of steel hitting steel had her heart thumping as she went down unceremoniously in the snow. Pain shot through her ankle and up her leg as whatever it was she'd stepped on held fast. Angling to get a better look, Kari leaned forward. The sight of the steel jaws clenched around her foot and ankle were enough to make her blood run cold. Some sort of animal trap, probably.

Uneasily, she looked behind her. She was more than a city block away from the barn where she knew Dillon was still working. He'd never hear her cries for help. Carefully, she got up on one foot, bracing one hand against the tree. She noticed that the trap had been anchored to the ground with a metal peg that had gotten loose. Pulling on it with two hands, she managed to yank it all the way out. With some difficulty and no small amount of pain, she tried dragging the injured foot along with the viselike clamp. It moved, but not without cost.

There was nothing to do but hobble back toward the cabin. She was certain Dillon would not be pleased that she'd wandered off without his permission and gotten hurt as well. Gritting her teeth, Kari started limping.

Each step hurt more than the last. Had those claws broken through the leather boot plus two pairs of thick socks? Had it broken her skin? Lord, it was probably filthy and rusty sitting out there for God only knew how long. When had she had her last tetanus shot?

Inching along, grimacing at the slow progress, she was halfway there when she saw Dillon emerge from the barn and turn to lock the door. His mind occupied most likely, he didn't look around, but headed straight for the house. She would have to further humiliate herself and call him.

"Dillon!" she yelled, thinking her voice sounded hoarse and weak. "Help, please."

Mercifully he heard her and turned in her direction, just as Zeus came racing out of the barn. Staying where she was, Kari raised one arm and waved, but the effort sent her sprawling in the snow, the steel trap digging deeper into her flesh. Involuntarily she cried out in pain.

Following Zeus, Dillon started running.

Chapter Six

"**Y**ou're really lucky you had on those heavy old boots and double socks," Dillon said, placing the ice pack on her bruised and swollen ankle. She'd given him a scare when he'd seen her wave and then go down. She'd even given Zeus a scare. "This may not feel too good, but it'll help bring the swelling down."

Stretched out on the couch, Kari felt like a fool causing such a commotion. Her hand drifted to pet the big dog who hadn't left her side since Dillon had carried her in. Odd how an animal senses someone who needs help. "I'm sorry. I had no idea you'd have rabbit traps in among the trees." She winced as the cold seeped through to her already-chilled foot.

Dillon raised a brow. "Rabbits? Those steel teeth would slice a rabbit in half. The trap is for coyotes and even mountain lions." He saw her face turn pale and wished he hadn't told her.

"Mountain lions? I had no idea." She shuddered at the thought.

Gathering her foot onto his lap, he sat back. "That's why if I'd known you were going to go wandering, I'd have stopped you. We don't often see wild animals, but there's the occasional one. If it's been a long, cold winter and food's scarce, they get more daring."

"What do you do with them if you spot one?"

He waved a hand toward a rifle leaning up against the fireplace.

"Oh," Kari said. "You shoot them?"

"Well, what else? If a mountain lion leaps on one of my yearlings or, God forbid, a newborn foal, he'd have him clawed open in minutes. I've got to protect my small herd."

"Of course you do." She sighed, shaking off the mental image of a mountain lion ripping open a small horse. "Ranching can be pretty brutal. I never realized."

Dillon thought that maybe she was beginning to see that this was no dude ranch where fake cowboys sat around a campfire and sang nice little songs every evening. "It can be a tough life, but also a good one."

Kari squirmed as the icebag all but numbed her foot. "Could we take that off now? It's really freezing."

Dillon dropped the bag on the floor and drew her foot more comfortably into his lap, rubbing warmth back into her toes with both his big hands, taking care not to touch the injured area. Back and forth, up and around, down the sole.

Kari felt warmth spreading, and it wasn't anywhere near her ankle. There was something very intimate about a man holding her bare foot, touching, stroking, that had her pulse increasing. Just like when he'd run to her outside, picked her up as easily as if she'd been a child, steel trap and all, and held her against his big body as he carried her into the house. He'd been so careful freeing the trap, then easing the boot from her already-swelling foot before gently rolling the socks off her foot. He'd helped her off with her jacket, propped pillows behind her, even poured her a small glass of brandy which she hadn't touched.

Her own mother couldn't have been more tender. And he hadn't even scolded her for carelessly getting caught in a trap.

Fascinated at the way his hands moved over her skin, she watched as his fingers moved up her leg halfway to the knee, massaging the tense muscles. She could have lain like that for hours, warmed by the fire and by his magic hands.

"I should really change out of these damp jeans," she finally said. But she felt too comfy to move.

"I can bring you the sweatpants and go into the kitchen while you change, so you won't have to walk on this foot just yet. Want me to do that?"

"I can't let you wait on me. You've done enough, and I promised I wouldn't be a bother." She started to sit up, intending to hobble to her room and get changed, but a sharp pain had her grimacing.

"You're not a bother." Dillon stood, setting her foot down on the sofa, wondering just when he'd stopped thinking of her as exactly that. "The brandy might help." He left and was back in minutes, tossing her the sweats and holding up a hand-tooled cane with an ivory handle. "You might want to use this walking stick to help you get around for a day or so. It was my uncle's."

"Thanks." Kari took a swallow of brandy and felt heat race down her throat and pool in her stomach. But as she changed, she heard him clattering around the kitchen and remembered the dumplings. Standing up on one foot, she tied the drawstring and made her way over, using the cane.

"Why can't you stay put?"

"It's time to add the dumplings." Picking up the wooden spoon, she hoped nothing had burned while she'd been outdoors. Stirring, she saw that things were at the almost-done stage.

Dillon had checked the pot himself and realized that she'd made the very dish he'd told her yesterday was his favorite. He couldn't remember the last time anyone had tried to please him with that kind of effort. "I can add the dumplings."

Standing on one leg, braced against the counter, Kari dropped the measured flour into the bowl. "You told me you hate to cook."

How is it she remembered every word he said? "I hate to 'not eat' more." He waved her and her cane to the kitchen chair. "Sit. Just tell me what to do and I'll do it."

Kari couldn't recall ever being coddled quite so thoroughly. Her father was definitely a no-nonsense man who had little use for self-indulgence. Even her mother used to say that if you get up and get moving, no matter how sick you are, you'll feel better. Both Kari and Dana had had perfect attendance in school because of their parents' attitude. And here this man was, being sweet and considerate, all over a slightly bruised foot.

She wasn't going to argue, though. Being spoiled was too pleasant a feeling to chastise him for.

Kari waited until he brought her the cookbook, then she read the directions aloud to him, watching with amusement as he carefully dropped gooey spoonfuls on top of the bubbling chicken and vegetables in the big pot.

Next he cut them each a wedge of lettuce, put out the leftover rolls and, in no time, they were eating. Mostly eating in silence, since Dillon seemed famished.

Finally he slowed down long enough to comment. "I thought you said you couldn't cook. This is wonderful." He debated about taking a third helping, then threw caution to the winds and scooped up another serving. Wrestling with large mounds of hay had made him extra hungry. Kari, on the other hand, was still working on her first helping. "Don't you like it?"

"Mmm, I do. I'm just not a big eater." She never should have had that brandy on an empty stomach. She felt so lethargic. She glanced at Zeus, waiting patiently for his dinner, and wished she could hand him the rest on her plate.

Dillon dipped a piece of roll in the last of the gravy as he noticed her yawn expansively. The fresh air, the scare, then the warm fire and brandy, now a heavy dinner—they'd all caught up with her. Shoving back from the table, he stood. "Come on, you're beat. Let me help you to your room."

Kari could hardly dispute his assessment. "I'm sorry to be such lousy company. I don't know why I'm so sleepy." She glanced at the stove, the sink. "I have to do the dishes. It's my turn."

"I'm on cleanup duty tonight." Bending, he scooped her into his arms and felt her tense up.

"What are you doing? I've got the cane."

He knew that; he'd gotten it for her. But she looked small and vulnerable, and he badly wanted to hold her close again. He decided not to question his motives, at least not right now. "Humor me," he said, and felt her relax, finally slipping one arm around his neck. Carrying her, inhaling that indefinable feminine scent, he wished he were really taking her to bed. To *his* bed.

"Stay," he told Zeus as the dog trotted alongside them. "I think you've got a new friend," he told Kari.

In her room he set her gently on her feet at bedside, then snapped on the table lamp. "Anything else I can do for you?"

"Thanks, but I can take it from here." She looked at his face in the soft light. It seemed he was reluctant to leave her, something she'd sensed earlier. Which was another reason she'd opted to turn in right after dinner. Sitting together cozily on his big couch in the firelight, stretched out with her foot on his lap, was a scene she was sure she couldn't handle tonight.

"I'll say good-night then. If you need anything, just yell." Dillon left her bedroom door slightly ajar.

In the kitchen he rolled up his sleeves and went to work on the dishes, his thoughts scattered. There was no denying his attraction to Kari Smith, or whatever her name really was. The feeling might be mutual; he'd caught her studying him and he wondered what she was thinking.

Was she wondering, like he was, about how the two of them had wound up together here in this time and place? Was she already getting homesick, or did the slower pace of ranch life hold a lot of appeal? Was she attracted to him as a man, or as some experiment, someone vastly different from the three-piece-suit types she undoubtedly spent time with? Did her rebellious interlude include a seduction scene playing out in her head, ready to set into motion?

Dillon blinked, annoyed with his mind's meanderings. Why couldn't he be like other men and be content to have a beautiful woman drop in his lap unexpectedly, to just enjoy her while she was with him, then forget her when she left? Why couldn't he trust her motives as easily as others would? Perhaps because he'd been lied to once too often.

A soft growl at ground level reminded him that he hadn't fed Zeus. He got the dog's food dish, added dry meal, then scraped the remaining chicken and dumplings on top before carrying his dinner into the laundry room. "Special treat tonight, boy." Zeus eagerly bent to his dish.

It was as he was walking back to the kitchen that he heard the crash, followed by a very female cry coming from the direction of the spare room. He raced over, pushed open the door and saw Kari sprawled on the bed, her hands wrestling with the shade from the small window alongside her bed. "What happened?" he asked, moving over to help her.

"The moon was shining in, so I decided to stand up and pull down the shade. Only it was stuck, so I tugged really hard and down it came, right on top of me." And she nearly twisted her sore ankle again, she thought, feeling foolish for the second time tonight.

Toeing off the fur-lined moccasins he wore around the house, Dillon stepped onto the bed and rolled up the shade. The soft bed underfoot made his reach a little wobbly, but he managed to hook one side in. But just as he was about to push in the other end, Kari moved, rocking the bed. Dillon lost his footing and dropped down onto the bed, narrowly missed landing on her, while the shade unrolled and went flying every which way, ending up on top of him.

Trying to get out from under the stubborn shade, Dillon glanced over and saw Kari's head bent down. "Are you hurt?"

She wasn't hurt, she was laughing as she looked up at him. "I've never seen anyone wear a window shade before." More giggles erupted as she grabbed one end to help disentangle him.

But as she did, the other end flipped and bopped him in the head. It wasn't hard and it didn't hurt. The absurdity of the situation had Dillon laughing, too. Finally he yanked the shade aside and saw the big rip. "I don't think this is going to do you any good tonight," he commented, tossing it aside.

Still smiling, Kari had to agree. "That's all right. I think the moon's drifted behind a cloud anyhow." Brushing back her hair, she met his eyes, saw they were dancing with good humor. She greatly appreciated a man who could laugh at himself. "You know, Mr. Tracy, I think I like you."

She was lying with her head at the foot of the bed, more or less where she'd ducked when he'd come crashing down with the shade, her hair spread out in an appealing tangle. She had on one of Aunt Edith's long T-shirts which, on her shorter frame, came almost to her knees. And she looked like every man's dream as she gazed up at him, her eyes sparkling.

"So you like me, eh?" Dillon shifted so he was leaning down to her. "How much?" he asked, and saw the smile slide from her, replaced by a sudden awareness that had his heart thudding. Silently she studied him as he moved fractionally closer. "This much?" he asked, and lightly kissed her chin.

Still, she just watched. "Or this much?" he asked again, kissing her forehead ever so gently. Her eyes widened, but she didn't speak. "Or perhaps this much?" he questioned, kissing first one cheek, then the other, trailing closer to her mouth.

Without her permission, Kari's hand rose and stroked along his cheek, caressing the stubble that seemed to charm her so. "I'm not good at playing games, Dillon. This sort of thing confuses me."

He placed his own hand over hers, drew it down to rest on the coverlet. "This sort of thing is a simple friendship between a man and a woman, that's all." That wasn't so and he knew it. From the first, friendship hadn't been on his mind, and it wasn't now.

She searched his eyes. "I don't think so. Our friendship isn't simple, and neither are you."

He should have guessed she'd see through his cavalier answer. "What are you afraid of, Kari? Me?"

She wasn't sure what he meant, but fear wasn't what she felt. "I've only known you three days."

Maybe three days was all it took for some people, Dillon thought. Certainly he was looking at Kari far differently now than when she'd first walked into his life. Then his only thoughts had been on how quickly he could get rid of her. Well, the snow had stopped and the roads were undoubtedly plowed by now. Still, he hadn't mentioned her leaving.

Because he wanted her—right here with him—but he didn't think it wise to mention that just now.

Giving her plenty of time to move away, he slowly lowered his head until his mouth was barely an inch from hers. Resuming the game he'd invented, he went on. "Just how much do you really like me, Kari?" He watched her eyes change again, darken. His lips barely grazed hers, gentle friction, slow movement, scarcely tasting. Then he raised his head.

Her eyes hazy with the first stirring of passion, Kari felt a delicious warmth spread. "I think I like you more than that," she whispered, and slipped both arms around his neck, drawing him nearer, opening to him. She felt his hands slip beneath her as his mouth came alive, his wild flavors exploding on her tongue. A gasp escaped from her as he deepened the kiss, taking her with the speed of light to places she'd never been.

Unleashed, his need flowed into her as the world slipped slightly out of focus. Her own needs, too long denied, swam to the surface as she held on. When his tongue slipped in to tangle with hers, she felt the room tilt.

Hadn't she sensed from the start that this man could awaken every dormant desire within her? Yet even so, she hadn't expected this swift freefall into passion as his hungry mouth devoured, his clever hands explored and his thundering heart pounded against hers.

Dillon felt her shudder with pleasure as he shifted his lips to flutter kisses along her satiny throat, then traveled up to breathe in her ear before returning to her wildly responsive mouth. She held nothing back, giving to him freely, as if she'd found something she'd been seeking all her life.

As he had. Here was honest reaction, unadulterated need, unbridled desire. When he pulled back from her and saw her lips tremble, it was almost his undoing.

Letting his breathing settle, he thrust shaky fingers through his hair as he straightened. "I...I didn't intend to do that when I came in here."

Her eyes were huge and luminous in the soft light. "Didn't you?"

"No, I—" Wasn't he the one who hated liars? "All right, maybe I had thought about what it would be like, once or twice."

Kari ran her tongue over her lips, tasted him. "I'm going to get really mad if you apologize for kissing me."

He almost smiled. The cuddly warmth of her reached out to him, as did her bed-mussed hair and fragrant female scent. How did she always manage to smell so good when he knew she didn't have cologne or bath powder with her? "How can I apologize for something I want to do again?"

Her small hands bunched in his shirt as she pulled him back to her. This kiss was slow, tender, leaving them breathless and wanting more.

"I don't know about whistling," Dillon finally managed, "but I do know one thing—you sure don't need kissing lessons." He eased from the bed, because what he badly wanted to do was crawl into his aunt's feather bed and make love to Kari until neither of them could move. "I'll let you get some rest." He waited until she shifted and crawled under the covers, then turned off the lamp and left, quietly closing the door behind him.

Kari lay awake, staring in the dark. Maybe Dillon was right. Maybe she was afraid. Of herself.

Something woke her, some sound from the big room. A glance around told her it was still night, still dark out. Curious, she shoved off the covers and stood, testing her foot. It hardly hurt at all. She walked out, pushing back her hair.

Fully dressed, Dillon was seated on a kitchen chair, pulling on his boots. Surprised, he looked up. "Go back to bed. It's only three."

"Where are you going?" Still wearing the socks she'd pulled on last night, she padded over to him.

"Calypso's dropped, ready to foal. I heard her on the monitor." He stood, reached for his sheepskin jacket.

"Oh, can I watch?" Catching his frown, she hurried on. "Please? I promise to stay out of the way."

He glanced down. "What about your foot?"

"It's better, really." To prove it, she took several steps without flinching. "I've never seen a birthing. Please, Dillon?"

What was it about this one woman that he found so difficult to refuse her anything? "All right, but hurry and get ready. Calypso needs me."

She hurried, pulling jeans on over the nightshirt, speedily tugging on boots, jacket and hat. Grabbing her gloves, she followed Dillon out into the silent night. Though it was cold, there wasn't that biting edge to the wind, and the sky was clear of clouds, a full moon lighting their way.

"I've read that pregnant women deliver more readily in the full of the moon," Kari said, aware of his impatience to get to his mare and trying very hard not to slow him down on the short walk to the barn.

"It's true for animals, too. The moon has a lot to do with cycles. I don't think even medical experts or scientists know exactly why."

"I hope we're in time." She'd caught his excitement.

"I'm sure we are. It's her first and just like with humans, the first rarely comes quickly." Dillon unlocked the big door, let her precede him, then closed it. Moving toward Calypso's stall, he shrugged out of his jacket, tossing it aside, then rolled up his shirtsleeves.

He'd been out to check on the mare several times after Kari had gone to bed, feeling as restless as Calypso. He'd finished in the kitchen, then sprawled out on the couch drinking coffee and staring into the fire. Thinking. Remembering.

Recalling the feel of her arms around him, the heady taste of her, the special scent of her. Reliving the kisses, the way she'd felt against him, her heart beating in time to his. Sleep hadn't come for a long while.

He'd barely gotten to bed, it seemed, and Calypso's sounds of distress had awakened him. Now, he opened her stall door.

The lighting throughout the stables was kept on dim at night, but now Dillon switched on a lamp over the mare's stall only. He ignored the snuffling of the horses nearby and bent to where Calypso lay on a thick bed of straw that he'd spread for her earlier. Her dark, expressive eyes shot to his, then shifted to take in Kari, hovering by the gate.

"It's okay, girl. I'm here," Dillon reassured her. "You can watch from there," he told Kari. "Too many people make a mare nervous."

Though she itched to help out, Kari stayed where he'd directed her. She saw Dillon slip on rubber gloves, then squat to examine the trembling horse, talking softly, reassuringly. She hadn't been aware of the sound before, but now she heard low music and wondered if that was on deliberately to soothe the animals.

"Won't be long now," Dillon spoke aloud. "She's fully dilated."

As Kari watched, the mare's huge belly heaved mightily as a contraction took her. Calypso's head shifted as she grunted. "Do you give her something for the pain?"

Dillon shook his head. "Not unless it looks as if there'll be problems. Pain medication makes a mare sluggish and unable to push. Plus it'll affect the foal. Nature can handle most births without medical assistance." He stepped back out of the way, aware that Calypso's water could break anytime. Getting a cloth, he wiped her sweaty body down, cooling her.

Kari saw the mare's eyes go wild as she shoved her

way through another contraction, watched her thrash her big head on the straw bedding. She couldn't stand it another minute. Slipping off her jacket, she entered the stall.

"What are you doing? I told you to stay…"

"I'm going to her head, to help her through this, woman to woman." Sitting down in the clean hay, Kari wiggled into position slowly so as not to startle the edgy mare. "You take care of your end, and I'll handle mine."

"You don't know what you're getting into. This is going to be very messy." The little rich girl with the manicured hands had no idea what to expect, he was certain.

"Life's messy, Dillon. I'm no hothouse flower." She turned back to stroke the mare's face. "You're doing just fine, sweetie."

Sweetie? "What is this, female bonding?"

"Males aren't the only ones who bond, you know." Kari was finding herself more than a little moved. She'd never seen a human birth, either, and had new respect when she thought of her mother going through this same thing. "This whole process is awe-inspiring. It's hard to imagine your mother suffering like this to bring you into the world, isn't it?" Her eyes on the mare, Kari didn't notice the way Dillon tensed. "For this alone, we owe them."

Dillon unclenched his hands, forcing himself to relax so Calypso wouldn't pick up on his tension. "Not all mothers are owed a huge debt of gratitude. Giving birth is only a tiny part of the mothering process, one any animal can do, as you can see. There's a hell of a lot more to it."

"Of course there is." Her hands stroked, but her eyes were on Dillon. Something with his mother had caused a deep bitterness in him. Kari wondered if he'd bring it out. Maybe if she skirted the issue, moved in from the back door. "There's a whole lot more to fathering than being there at conception, too, but some men walk away from further obligation to the child they've created." Her college roommate had never gotten over her father taking off.

Dillon gentled his touch as he wiped the mare's bulging side. "I don't know why, but somehow it seems worse when a mother walks away from a child than when a father does." Or was he letting his personal experience color his viewpoint?

"Is that what happened to you?" she asked softly.

Only the hum of the generator and the snuffling sound of the animals could be heard as the question hung in the charged air. Kari wondered if she'd overstepped her boundaries.

Dillon's jaw clenched hard as he ground his teeth. "It would have been far better if she'd walked away right after my brother and I were born. As it is, she put us through ten years of hell before the booze killed her."

Kari hardly knew what to say. She had friends whose parents drank a great deal and had known a few people in college who were drawn to excesses. But never one who'd died from it. "I'm so sorry, Dillon."

He guided Calypso through another contraction, then shrugged. "It was a long time ago."

He wasn't fooling her by pretending it didn't matter. Ten years. He'd been a child and he'd seen too much. "She must have been very unhappy to drink herself to death."

Dillon made a sound, like a bitter grunt. "That's not how it happened, though it probably would have in time. She used to leave Terry and me and go barhopping. Dad would be working in the grocery store he still owns, and we'd have to phone and tell him we were alone again. He'd come get us, and we'd play in the back room until closing time. As we got older, we'd help out, stocking shelves, filling phone-in orders. Finally, he'd lock up, take us home, make us dinner, put us to bed.''

Kari's heart went out to the two little boys, though she kept her features even, sure he'd hate knowing she felt sad for the child he'd been.

Dillon stroked the mare's flank, but his stormy eyes were seeing another scene. "She always came home, staggering, smelling terrible, sometimes falling-down drunk. Until one night.''

"She walked away and never came back?"

"No. She got hit by a car walking home along the side of the road. Prescott's a small town, even smaller then. Everyone knew that Mary Tracy was a drunk, that Dad kept the family going. You should have seen her funeral. Everyone came who'd ever spoken to Dad or stepped in his store. They came not for her, but for him.''

"Perhaps it's small consolation, but at least you have a strong and loving father. Some don't even have one parent who cares." She'd visited abused and abandoned children at several shelters in Phoenix. The sights she'd seen had truly opened her eyes.

Dillon drew in a deep breath. "Yeah, I know. That's why I hate disappointing Dad by not sticking with the law the way he wanted.''

"It seems from what you've said that he loves you a great deal. He wants you to be financially secure, maybe because he had to struggle. When he sees how you love this ranch, he's bound to come around." At least, she hoped so, like she hoped her father would understand that she needed to step away from working with him, to live her life as she saw fit. "Parents usually want what's best for their children. They just go about it the wrong way at times.''

Dillon wasn't a man who talked about his life, past or present, easily. Perhaps he'd confided in her because he'd guessed she would understand, since she seemed to be having similar problems with her own father. Or perhaps it was that their relationship had shifted to a new level after sharing those soul-shattering kisses. Or maybe it was the emotionally charged atmosphere of impending birth that had him in a revealing mood. Whatever, he didn't regret speaking up.

She was easy to talk with, easy to be with. Maybe too much so.

Just then, the amniotic sac broke, signaling the birthing was underway. Dillon shook himself free of his tangled memories and knelt into position. ''Hold tight,'' he told Kari. ''Let her know you're there, but don't let her move too much.''

Startled back to reality, Kari did as he said, her heart thumping almost as wildly as the mare's. ''Poor thing, she's exhausted.'' Would she go through this one day? she wondered. Would she be a participant in bringing a new life into the world? She'd always wanted children, and watching the process up close hadn't changed her mind. She was certain that she, along with millions of other females, would know the pain was worth the wondrous results.

Bending to the mare, Dillon saw that the foal was in diving position, head tucked low between front feet. Calypso gave another mighty push as Dillon made sure the legs weren't twisted. ''This is the touchy part,'' he explained in a low voice, feeling that Kari wanted to know. ''The foal's hooves are razor sharp and so they've got this waxy protection on them in the womb. But sometimes an active foal can wear that wax off, and if it isn't in correct position or if it's too large for the mother to handle easily, those hooves can tear her uterus or even do more extensive damage. That's why I like to be there when the legs start out.''

"Have you ever had that happen?''

"Only once, one summer when I was helping my uncle with a birthing. The mare wound up so badly cut that we had to put her down." He reached inside the birth canal to help the foal along, guiding, assisting. "Come on, girl," he coaxed the mare. "Another good push should do it."

But Kari was thinking of the poor damaged mare. "You couldn't save a damaged mare like that, let her heal naturally?"

"No, she was too far gone, lost too much blood."

Rising to her knees, Kari saw the front feet slipping forward, then the shoulders cleared. She wasn't even aware of the tears dampening her cheeks as she watched a small miracle in motion. Dillon was cleaning the wet foal, waiting, then easing back as the rest of him slid out. In seconds, she saw the birth sac drop away and the new-born struggled to his feet.

"Look at him, Calypso. You've got a son." Dillon's voice was clogged with emotion, with excitement. A birth never failed to move him, but this one more than usual. Was it because of the way Kari's damp eyes gazed into his across mother and son?

The colt's spindly legs wouldn't hold him upright on first try, so he gave up for the moment and sank back down near his mother's head. While Dillon tied off the ends of the umbilical cord and put iodine on immediately, Calypso sniffed at her new son, getting acquainted.

"He's got two white streaks, one on each front foot,

like socks,'' Kari commented, still enthralled. She watched the two horses as Dillon took care of the after-birth.

When he returned, she was outside the stall, watching as Calypso stood proudly while her son nursed. The hungry sound of suckling seemed loud in the quiet barn. Wiping his hands on a towel, he saw that Kari's eyes were still shiny. "Some production, eh?"

She turned her glowing face to him. "It was wonderful. I can't thank you enough for letting me be here."

"You were more than just here. You were part of things." Flipping the towel onto the stall, he stepped over and took her into his arms, giving her a swift, hard hug. "We did it together."

"I think Calypso deserves some credit," she said with a chuckle, but when he pulled back and looked into her face, she forgot the mare, the colt, the barn, her own name. His eyes were hot, hungry, needy. She felt that same surging need swell inside her, stronger than before in her room.

Dillon's feelings whirled and swam, churning, heating his blood. He crushed her mouth with his, wrapped himself around her and took. Took from her in the most elemental way, her sweetness, her beauty, her heat.

And she clung to him in a way he'd been dreaming of, her arms circling his neck, her mouth as eager as his, her body perfectly aligned with his, making him crazy. She'd discarded her jacket earlier and wore only the nightshirt and jeans. His hands moved between them with sensual purpose, finding her breasts swelling to his touch, fanning the flame.

He wanted nothing more than to carry her up to the loft where sweet-smelling, clean hay was spread about, and to lay her down there, to feast on her, to love her.

But his clothes were damp and stained from the birthing, and he still needed to clean out Calypso's stall, for soon she and her colt would want to sleep.

He needed to let Kari go, and he would, in just another moment. His hands kneaded and caressed warm, willing flesh as her knees buckled. When she sighed into his mouth, he knew he had to stop now or he never would. Breathing hard, he eased back, still holding her, resting his forehead against hers.

Dazed, shaky with an overwhelming desire, Kari gasped for air. "You...you make me forget everything, everyone." Her whole body trembled as she inched back, denying herself the release she craved almost more than the air she drew in, in deep, greedy gulps.

"Another time, another place," he whispered. "I need to see to Calypso and the colt."

She took a staggering step backward. "I know." And what would she have done if there'd been no urgency to see to his mare? Would she have taken that tumble in the hay with him? Kari thought she knew the answer, and it stunned her.

Dillon helped her into her jacket. "Go inside, go back to bed. The fun part's over and the foal's here." At the barn door he whistled for Zeus, and in seconds the big dog came galloping up. "Go with her, Zeus," he commanded.

"I'll be all right." Oddly, she wasn't afraid of the night, not out here in the country. Then she remembered the mountain lions and coyotes, and decided walking with the German shepherd was a good idea.

He squeezed her hand, watched her go, looking back once over her shoulder, her silken hair shifting in a night breeze. He stood there until he saw them both go inside, the door close. Trying for control, he pulled a long breath. The last thing he wanted to do was clean that stall tonight. But he knew he had to.

Slowly, tugging on his leather gloves, Dillon walked back and went to work.

Chapter Seven

"Norma, is that you?" Kari said into the phone.

"Kari? Of course it's me. Where are you?" Intense days of constant concern, for Kari's safety and for her own job security, made Norma's voice almost shrill.

"I called the office and they told me you were still in the Bonaventure suite. Why?" Kari was truly puzzled. She'd been gone four days.

"Because your father thought you'd call here again and that's exactly what you're doing." Norma struggled to keep the whine from her voice, but it still sounded pleading. "Won't you please come back, Kari? Everyone's worried sick."

"Well, they shouldn't be. I told you I'm fine." She paused a moment, picturing James Sinclair during a crisis. It wasn't a lovely scene. "How's Dad taking this?"

"About like you'd imagine. Not good. He wants me

to patch you through to his cell phone no matter when you call. All right?''

''Go ahead.'' She'd guessed that her father would want exactly that, and braced herself as she sat down at the kitchen table and waited. Dillon was in the paddock exercising the horses. It was a beautiful day, cold but filled with sunshine that was rapidly melting the snow.

Kari had checked on Calypso and her new colt twice already this morning. And, since she was already there, she'd strolled by and visited the other horses, as well, passing out apples and carrots the way Dillon had shown her. She was especially drawn to Rainbow, the gentle Appaloosa whose ears perked up the moment she heard Kari's voice. She'd never considered the fact that horses had their own personalities. Which was just one reason she steered clear of Domino. The huge stallion, always huffing and blowing, pawing the floor of his stall, frightened her.

''Kari, are you there?'' Her father's voice tugged her attention back to her call.

''Yes, Dad, I'm here. How are you?'' She could picture his impatient frown, the way he paced when he talked on the phone, stabbing the air with his Mont Blanc pen to make his point.

''Never mind how I am. How are you? Is anyone with you? Tell me, did someone abduct you and is keeping you against your will?''

She almost smiled at the high drama. ''No, nothing like that. I'm fine, really I am.''

''Well then, what in hell's gotten into you, Kari? Why'd you run off like that, scaring your mother half to death?'' James always used his wife to bring his girls up short, knowing they hated worrying her more than him.

Kari wasn't buying his bluff. ''Dad, I need you to listen to me, *really listen.* I needed some time away, to think things through. And…"

"Why can't you think here at home where I know you're safe?"

"Let me finish. At home there're too many distractions." And her father was the main one. "I'm always being dragged off to some luncheon or meeting or trip. I've been doing a lot of soul-searching and that's not the life I want, Dad."

There was the briefest pause as James tried to think how best to answer her. "All right, then, you come back and we'll talk things over and you can tell me exactly what it is you do want."

Kari ran her hand idly over Zeus's thick coat as the dog gazed up at her. Ever since the trap incident, he'd stuck close by her. "I'm not ready to come back just yet," she finally answered, and waited for the explosion.

James Sinclair was never one to disappoint. "Damn it, Kari, I've had enough of this. I'm fending off the press everywhere I go, trying to explain away your absence. Your mother and sister have to do double duty to take over your schedule. And I can't concentrate on work because I'm worrying about you."

In contrast, Kari's voice was soft and low. "See, Dad. That's just what I mean. You're used to running the show and the lives of everyone around you. I can't let you do that anymore. I'm not coming back until I'm ready, and you'll just have to live with that."

A shrill whistle from outside caught Zeus's attention. He gave a short bark and rushed to the door, wanting out.

"Is that a dog I hear?" James asked. "Where are they keeping you?"

It was as if he hadn't heard word one she'd uttered. "Give my best to Mom and Dana. I promise you, Pinocchio's fine. I'll call again.'' Quickly, before he could persuade her otherwise, Kari hung up.

In his Washington office, James scowled at the dead phone in his hand. He turned toward his aide. ''Well?''

''Sorry, Senator, she didn't stay on the line long enough to trace.''

''Damn,'' James muttered before storming out of the room.

Kari left the barn with a smile on her face. The young foal had pranced about, showing off for her, then nuzzled her neck and fallen asleep with his head in her lap. She'd stayed awhile, listening to Dillon's terse commands to Remus and Caesar as he worked the two colts out back. Sitting on a bed of straw, Calypso lazily watching her with her son, Kari had felt at peace. After a while, she'd gotten up and walked out into the sunshine.

On her way to the house she intercepted Mac heading for his old truck, carrying a bundle inside a pillow case. ''Lovely day, isn't it?''

''Yup,'' the man of few words said.

''Are you going into town?'' She didn't really care, just wanted to make conversation.

''Yup. Goin' to the laundromat.'' Mac shifted his tobacco plug to the other side of his mouth.

Kari looked at the overstuffed pillow case, then back at the old man's grizzled face. ''You don't have to do that. I'm doing laundry right now. I'll be glad to add your things to our load.''

Stopping, he eyed her from beneath the brim of his brown hat. ''Can't have you doin' that. Wouldn't be right.''

She dismissed his refusal. ''Of course it would.'' She reached for the bag, but he held on.

"You sure? I mean, well, you don't look like someone's washerwoman." Which was one of the longest sen-
tences he'd said in quite some time.

Kari laughed, enjoying his puzzled look. "I'm not a
washerwoman. I'm a woman who washes when it's necessary." She tugged the bag free of his grip. "I'll bring
your clean clothes to you as soon as I'm finished." She
continued on to the house and went inside.

Mac shoved his hat back a bit on his balding head and
scratched his forehead. He couldn't figure what the
woman was up to, but he might as well see it out. He
hated going into town.

By two o'clock, Kari's spaghetti sauce was simmering
on the stove and the laundry was done. She set her own
things in her room, put away the clean towels and stacked
the old ranch hand's clothes in a basket she'd found in
the closet. She hadn't set out to wash more than a few
things today, but she'd volunteered to do Mac's after
watching him hobble along, looking as if every step he
took was painful. She knew better than to ask how he
felt, sure his answer would be a stoic "Fine."

Helping out in a small way like doing his laundry
might ease things for him. In many ways he was a great
deal like her father, she thought. Mac probably felt that
washing and the like were women's work, but he'd do it
if he had to. And he'd sooner chew nails than admit he
hurt anywhere, as if doing so would reveal a weakness.

Carrying the basket and humming a show tune, Kari
walked over to Mac's trailer and knocked. She heard
shuffling footsteps a few minutes later, and the door
swung open. The old man's small eyes widened, and he
appeared speechless as he stared at the neat stack.

"Here you go," Kari said, handing over the basket.

Mac took it from her and continued to stare as if she

were some sort of alien. "Used to be a woman here when first I signed on with Dillon. Lisa. Engaged they were. She never washed his clothes, never mind mine. Can't figure you out nohow."

As speeches went, it was brief, but long for a taciturn old man. "There's nothing to figure, Mac. I like to pay my way, if not with money then by helping out. Besides, it gave me something to do."

Earning his keep was something Mac could relate to. The look on his face was almost a smile. "I appreciate this."

Kari smiled. "Don't mention it." With a wave she slowly strolled toward the barn, careful to stay on the beaten path where no dangerous animals or deadly traps lay hidden. But most of all, her thoughts were on Dillon.

Dillon with those marvelous hands. She'd never known how drawn she could be to a man's hands. His were strong and powerful, showing the unmistakable nicks and scars of his rugged life-style. Yet how gentle they'd been when he'd soothed Calypso, how carefully he'd helped the colt through the birthing, how tenderly he'd cleaned the newborn.

Then later he'd taken Kari into his arms, and those same incredible hands had roamed over her body, thrusting into her hair, then shifting to caress the sensitive skin of her breasts, causing them to ache and yearn ever since. Was it possible to fall in love with a man's hands?

Or was it his eyes that were his best feature, the way his many moods changed them from dark and smoky to bright and mischievous? She'd seen them grow stormy as the sea at Big Sur during a heavy rainfall, then tame to a robin's egg blue, the color of the sky the morning after the storm. And when he looked at her with those fascinating eyes, she saw heat and passion, barely held in check, sensual awareness and need. Yes, it would be easy to fall in love with Dillon's eyes.

In her mind's eye, her thoughts slid down to focus on his mouth, soft and pliant one moment and turning hard as steel the next as he crushed her to him. Who could ever forget that mouth once those full lips had branded you?

Perhaps then it was the whole man that she admired, that she wanted, that she loved. Kari slowed her steps, watching out for melting puddles of dirty snow. Love, she thought again, the word floating to the surface. Was she in love with Dillon Tracy? Love was such a nebulous concept, everyone's description just a shade different. She knew people who'd been in love three, four times. Did that mean love was born only to die shortly after? She didn't want that, wanted instead a love for all time. Or was that just a romantic dream?

Her father had always told her a marriage would work really well only if two people came from the same background, liked the same things, had the same goals. So where did that leave her and Dillon? He wanted to ranch, to work his horses, breed and sell, live a simple life. She wanted…what? Well, for starters, she wanted a simple life, too. She'd lived a complicated, overly busy, crowded one so far, and that held little appeal for the future. She wanted a home, a sharing relationship, a lasting love, children. She had no idea if Dillon's needs encompassed all that.

Then there was the problem of his family accepting her and, perhaps even larger, hers accepting him. But you marry the man, not his family, she remembered reading. True, but getting along made things easier. Or was easy another romantic dream?

But a bigger problem loomed. What about the lie she'd

never spoken aloud but that hovered between them nonetheless? She hadn't revealed who she was, and lying by
omission was just as damning. She got the feeling Dillon
would consider her omission a breach of faith. He'd been
lied to before, he'd said. By his mother? Or was it this
Lisa person Mac had mentioned? Lisa had lived here
briefly, it seemed, but didn't do laundry. What had she
done, besides warm Dillon's bed?

None of her business, Kari thought, but the question
nagged at her. Perhaps Dillon would tell her if she
nudged him.

She was almost at the barn door when she heard a loud
whinny from the direction of the paddock, a sound that
sent shivers down her spine. It was like nothing she'd
heard before, surely not a sound any of the mares had
made.

Curious, she circled and headed for the paddock fence.
There were only patches of gray snow here and there on
the dormant grass within the fenced area. She saw one
of the chestnut broodmares that looked so much alike
near the center, either Holly or Dixie, Kari wasn't certain
which. She appeared nervous and twitchy, suddenly
throwing back her head, her dark mane flashing in the
sun as she pawed the ground. A feeling of anticipation
hung in the late-afternoon air.

Suddenly the barn door slid open noisily and the huge
stallion came thundering out into the paddock, his nostrils
flaring. The mare sensed him before she saw him and
became very still. Slowly, almost lazily, he circled her,
drawing ever nearer. She swished her tail and took a few
steps forward as Domino passed behind her, his nose
twitching.

Kari moved closer to the fence as realization sunk in.
Dillon had told her he'd be breeding his stallion to one

of his mares soon. She saw him walk out of the barn and move along the fence on the opposite side from where she stood, his eyes on the two horses. She shifted her attention back to the age-old mating ceremony.

Domino snuffled as he moved in front of the mare, then leaned down to nip at her neck before dancing quickly away. He was playing with her, Kari realized, enjoying the little ritual leading up to the main event. The mare moved her head as if acknowledging the love bite, then pranced away just out of reach.

Fascinated, Kari leaned her arms on the top rung of the fence, feeling the heat of the sun dampening her face. Or was she warmed by the scene in front of her? Suddenly Domino reared up on his hind legs, his front feet stabbing the air in a mighty show of power, then circled back to the mare. As if answering him in kind, she reared back, too, then skittered away, her teeth bared, her wild eyes looking everywhere but at the stallion.

Kari found herself smiling. She was flirting, playing coy, yet inviting him to get closer. She'd had no idea animals courted before coupling, much as humans did.

Finally Domino grew impatient, moving closer to the mare. In a calculated move, he reared back and brought his front feet down over her, causing her to sink to her knees. Again he took the time to lean forward and take several nips along her thick neck. The mare visibly trembled as the stallion pulled back and plunged into her with a wild and primitive whinny.

Hands damp and her heart beating furiously, Kari gasped as the sound of the mare's scream echoed in the thick afternoon air. Then in moments it was over and there was only silence.

Removing her shaky hand from the top board, Kari gazed across the paddock to where Dillon waited, and their eyes locked. He stood perfectly still and unsmiling. She saw the passion in the intense blue of his gaze and wondered if he could read the same in hers. There was no denying the depth of her arousal.

Finally Dillon broke contact and went over to the once again docile mare to lead her back inside.

Swallowing around a dry throat, Kari wiped her hands on her jeans and walked toward the house, unsettled by what she'd seen. She hadn't been expecting that sort of breeding. Some time ago she'd read an article about how many horse and cattle breeders used artificial insemination so that the over-eager males wouldn't hurt the females. But apparently Dillon preferred to let nature take its course.

Entering the laundry room, she hung up her jacket and shoved up the sleeves of her sweatshirt, feeling warm all over. Tugging off the boots Dillon insisted she wear outdoors, she padded to the kitchen wearing only thick white socks. After washing her hands, she checked the spaghetti sauce and found it just right. She had the pot of water already on the stove for the pasta, and a salad made, but she wasn't sure what time Dillon wanted to eat dinner.

Restlessly she prowled the big room. She didn't feel like watching a movie or even reading a book. Instead, she stood at the front window, gazing out as the sun slowly lowered in the sky.

Funny what a difference a few days could make. Changes in the weather—the snow was disappearing and the days warming gradually. Changes also in herself. She felt different from when she'd arrived. Less tense, more focused. Except perhaps for the last half an hour.

She hadn't really needed to witness Domino and the mare to become aware of Dillon Tracy. She'd been getting there on her own, more each day. The kisses they'd shared in her room over the fallen shade incident and again in the stables after the birthing had awakened her body in such a way that whenever she saw him, her thoughts shifted to sensual possibilities.

This wasn't usual for Kari. Her one youthful fling in college with a musician she'd outgrown almost immediately had been more a rebellion against convention than any deep feelings on either of their parts. There had been one other man she might have gotten serious with, but she'd discovered that he was using her as a stepping stone to her father, a fact that had hurt for at least two weeks. She wasn't used to thinking of men in the physical sense as much as on a cerebral one, since those were the types she knew.

But Dillon was different.

He made her aware of herself as a woman. His eyes as they wandered over her were hot and hungry. He had her mouth watering for another taste of him, another—

The back door opened noisily.

Turning, Kari rearranged her features and walked back to the stove, busying herself by stirring the sauce that needed no stirring. She heard the water running in the laundry room sink where Dillon usually washed up. But she didn't hear him come into the kitchen, because he'd removed his boots.

"What did you do with all the towels?" he asked.

Startled, she dropped the spoon and swung around, then felt the breath catch in her throat. He was shirtless, his face and hands wet, the hair on his chest damp. She couldn't seem to take her eyes off the water glistening in the dark curls liberally sprinkled across the muscular expanse. When finally she did, sliding her gaze up to his, she knew he saw everything he needed to know.

Her hands flew to her flushed cheeks as she tried to

remember his question. "Towels. I washed them all and put them in the linen closet. I guess I forgot to leave one in the laundry room." She started past him to get a towel, but he stopped her with a hand on her arm.

"Forget the damn towels." Dillon pulled her to him, his mouth finding hers. Passion was like a hot, bubbling stream coursing through him. He was so aroused he could scarcely stand upright, had been since he'd seen her across the paddock while a primitive mating had taken place mere yards from both of them.

He hadn't needed the extra stimulus, Dillon knew. He'd been wanting her from almost the first moment she'd stepped into his home, though it had taken some time for him to admit that. His hands traveled down her back and lower, pressing her softness into his granite hardness. He felt her jolt as she realized how ready he was, and wondered if he'd frightened her. But instead, she leaned closer into him, reaching for his heat.

Sounds Kari didn't recognize as her own came from deep within her as, at first tentatively, then more boldly, she explored the wonder of his mouth with her searching tongue. He dueled with her, then shifted slightly and took her deeper. She was lost, totally lost.

A ripple of desire so strong that his knees nearly buckled raced through Dillon as he picked her up, never breaking the kiss. His long, hurried strides took them to his room where he laid her on the burgundy comforter that covered his bed, and followed her down. Still his mouth was locked to hers, his breath mingling with hers.

Kari's hands were free to roam, free to touch the smooth skin of his shoulders, his back. In wonder, in delight, she traced the hard muscles, then moved to the front where her fingers tangled in the dark, damp hair of his chest. How good he felt, how strong and powerful.

She felt him shift to nibble at her neck, much the same as Domino had nipped at the mare. An answering need inside came alive and she raised one knee, squirming as a fire spread low in her belly. She'd never wanted like this, never been wanted like this.

The need to be flesh-to-flesh with her was huge. Dillon touched the hem of her sweatshirt. "I need to touch you," he said, his voice husky.

"Yes, touch me."

When she raised slightly to give him access, he pulled the shirt off over her head and tossed it to the floor, surprised and pleased to find she had nothing on underneath.

First his eyes looked their fill, followed by his hands as he gently caressed her breasts, watching the peaks harden. When he bent his head to put his mouth to her, he heard Kari suck in a deep breath and then jolt as he drew on her.

Kari's eyes fluttered closed as she let the first wave of pure pleasure race through her. His fingers were rough and callused and terribly arousing as he rubbed and circled, the slow friction causing heat to surface everywhere. When he shifted to the other side, she cried out his name, thrusting her hands into his thick hair, holding him to her.

Floating. She was floating, the mists closing in on her, making her forget the outside world, all her worries and concerns. There was only this room, this man, this overpowering passion. He moved back up to her welcoming mouth, stealing the very breath from her. She felt his busy hands shove down her jeans quite easily, since they were too large for her, then pull off the last barrier. She was naked to his eyes, his touch, but surprisingly she felt no shyness, only a desire to please him. As she watched his gaze skim over her, she realized she had.

His hands moved over her slender frame, skimming down her sides, along her restless thighs. Kari felt his mouth follow his fingers and found herself whispering soft words to him, incoherent mumblings as he journeyed over her. But she didn't care if she made sense or not. Her own hands went exploring, and she heard his groan as she touched him, glorying in the power that could make him tremble. Her skin tingled everywhere he touched, her kiss-bruised lips ached and her swollen breasts yearned. And still she wanted more.

As if he'd read her thoughts, his fingers moved inside her. A powerful, raw hunger had Kari in its insatiable grip as she felt the threat of explosion building. Her body moved without her permission, seeking release, reaching. Then she was flying, hurtling. Lost in a primitive passion she'd never known quite like this, Kari bit her lip to keep from crying out as wave after wave ripped through her. Clinging to him, she buried her face in his neck, her breath coming in gasps. The pulsing shock waves slowly subsided as he held her close.

Dillon watched her open eyes still hazy and not quite focused, her face flushed and very lovely. He'd never known a woman so responsive, so open to each new pleasure.

But his own needs were clamoring for attention. His hand fumbled at the snap of his jeans and he quickly removed the rest of his clothes, then returned to her. Tenderly, he kissed her.

The kiss went on and on, patient, loving, arousing. Kari was shocked to find herself wanting more, wanting again, needing him. When he reached into the nightstand for the protection she'd been too involved to remember, she found herself marveling at his caring nature. Then he was poised above her, as if waiting for permission.

Dillon saw her smile, that womanly smile that seemed to contain a million secrets, then she reached out her hands to welcome him. Softly she whispered his name as he slipped inside her as if they'd been lovers for years. Hadn't he guessed that they'd fit together perfectly, beautifully, as if each had been waiting for the other half to complete the whole? With iron control, he slowly began to move.

Sighing, Kari's hands on his back held him close. A feeling of utter rightness enveloped her, of coming home, of total completion. She swallowed a gasp as he picked up speed, thrusting powerfully now, reaching together. Hot and trembling, she let him take her to places she'd never been, holding on to him as if to a lifeline.

Kari came back to reality slowly, her eyes opening, looking around the unfamiliar room, becoming aware of the unfamiliar weight on her. Still, nothing had really changed. Yet everything had.

A silly cliché perhaps, but she truly hadn't known making love could be quite like what she'd just experienced. Shattering, stunning, mindless. Then lying here feeling languid, peaceful, loving. She was not totally without experience, but the few she'd had never led her to even imagine the powerful passion she'd felt with Dillon. She was afraid to think of the future, to plan ahead. But at least she would always have this.

Dillon shifted, turning onto his back, taking Kari with him, tucking her head onto his shoulder. He wasn't ready to get up or to face her just yet. He had to sort out his feelings.

Four days she'd been in his life. Only four. Yet hadn't

he been the one to tell Kari that sometimes it only took a short time—*it* being strong, deep feelings. The *L* word. Love.

Did he, in fact, love Kari? Or was it just sex? Sex was a powerful pull to a man who'd been without a long while. But to be honest, sex he could have had easily enough. A phone call, a drive into town, a meaningless release. What he'd just experienced with Kari was light-years beyond that.

He'd wanted to please her, to watch her expressive face as he touched her, to see her climb with him. He'd wanted to hear his name on her lips as she exploded, to listen to the soft sounds she made as he loved her, to truly make love, not just have sex.

Short as the time had been, in these last few days, she'd made changes in him, made him realize there was more to life than just his horses and hard work. He'd begun looking forward to her attempts at cooking, which actually hadn't turned out badly. He'd begun to listen for her laugh, to look for her visits to the stables to bring him coffee. She'd won Zeus over, something no woman had ever managed. And several of the mares, to say nothing of his new colt, all perked up when she came on the scene.

There was so much to the woman, her desire to please, her intelligence, her wit. Yet what about the life she'd walked away from? To her, this was a time to regroup, to reassess her life, an interlude. Did he even know what she'd told him was the truth? Was she hiding more from him than her true name?

And yet now that he'd tapped into her passion and experienced her wholehearted response, how could he let her go? And the biggest question of all: how had he let himself fall for a woman just passing through his life?

Kari shifted so she could look into his eyes, needing to know if she'd find regret there. But when he met her anxious gaze, he smiled in that wonderful, warm way he had. "I was wondering what you're thinking."

Lazily his hand caressed her lovely back. "I'm thinking I'd like to try that again, just to make sure we got it right."

She smiled. "Oh, I think we got it right."

"Then you don't want a rematch?"

"I didn't say that. I just figured men needed to rest before resuming. Am I wrong?"

He wiggled onto his side facing her. "Let's find out."

Kari laughed, but her heart wasn't in it, not really. Something was bothering her, something she needed to ask Dillon. Perhaps her timing wasn't the best, but sometimes pillow talk was the most honest of all. "Can I ask you something first?"

Setting aside his misgivings, he stroked her soft cheek. "Go right ahead."

"Who's Lisa?"

Chapter Eight

The smile slid from Dillon's face as he eased back to look at Kari. "Where'd you hear about Lisa?"

"Mac mentioned that, when he first came to work for you, a woman named Lisa lived here with you. Was he right?"

The mention of a conversation with Mac had Dillon raising a puzzled brow. "You talked with Mac? About me and Lisa?"

"Sort of." Adjusting the comforter over herself, Kari found it easier to face him at least partially covered. "I did his laundry and—"

"What?" At that piece of news, he sat up. "Did I hear you correctly? You did Mac's laundry?"

She frowned, wondering what all the fuss was about. "Yes. I ran into him when he was on his way into town to do his washing. I was throwing some towels in, anyway, so I offered to do his stuff, too. No big deal."

Shaking his head, Dillon laughed. "I'll bet Mac thought it was a pretty big deal."

"As a matter of fact, he did. That's when he said that Lisa used to live here and she never did *your* laundry, much less his. So I got to wondering just who she was. Or is. If I'm out of line, you can just ignore the question."

Dillon flopped onto his back, raising his arms and putting both hands under his head, oblivious to his nakedness. "I have no problem telling you about Lisa Morgan, and she's definitely in the past tense. We met at college my last year of law school. We seemed to enjoy the same things, had a lot of laughs together—when I wasn't studying or working my two part-time jobs or sleeping. We decided to get married."

That sounded a little too simplistic, but Kari kept quiet.

"We got engaged the week before I graduated, the same week my uncle died and left me this ranch. I immediately wanted to work the ranch and forget the law. But Lisa had been trying to persuade me to set up a law practice in Phoenix or Tucson, saying Prescott was too small a town. Provincial, she called it. That was before I drove her to DeWitt and she saw what small really was."

"She didn't like DeWitt?" Kari kept her eyes on his face, wondering how he could lie there without a stitch on and chat so nonchalantly. It was one of the vital differences between men and women, the way a man strolling around in the nude seldom seemed bothered.

"She hated it, I found out later, but that's not what she said at the time. She said that if I wanted to ranch, she'd ranch along with me."

"Did you believe her?"

He gave a mirthless chuckle. "I wanted to, but I had

my suspicions. Lisa was very fond of nice clothes, good jewelry, traveling. Her father's a successful lawyer and she was used to the good life. I told her what to expect living on a ranch, that her life would be very different. However, she insisted that she loved animals and the outdoors. Just in case, I postponed the wedding, saying I wanted us to wait until the ranch got going. See, my uncle had been sick for a couple of years after his wife died and he'd let the place get run down. There was a lot of work needed doing.''

"And you did it all alone?"

"Actually, much to my surprise, Lisa worked alongside me. She ruined her perfect manicure by pitching in, cleaning windows, painting, scrubbing floors while I hammered away, mending fences, shoring up the barn, all but remodeling the house.''

"Then she did take to ranch life?"

"So she wanted me to believe, but unknown to me, she was plotting behind my back to get me to give up ranching and return to the law. A couple of suspicious things happened—repairs I'd made suddenly became broken again while I'd been in town. Brand-new feed I'd bought got soaked in a rainfall, when I knew I hadn't left the barn window open. My tractor suddenly turned itself on and rammed into the storage shed. Too many incidents for me not to wonder what was going on.''

"Was Mac already here?"

"Yeah, but he stayed away from Lisa. He made it clear he didn't care for most women, and especially Lisa." He smiled, remembering. "He asked me once, when he saw me doing the wash, why I'd want a woman who wouldn't even do that much. Said she must be pretty good in bed." Dillon turned to her. "I'm still not sure how you got Mac to loosen up. He's hardly spoken two words to a woman since I've known him.''

Kari shrugged. ''I wasn't trying to pump him for information about you. I took him his clean clothes and he mentioned Lisa.''

''Interesting. Well, anyway, as I said, I had a feeling Lisa was up to something. I sure as hell didn't suspect Mac, since he'd have no reason to sabotage the first solid home he'd had in years. And Rich wasn't working here yet. So I began to watch her when she didn't think I was looking. Finally, one night she snuck out of the bedroom when she thought I was asleep. It was a summer night, quite warm. I followed her and saw her open the corral gates, freeing all four of the mares I'd saved up and purchased just that week.''

''You must have been furious.''

''I was. I jumped on Henry and rounded up three of them, but the fourth had run into the forest and broken a leg. I had to put her down. I locked the horses in the stables and went into the house. Lisa was already packing, knowing full well what was coming. I asked her why she'd done it all. She had no apologies, merely said she didn't want to be a rancher's wife and she was determined to show me I wasn't cut out to be a rancher, either. By then it was the middle of the night, but I didn't care. I drove her back and dumped her on her parents' porch. I never saw her again.''

''What she did was pretty underhanded,'' Kari commented.

''Yeah, you could say that. It wasn't just the hurt and disappointment. What really infuriated me was the deception, the lying. My mother had lied to my father, my brother and me for years—about not drinking anymore, about not using the grocery money for booze, about all manner of things. Then along came Lisa and she turned out to be basically the same." He propped up on one elbow, looking at her. "I guess you can understand why I hate lying."

Unable to meet his eyes, she nodded. Should she tell him now who her father was, Kari asked herself, and lose him before she really had him? No, she needed to get their feelings for each other on more solid ground. Then she'd tell him for sure.

She was quiet too long, Dillon decided. He'd given her an opening to confess, if she had anything she'd been hiding from him. Only she hadn't, so maybe he was wrong. After all, millions of people really were named Smith.

Rolling over, he pinned her beneath him, smiling down into her serious face. "Turnabout's fair play, you know. I've told you about the only woman who's ever even gotten to first base with me. How about the men in your life?"

"My story won't take but a minute to tell. I went through a rebellious stage in college, met a guitarist from a rock band named Will Sloan, and had a brief fling with him. No one else until Tom Reynolds." Kari stopped there, wondering if the name might ring a bell with Dillon since Tom's name was often in the papers on the Washington scene. Then again, she hadn't seen a newspaper enter the house since she'd arrived.

Skimming a finger along her breastbone, he waited till she looked at him. "And what happened with Tom?"

"Not much. After a few months I figured out that he was more interested in getting connected with my father than with me, using me to gain his favor, so to speak."

"Your father must be an important man." Who would probably take one look at him and wonder how he had the nerve to even approach his daughter, Dillon thought.

"I suppose he is." Kari felt a shiver take her as his hand inched below the coverlet that was draped over her breasts. "Importance is in the eye of the beholder, don't you think?"

"Probably." He dipped to kiss the swell of one breast.

"So tell me, was Mac right? Was Lisa good in bed?" She probably shouldn't have asked, on such short acquaintance. But lying naked with him lent an intimacy that seemed to invite personal questions.

"So-so. She didn't seem all that interested in sex. I often felt as if her mind was elsewhere." He touched his tongue to the pulse point in her throat and heard her draw in a sharp breath. "Mmm, you like that?"

"Yes, I like that." Kari felt the sensual tug again, aware that once was not enough, not with this man. Resolutely she put their rocky relationship on hold for this moment, this short space of time. She knew without a doubt how compatible they were in bed. The rest could wait.

Slipping her arms around him, she drew him closer, stretching to place a warm, moist kiss in his ear. "Do you like that?"

Dillon shifted, rearranging their bodies so she was poised above him. "I like everything you do to me." Carefully he joined with her, then took her mouth for a long, slow kiss.

"Come on, Phil, how long can a healthy young woman be laid up with the flu?" Ted Conway shook his head as he stood in front of his managing editor's desk. "I'm telling you, Senator Sinclair's office is stonewalling us."

Preoccupied, Phil Norris scribbled a note on a file and set it aside before leaning back in his chair. "Why would they do that?"

Ted shrugged, his slim fingers toying with his trademark red suspenders. He'd been a feature writer specializing in the political scene for the *Arizona Republic* for six years, long enough to know when some flunky was trying to mislead him. "That's what I want to find out. Kari Sinclair hasn't been seen since a week ago tomorrow when she gave that talk at the Bonaventure. No one saw her anywhere on the grounds, yet her assistant, Norma Brice, stayed on for four days. She hasn't checked in at any area hospitals, even under an assumed name. I've got a source who works for Kari's doctor, and she hasn't been seen by any physician since sometime last year. Something fishy's going on, I tell you."

Phil dug his pen out of his top drawer. "Maybe she's got a new boyfriend and she's holed up with him."

"If that's the case, I want to know. I can easily do a column on that, providing he's interesting at all. But I doubt it. Kari's not the one who would do something like that. That would be *Dana* Sinclair." Ted dropped his lanky frame into the chair opposite his boss. "How about this? I do a short feature speculating on where Kari Sinclair is? If she's ill, why the secrecy? If not, where is she? I'd run it alongside her latest picture, see if we get any calls. Let's shake the bushes and see if anything falls out."

Toying with his pen, Phil was thoughtful. "Might turn into something. But we can't afford to upset the senator.

He spends a lot of time in Washington, but he's got a long reach and Phoenix is his home base.''

"I hear you." Ted jumped up, anxious to get to it. "Inquiring, but not implying. Gotcha. Thanks, boss.''

Sighing, Phil hoped he hadn't made a mistake in letting Ted run with that particular ball.

Dillon moved Maisy, his big sorrel, into a slow trot as he rode the fence line, checking for breaks, for loose posts, for damaged wood. The winter hadn't been particularly harsh, so he found very little needing repairs. Lazily he moved along until he got to the west section. He eased Maisy to a stop and gazed at his land.

Another week, possibly two, and he'd be able to till the soil here. Last week's storm had definitely been the last of the season. Already the days were warmer, the sun staying out longer. Nearly all of the accumulation had melted, leaving the ground damp and almost pliable. He'd plant a larger garden this year, maybe even some root vegetables. He needed to build that root cellar he'd been planning. Tomatoes hadn't done very well last year, but he'd take another shot at them, anyhow.

Peppers were always good, and cucumbers. The squash had really taken off, and some of the pumpkins had weighed over ten pounds. Maybe he'd get Kari a book on canning and she'd give it a try. He already had Edith's jars and—

What in hell was he thinking? Dillon wondered, as he reined Maisy around and resumed his inspection. Kari would be long gone before this crop was in, much less ready for the picking. He'd share with the Martin family up the road, fifty-fifty, and Mrs. Martin would do the canning, like last year. He knew that Abner Martin couldn't do much farming since his tractor accident a while back. They had three children, so they appreciated the help.

Still he couldn't help picturing Kari in his kitchen, two big pots on the stove, cooking and blanching, then pouring the finished product into sterilized jars. Her face would be flushed from the heat, her hair held back by a rubber band like she so often wore it during the day. Each time she tried a new recipe and it worked, she was so happy, so eager to have him taste it.

And she was good...a natural cook. If she hung around much longer, he'd undoubtedly gain weight. But that thought led him to a slice of reality. She wouldn't be here much longer, he was certain. Already she was showing signs of restlessness. He'd catch her staring off into space, lost in her thoughts. Or standing at the window and gazing out for long periods of time. What was she thinking? Had she figured out what she wanted to do after this time in the country, this break from routine?

A bigger question was, did he figure in her future plans at all? Dillon slowed Maisy to a walk as he pondered that. She'd never once mentioned leaving, nor had he, even though they both knew the snow was no longer keeping her here. Then what was?

She honestly seemed to enjoy just about everything—the cooking, the time she spent with the horses, walking with Zeus who was now her steady companion, even doing the laundry. Last night she'd dug up Aunt Edith's old sewing basket and sat on the couch, mending after dinner, humming a song from *The Sound of Music*. He'd told her that mending his clothes wasn't part of their arrangement, but she'd said it was the one domestic chore her mother had taught her.

Her mother. What was the woman like? Dillon wondered. And the important father, what exactly did he do? Apparently he had a strong influence on Kari, the kind of paternal smothering that he'd experienced, as well. Maybe now after this time away from her family, Kari would have the courage to leave their home, to strike out on her own. Maybe she'd even choose to stay with him.

Whew! There was a thought. Dillon stopped Maisy and slipped down to the ground, checking out a leaning fence post. But he found himself staring up into a cloudless blue sky instead. It shocked him that he wanted her here with him. Not just to warm his bed, though he wouldn't discount that aspect of their relationship.

But he wanted more. He wanted love, and the thought stunned him, since he'd never allowed himself to admit that before. Maybe he'd been afraid to want something he wasn't sure he'd ever find. Because no woman had ever loved him.

His mother had loved only her bottle, not Dad or Terry or him. Lisa had loved the idea of being married to an attorney, to more or less continue the life she'd grown up knowing. There were a few mares in the stable who were quite fond of him, but no female person had ever loved him. Was Kari falling in love with him?

Hard to tell. She was wonderfully responsive in bed and genuinely affectionate out of bed. But love? That was another more serious ball game. If Kari loved him, she'd have to go against her family's wishes, since he probably wouldn't pass muster with them. Since she still hadn't had the courage to move out of her father's house at twenty-six, would she be brave enough to buck them over a man? Doubtful.

Dillon propped a booted foot on the bottom rung of

the fence and shoved back his hat. Why should she trade an undoubtedly good job and probably a nice house and all the amenities for a hard life as a rancher's wife? There were rewards aplenty, he knew, but would Kari see that? Most people were for instant gratification, not working through the long haul for something that gave them pleasure and satisfaction. How could he judge how she'd stand up to this tougher life by watching her for only a week or so?

Moving slowly, still lost in his disturbing thoughts, Dillon mounted and continued on, keeping Maisy to a slow pace. It was getting warm, and he wished he had a glass of iced tea. He'd dressed for the chilly morning, but the sun had changed that. He would check the east section, then head back for a drink.

And he'd keep his mind on fencing instead of on what was an impossible situation without an answer in sight.

Cinnamon was frisky this morning, Kari saw, watching the new colt show off for her. Dillon had let her name him, although he'd said that Cinnamon was a girl's name. She'd pointed out that cinnamon was a spice, not a gender, and that he was a sexist. He'd laughed then and hugged her close.

Leaning back against a barn support, her eyes on Cinnamon's stall but her mind elsewhere, Kari grew thoughtful. She was growing awfully fond of those hugs and more. His kisses, his affection, his lovemaking. It had been only three days since he'd carried her to his bed the first time, and Kari honestly couldn't remember three nicer days in her life.

To lie in his arms after the loving, to fall asleep with a lover's heartbeat against her ear, to feel warm and safe and content—all were experiences she'd never had quite like this. The sex was wonderful, but merely the icing on the cake. Dillon was the cake.

He seemed to honestly enjoy being with her, and she found him fascinating. He took her into the tack room, explained the different saddles, the bridles, the bits. He walked with her down by the stream that bisected his property, and they'd stood watching the clear water racing over the smooth rocks, listening to the birds flutter around in the trees. He sat with her by the fire and talked about his dreams, about adding to his stock, finishing the indoor arena, maybe hiring another trainer, expanding the house. A man who relaxed enough to share his dreams was also one she'd never known.

In the week and a half she'd been with him, he'd changed, softened, mellowed. He laughed more, touched more, was even playful at times. Gone was the almost-perpetual frown, the tension, the stubborn tilt to his big shoulders. He found more reasons to finish his work quickly and come looking for her. He thought up ways to please her, like teaching her to ride, first on the gentle Appaloosa and then on the docile gelding. For a man who had a great deal to do, he found time for her, which was a big gift in itself.

Kari bent to pick up a piece of clean straw and stuck one end in her mouth, chewing on it as she chewed on her rambling thoughts. She needed to tell him about her father and all the reasons she'd wanted time away from that whole political scene. She needed to find just the right moment, and she'd honestly been trying. She'd actually had her mouth open a few times, on the verge of confessing. What stopped her was fear, fear that Dillon would think she'd deliberately deceived him and would want nothing more to do with her.

He hated liars. He'd told her that on more than one occasion. In the beginning, not telling him everything hadn't seemed like a lie, but rather like something she simply hadn't felt like explaining. But since hearing the story of his mother and then Lisa, knowing firsthand how he felt about the smallest duplicity, she felt worse than ever, yet unable to think of an opening.

He would hate her, Kari was certain. He'd dumped his fiancée, someone he'd known for long months, back on her doorstep in the middle of the night when he'd discovered the truth about her, unable to stand the sight of her another minute. He'd do the same to her.

Kari felt tears well up. Why hadn't she been up-front from the start? Because he wouldn't have let her stay an extra minute if he'd known her father was a United States senator who was less than happy that she'd taken off without notice. And because she hadn't wanted her father to know she'd skipped out on the Secret Service to wander about alone, winding up in a stranger's truck miles from home. It had seemed a small evasion. She wasn't a liar by nature, had always been painfully honest. But would Dillon ever believe that, after he heard her story? Not a chance.

Enough of this mental meandering, Kari decided as she tossed aside the piece of straw. She'd make herself useful and add clean straw to Cinnamon's stall. She spotted a pitchfork leaning against the next pillar and started over. But she hadn't gotten far when she noticed a man separate himself from the shadows around the empty stall.

"Hey, there, sweet thing," Rich Morley drawled. He

shoved his black hat to the back of his head and smiled at her. "I've been hoping I'd run into you."

Her first thought was that she was alone in the barn with this man and his eyes were hot and menacing. Where was Zeus? Then she remembered that he'd run off to chase a rabbit on her way in. Taking a step back, she knew she shouldn't show him even a hint of fear. "I was about to add fresh hay to the colt's stall, but you can do it instead. I've got to get back to the house." Turning, she headed for the double doors.

In three long strides, he was beside her, his hand grabbing her arm. "Hold on. What's your hurry?"

Kari swallowed hard. "I've got something on the stove."

"It'll keep." He leaned in closer, his other hand skimming her hair. "You're sure a pretty one, aren't you?"

She could smell sweat on him and cherry tobacco. "Let me go," she warned, wrestling her arm from his grasp.

But he held on, squeezed tighter, his strong workman's fingers circling her arm easily. "Don't be in such a rush."

Her heart thumped loudly in her chest as icy fear clutched at her. "Dillon will be looking for me."

"Not for a while he won't. He's way out yonder riding fence." He bent his head, aiming to nuzzle her neck, but she twisted away from him.

"Stop this. Let me go. Dillon's going to be furious with you." Where was he? Oh, God, why wasn't Dillon here?

Rich's laugh was deep, knowing. "I know what's going on between you two. I figure you got enough for both of us."

Angry now, her eyes blazed into his. "I'd die first." Behind her back, her hands groped for something, anything, to hit him with as he backed her against the stable wall. She heard the high whinny of one of the mares, who sensed the danger, but it seemed no one could help her. Why hadn't she at least left the door open so she could yell for Zeus?

Rich's thin lips curled into an ugly smile. "We'll see about that, Miss High-and-Mighty." He pulled her close to his big body and clamped his strong arms around her.

Kari could think of no other way out. She opened her mouth and let out a blood-curdling scream.

Dillon was slowly trotting Maisy back to the barn when he heard what had to be a scream. Only one person he knew would scream like that. Leaning forward, he dug his heels into Maisy's sides and moved her into a full gallop. The big sorrel easily jumped the fence into the paddock and kept going. In less than a minute they'd reached the open sliding door. Dillon slid off before Maisy had fully stopped, breaking into a run. He was pretty sure the scream had come from the direction of the barn, not the house.

He ran into the dimness looking every which way while his eyes adjusted. His boots pounded on the cement walk as he heard several of the horses snuffling. "Kari?" he called out.

Pausing, he thought he heard a muffled sound from the vicinity of the new colt's stall. Switching directions, he moved to the male side, still unable to see anyone. Again he called her name. Then he heard Zeus barking like fury at the other door and knew he was headed right.

Kari struggled and fought as Rich wrestled her to the

ground in the empty stall. She heard her name called, heard footsteps. She kicked mightily, trying to reach the stall wall so Dillon would know where she was, but she couldn't quite manage that. Rich's hand over her mouth and nose was horrible, but she had to use what she had. As she shoved an elbow into his stomach, he loosened his grip enough so that she opened her mouth and sank her teeth into the flesh of his hand. He let out a yelp, then cursed her ripely.

Dillon got to the stall door, opened it quickly and summed up the situation in moments. Rich had his back to him, his open hand drawn back, obviously intending to slap Kari so she'd stop struggling. Dillon grabbed his shoulder, swung him around and yanked him backward so that he landed hard on his rump. Rushing him, Dillon slammed his fist into Rich's chin, his rage adding to the power of the punch. "Move out!" he ordered Kari.

But the two men were grappling by the stall door, so she couldn't. Instead, she went to the far corner and stayed there.

Lean and mean, furious and frustrated, Rich scrambled up and rammed into Dillon from a low crouch, sending both of them crashing to the floor. On top now, straddling Dillon, Rich began punching. As Dillon tried to get free, he paused, his big fist held high. "Hey, man, come on! She came on to me, honest. What's the big deal? We can share her, you know."

Dillon saw red, literally. Jabbing a right into Rich's smiling face, he felt a couple of the man's teeth loosen. Taking advantage of Rich's pain, Dillon reversed their positions. With both fists, he vented his fury until he drew blood, then paused as Rich held up both hands to ward off more blows. "You're not worth it," Dillon said, pushing to his feet.

Relief washed over Kari.

Grabbing the pitchfork that had been leaning against the outer wall of the stall, Dillon held the prong end out toward Rich as he slowly got to his feet, one hand holding his bloody jaw. "Get out. You're through here. Don't ever come back."

Suppressing a moan, Rich picked up his hat, dusted it against his pant leg before sending a withering glance toward Kari. "You're probably a cold fish anyhow."

Unable to resist, Dillon poked the prongs of the pitchfork none too gently into Rich's back as he left the stall. Limping to the door, Rich shoved it open only to have Zeus hurl at him and knock him to the ground. The big dog had the man's wrist in his mouth in seconds, tossing his head back and forth, ready to maul. "Hey, get him off me!"

"Zeus!" Dillon's short command caused the German shepherd to reluctantly open his jaw, but he stayed there, growling low in his throat until Rich made his way to his truck and drove off.

By then Dillon had Kari in his arms, pressing her cheek against his chest, his heart pounding with the remnants of the adrenaline rush. He felt her quiver and pressed his lips together in anger that this had to happen. "Shh, it's all right. He's gone now."

"Thank God you showed up when you did." She was having a little trouble getting her breathing to slow. Making a face, she wiped her mouth on her sleeve after biting his hand.

Zeus came charging over, barking worriedly, sniffing at her. Kari reached to pet his head affectionately.

"He feels bad he wasn't inside with you," Dillon commented.

"It's my fault for shutting the door."

Dillon's face was grim, his mouth bleeding from a split lip which he ignored. "No, it's Rich's fault for being that kind of man." He stepped back, checking her over. "Are you all right? Did he hurt you?"

"I'm fine, but you're bleeding." She dabbed at his mouth and chin with a tissue she found in her pocket.

"It's nothing." Dillon stepped back, blaming himself for not warning her to keep Zeus with her at all times. It would seem that four-legged creatures weren't the only predators she had to worry about.

"Let's get you inside." But he winced as he started out, rubbing his jaw. "He packs quite a punch."

"You pack a bigger one," she said, smiling up at him.

Chapter Nine

Today was the day, Kari decided as she poured hot coffee into Dillon's favorite mug. Today, she had to tell him everything.

She set the pot down with unsteady hands and noticed she'd spilled coffee on the counter. Grabbing the dish towel, she wiped up, wondering if she'd have the courage to go through with this.

Unquestionably, he deserved to know. And she'd feel better once everything was out in the open. All right, she told herself, worst case scenario: he becomes angry. She'd rehearsed her explanation in her head innumerable times. She'd make him listen, make him understand. He was a reasonable man. He'd know she hadn't intended harm with the small omission.

A ripple of fear skittered up her spine. Maybe he wouldn't think it was so small. Then again, after last night, maybe he'd willingly forgive her.

By sending Rich Morley away, Dillon had made her feel safe again. The whole experience had left her trembling. The man had been dirty, smelly, cunning. Kari wasn't sure what would have happened if Dillon hadn't arrived when he had, but she had a feeling Rich was the sort who'd force a woman without a second thought. She shuddered at the recollection.

After Rich had left, sensing how upset she was, Dillon had taken her back to the house, held her in his arms on the couch until she'd calmed down. With her head resting on his shoulder, feeling his heart beat beneath her hand, she'd felt a comforting peace she'd seldom known. Here was a man who would always fight for her, who'd do everything in his power to keep her safe. Then Dillon had said something that had confirmed her own feelings.

"I don't know what I'd have done if anything had happened to you," Dillon had confided. "You've come to mean more to me than I'd planned, Kari."

She'd looked into those compelling blue eyes and kissed him, letting her actions speak for her. He'd taken her to bed, then, and they'd made slow, tender love for a very long time. Afterward, Kari had lain in the dark, knowing she loved him, yet unable to say the words out loud.

Slipping on her jacket, she picked up the mug and left for the stables where she knew Dillon was working this morning. Zeus jumped up from his spot by the fireplace where he'd been dozing, and trotted alongside her. Dillon had warned her to *never* go anywhere without the big dog. He didn't have to convince her, after the incident with Rich.

Kari had a feeling that somewhere along the line, Dillon had come to accept her story as fact, maybe because his feelings for her had deepened and he badly wanted to believe she was telling the truth. She dreaded having to burst his bubble, but sooner or later everyone had to face up to things. And this was her time.

She found him in the hayloft shifting huge mounds of hay with his pitchfork after having undone the bales that had been delivered yesterday. It was hard, hot work, Kari noticed, thinking she should have brought him something cold instead of coffee. "Anyone up there?" she called out, standing at the base of the runged ladder and looking up.

Dillon paused, shoved back his hat and swiped at his damp forehead with his forearm as he jammed the pitchfork into a solid pile. "Want to take over, give me a break?"

He'd rolled up the denim sleeves of his shirt to reveal strong arms rippling with muscles, the same ones she'd caressed last night in bed. His snug jeans were dirty and his boots badly scuffed. He looked wonderful to Kari.

"Mmm, I'm not sure how good I'd be at manual labor. But I did bring you some coffee."

"Great. Carry it on up."

She had a moment's hesitation, not sure she could climb the steep ladder without spilling the coffee. But she started up while Zeus stayed below barking. It was the one place he didn't go since he couldn't get a good foothold on the skimpy rungs of the ladder. Near the top Dillon leaned down to take the mug from her, then helped her over the top rung.

Stepping onto solid hay-covered flooring, Kari looked around. He'd broken up most of the bundles, releasing the sweet scent to mingle with the smells of oiled leather and clean horses. Dust motes danced in the sunshine rays pouring in through two long, narrow windows. It was warmer up here and she could see why he'd removed his jacket.

"So this is where you spend so much of your time. Nice."

"I think so." Dillon wandered over to a thick mound of hay by one of the windows, pulled off his gloves and sat down to drink his coffee. "I used to come up here when I was a kid spending summers with my uncle. A great place to read or daydream. I did a lot of both." He waited until she took off her jacket and walked over, sitting down alongside him. "A good place to coax a girl into making out, too."

She smiled at him. "I'll bet you managed that a time or two."

"Yeah, you could say that. I especially remember Mary Jane Donnelly. We were both fourteen when I convinced her we could see the whole valley from the loft windows."

"Fourteen! You were a little advanced for your age."

Dillon sipped from his mug, leaning back against the hay stack. "I hadn't planned on doing The Big Deed. Just a little kissing, a little touchy-feely stuff. That's all we did, all I could talk her into, at any rate. The problem was that when we climbed down and Mary Jane's mother came to pick her up, we hadn't gotten all the hay out of our clothes and hair. Mrs. Donnelly hit the roof, called me depraved and went right home to phone my dad."

Leaning back against the hay, Kari turned to face him. "What did your father do?"

Dillon shrugged. "Not much. Lectured me. The thing was, he believed me when I told him nothing much had happened."

Even then, he'd been honest as the day was long; his father knew it and probably everyone else did, too. "So that was the end of your making out in the hay loft, eh?"

"Not really. I just got better at picking hay off clothes and hair." He finished his coffee, set down the mug and turned toward her to nuzzle her neck.

She shivered, but kept her mind on track. "Aha! So how many other girls did you coax up here?"

"Hundreds." He placed a moist kiss in her ear. "Maybe thousands."

"I believe you."

He pulled back to look into her eyes. "You shouldn't. I did a little fooling around with one or two, but I never once made love with a girl up here, and I always wanted to." His hand moved to the buttons of her shirt. "How about we fulfill one of my fantasies?" The backs of his fingers stroked the rise of her breasts as he watched her flesh react.

But Kari's good sense, mingled with a dose of modesty, intruded. "This isn't exactly a private place. Mac could wander in and we might not even hear him. Or a delivery person, a neighbor."

"Mac's out in the pasture, mending the broken fences I found the other day. I'm not expecting any deliveries, and around here, neighbors rarely just drop in." He bent to nibble on her neck.

Before things got out of hand, Kari remembered why she'd come out to the barn. "Actually, I think we should talk."

But Dillon's jeans were already uncomfortably tight, and talking wasn't high on his list of priorities just now. "You don't really want to talk now." To prove his point, he took her mouth in a deeply intimate kiss as his busy fingers began unbuttoning her shirt. Though her mind may have wanted to talk, her body wanted something altogether different, he was sure. "Do you?" he whispered, trailing kisses along the silken line of her throat, then returning to plunder her mouth again.

Kari was lost, powerless, drifting. Amazed at how easily, how quickly, he could do this to her, she found herself forgetting everything but Dillon and the pounding need he'd resurrected inside her yet again. "But I...I want to tell you something," she managed, a final attempt to break through the haze.

"Not now. Later," Dillon said as he unzipped her jeans and shoved them off. He felt her shiver and raised his head. "Are you cold?"

Nothing could be further from the truth, for she was on fire everywhere he touched, and he was touching her everywhere. "Cold, lying here with you? I don't think that's possible, not even in a pile of snow."

"Are you trying to flatter me?" He smiled as his hands slid up and down her legs, warming, stroking, arousing. She was small-boned yet long-limbed and her dark eyes reflected the passion inside her that he was about to set free.

"I don't need to flatter you. From the first time you touched me, I knew no one else had ever touched me like that, made me feel what you do." Moment of truth, the most important truth of all, Kari thought as she raised both hands and framed his face, looking deeply into his eyes. "I didn't come here looking for this, Dillon, but I can't deny it, either. I love you."

He went still, perfectly still, savoring the words and the feelings they evoked. Yet he was wary, both by nature and from experience. "Don't just say that because you think it's what I want to hear."

"I wouldn't. I've never said those words to any man before."

Dillon swallowed around a huge lump. "No woman has ever loved me before." It was a difficult admission for a proud man to make.

"A woman loves you now, deeply. This woman." She watched his eyes change, the wariness replaced by something resembling hope. Then he lowered his head to kiss her.

The kiss started out sweetly but escalated swiftly as he pulled her closer. Dillon felt her respond instantly, her arms encircling him, her mouth open and seeking. This was what he needed in a woman, this unashamed passion that he never had to coax from her, the answering desire, the consuming hunger.

He could now admit it had been like that from the start for him with Kari. Wherever he was, whatever he was doing, he had only to look up and see her, and he wanted her. His eyes would lock with hers and he'd see that slow, smoldering look, and it was all he could do not to race over and carry her off. He had no idea if it would always be like this, just that it was now and he was grateful.

He eased back to open the shirt he'd unbuttoned, leaving it in place at her back against the prickly hay. She'd taken to wearing no bra since she had only the one she'd arrived in, a fact that drew his eyes to her repeatedly. He made love to her breasts with his eyes, then his hands and finally his mouth, drawing deeply on her. The soft moan she made was music to his ears.

He felt her fingers at his belt buckle and eased back

to help her. It was then that he noticed that his clothes were far from clean. "I'm dirty. I should—"

"It's just your clothes. Take them off." Impatience was like a hum in her ears, like a drumbeat in her blood. For days now, and for glorious nights, they'd made love regularly and often, so much so that now the sight of him undressing and fully aroused had her squirming with the need to be one with him.

Dillon yanked off his shirt and saw the blush of anticipation steal over her face. "You're something else," he whispered.

Meeting his eyes, she knew what he meant. "I can't deny how much I want you nor my response to you."

He reached for her hand and placed it on the zipper that strained over the throbbing evidence of his desire for her. "Nor can I," he said in a husky whisper as her fingers tightened on him. Edging back, he shed the rest of his clothes, then leaned back to her.

He touched her intimately, as if she were fragile, delicate, precious—when she knew she was none of those. He kissed her as if he couldn't ever get enough, as if he could go on for hours, and she wanted him to. He held her as if she might break, and she loved him for it.

His fingers found her, and he felt her jolt in response. There was no need to prepare her, to wait any longer. Dillon captured her mouth as he slipped inside her. He swallowed her soft sigh of pleasure as her muscles tightened, welcoming him. He began to move.

For Kari, the loft with its prickly hay jabbing at her disappeared. Eyes closed tightly to hold in the feeling, she let Dillon lead. Everything centered on this man who was wrapped around her, who was deep inside her, who was taking her to the heaven he'd already shown her. She held on, feeling the world as she knew it about to shatter.

Then suddenly, she was soaring, flying out of control, rising on a tidal wave of feeling. She opened her eyes to gaze into his and saw the intensity, the passion.

"I love you, Kari," he whispered, then he let go and joined her in that special place of their own making.

Afterglow. As never before, Kari understood what the word meant. She felt as if she were literally glowing after making love with Dillon, noticing the rosy hue of her skin which was like what she felt inside. She was lying with her head on Dillon's chest and had no recollection of him rolling over onto his back and taking her with him, yet keeping them deeply joined. Perhaps the three little words he'd said at the crucial moment had overshadowed everything else for her.

He loved her. She knew because he'd told her repeatedly that he didn't lie, so he had to mean it, to feel it. Since her early teens, she'd longed for someone of her own, someone who'd love her unconditionally. But would he, once he heard what she'd come up here to tell him?

Shifting, she looked into his face and wondered if this was the right moment to bring up a disturbing topic. She saw him smile, and the corners of his eyes crinkled.

"Are you as happy as I am?" he asked her.

Oh, Lord, she couldn't tell him now. "I never knew I could be this happy," she answered, ignoring that small voice, postponing yet again the inevitable. Keeping her gaze lowered, her fingers played with the hair on his chest, hoping he couldn't read her thoughts. She felt him move to adjust her weight more comfortably. "Am I too heavy on you? I can roll over and—"

"No, don't go. Not yet." His arms tightened about her. "I could stay here just like this the rest of the day." Even with several sharp pieces of hay poking into his backside.

Later, Kari swore to herself. She definitely would tell him everything later, before this day was over. For now she crossed her arms over his chest and rested her chin on her hands, gazing at the face he hadn't yet shaved. "Have you ever grown a beard? I think you'd look good in one."

"I have occasionally, in the winter." The winter. Next winter, with Kari here alongside him. The very thought warmed him. Maybe dreams do come true, even the ones you're afraid to acknowledge. "I'll grow one, if you like."

"Hmm, you're awfully agreeable. I don't recall you being *this* agreeable yesterday afternoon."

His hands on her buttocks pressed her closer, reinforcing their joining. "I don't recall feeling this good yesterday afternoon."

But Kari couldn't ignore her worried thoughts. "It's good between us, isn't it, Dillon?" Maybe if she got him to admit that, if he kept that thought uppermost in his mind, her news when it came wouldn't upset him too much.

"Good?" Lazily he stroked her back. "It's fantastic, wonderful, mind shattering."

She didn't think they were talking about the same thing. "I don't mean just the sex."

He thought that over a moment. "Yes, it's very special, what we have between us." Love. He was still getting used to the idea. He raised a hand to touch her hair, and with just that small gesture, felt himself harden. Trailing his fingers along her cheek, he waited for her to notice.

She did, her gaze flying to his. "You're…amazing."

He smiled, then touched his lips to hers, hungry again for her kiss.

As Dillon began to move within her, Kari rubbed her cheeks against his, delighting in the scratchiness of his unshaven face. With their positions reversed, she felt invigorated, testing a control she'd never experienced before. She felt her blood heat, her pulse pound, her body come doubly alive. Taking over, she moved against him in the familiar dance of love.

Dillon let her lead, let her do what she would, let her take him up and over the rainbow. Astride him, she was all flash and fire, her small, searching hands racing over him while her mouth nipped at the fullness of his lip, then kissed away the small bite. In moments she had him straining, groaning and she let out a small laugh of victory as she returned to capture his mouth.

Finally she had him striving, cresting, pouring into her. Struggling for breath, he felt her body pulse as he cradled her close in his arms. When at last she lifted her head, she couldn't hide a secret womanly smile.

"Surprised you, didn't I?"

"You could say that. You're not nearly as inhibited as I thought you were at first." He grinned. "I like it."

The laughter left her eyes and she became serious. "Only with you, Dillon. Only you." On a wave of unexpected sadness, she laid her head on his chest and struggled not to cry.

"You're supposed to be able to stand in the stirrups so your rear end just clears the saddle. Then you know

your stirrups are properly adjusted to the right length.''
Dillon secured the buckle and stepped back, looking up
at Kari sitting in the saddle on old Henry. ''There now,
slide your boot in there and try standing up.'' He watched
as she did as he directed, saw there was just the right
amount of space between the seat of her jeans and the
saddle. ''How's that feel?''

''Good.'' She was excited about riding out with Dillon,
yet just a shade nervous.

Dillon mounted Holly and reined her in alongside the
gentle gelding. He'd picked the quiet mare rather than
his jumpy stallion so he could easily control her on the
ride and not have Kari spooked. ''Don't worry, we're
going to start off with a slow walk and maybe move into
second gear if you like. Nothing fancy.''

She held Henry's reins loosely in her gloved hands the
way Dillon had taught her. ''Second gear?''

''That's a trot. We'll do that only if you're ready.''
Making a kissing sound with his lips, he nudged Holly
into a walk, noticing that Henry fell in step alongside.
Good old Henry, he knew just what to do. ''That's it, sit
tall, let him know who's in charge.''

Kari knew exactly who was in charge, and it wasn't
her. She suspected Henry knew that, too. Cautiously she
flipped the reins a tiny bit, pleased when Henry responded.

Dillon watched Kari chew on her lower lip as she concentrated hard, and he smiled. He'd had her on Henry or
Rainbow nearly every day, but that had been only in the
paddock. This was the first time they were wandering out.
He looked up at a clear blue sky with only a few puffy
white clouds lazily floating about. The weather was

warming, he was caught up on his most pressing chores, his horses were doing well, and he had a beautiful woman who cared about him riding by his side. What more could a man want?

"It's a beautiful day, isn't it?" he commented.

Forcing herself to relax, Kari looked up and decided that he was right. It was a great day. "Yes, it is." They were skirting a copse of tall evergreens, skinny fir trees, big cottonwoods. The air was fragrant with the scent of pine and sunshine. The stream on the far side of them was so clear she could see the individual stones in the creek as it gurgled and rushed downhill. Birds, sensing spring approaching, flitted through the treetops, chirping their pleasure at the warmer weather.

Kari allowed herself to take it all in, to absorb the sights and sounds and smells, smiling. "It really is lovely up here. And it's so quiet, except for nature. I can see why you'd prefer this to a busy city."

Yes, he did, but did she? Dillon wondered. Despite her stated feelings for him, was she growing anxious to return to all things familiar, her active urban life, her family and friends? If so, she'd shown remarkably few signs of it.

He inhaled deeply, drawing in the clean air. "I can't imagine living anywhere else."

Kari decided to keep quiet. If she showed him just how much she loved this place, he might get the wrong idea, that she was trying to tie him down. This was the nineties, and a declaration of love didn't necessarily mean marriage and forever. She still had a lot to discover about Dillon, such as did he want children, did he want a stay-at-home wife or one who also worked, did he plan to stay here and expand this place or move elsewhere and build again?

But if there were gaps in her knowledge of him, she knew he lacked even more information about her. They'd never discussed what she wanted, mainly because she'd arrived there with the express purpose of deciding just that for herself. She'd never in so many words told him she wanted off the merry-go-round that was her former life and instead have a quiet life, a home and family, nor had he asked.

All of that would have to wait until she told him everything about the deception she'd lived under all this time and got his reaction. They couldn't make future plans until they'd cleared up the past.

"Look up ahead!" Dillon stood in his saddle, gazing toward the bend in the stream as it flowed into the Hennessy River. "The water's really high, for this early in springtime."

Tugging her attention away from her disturbing thoughts, Kari followed his gaze and saw a wide river that seemed to go on for miles as it swallowed up the shoreline. "Isn't this how it usually is?"

"Not exactly." Dillon walked Holly to a few feet from the edge and drew to a stop, making sure Kari followed suit. "See how the river water's churning? That means there's more water flowing in way up ahead, probably from early spring meltdown of the snow in the mountain areas. Notice how the water's soaking the scrub grass along the edge here? It shouldn't be, not yet anyhow. There're stones and rocks along the bank that help to keep the shoreline from eroding, but already the river's too full."

"It must have been a snowy winter up north of here," Kari said as she watched the river lap at the grassy bank.

"Yeah, it was. Hopefully, it'll be a warm spring, and

some of this will evaporate before it gets to be a problem."

"What kind of problem?" Obviously she knew far too little about this area.

"Flooding. If instead of sunshine we get a rainy spring, and the water in the river mounts, it'll overflow, seeping into the forest area. Six or seven years ago, the Hennessy flooded so badly that it flowed all the way to the houses on the other side of this tree cover. People had to be evacuated from their homes. Very few ranchers have flood insurance. Quinn and I worked alongside the other residents practically night and day, trying to hold the water back."

Her hands on the horn of the saddle, Kari leaned forward, interested in how anyone holds back nature. "How did you do that?"

"Sandbags, mostly. We've still got some in the barn, and so do most of the ranchers around here. The town called for help and others came with more bags. We piled them along the treeline, high as a man's shoulders in some spots." He frowned at the river as he squinted up ahead. "I sure hope we're not going to have a spring like that one this year."

"Did it work? Were you able to hold back the river?"

Dillon sighed, remembering. "Yeah, barely. I lost track of how many hours we hauled those heavy bags around, sleeping in shifts, then coming back to do more. A week, maybe ten days. There are never enough hands to help out at a time like that, because it's basically back-breaking work. I was one of the younger ones, and even I was exhausted. The older men, like Mac, they had a bad time of it."

"It's really great though, that everyone pitched in,

neighbor helping neighbor.'' Kari wasn't so certain that spirit of cooperation would hold true in her own neighborhood in a time of crisis. The problem might not be an overflowing river, but even urban areas had their troubles. Yet people were so busy, rarely finding time to help others, except maybe at the holidays when a friendlier spirit prevailed. Up here, in the country, everyone relied on his neighbor because they never knew when they'd have a serious problem. ''I like that, knowing you can rely on people around you.''

Dillon nodded. ''I like that, too.'' He edged Holly closer, reached for Kari's hand. He was wondering something, wondering if she missed having her hair done, her nails polished, makeup on—things she hadn't had since moving in with him. He wondered if she was tough enough to handle country life and all that implied. Or would she soon tire and try to persuade him to leave for the big city? Was she made of the right stuff? ''Would you jump in the fray, help out your neighbors, if you lived up here?''

Kari looked wounded that he'd think otherwise. ''Of course I would. I'm surprised you asked.'' Did he think her cold and callous?

''It's just that you're city born and bred and...''

''So are you, for that matter. Where we're born doesn't define us, nor does where we live. You wound up in Prescott because your father lived there, but you moved to a place you like better. What makes you think I couldn't do the same?''

Maybe because at twenty-six she still lived with her parents. Would she have the courage to stand up to her father, to trade an easier life for a harder one? But he wasn't about to let her see his doubts, not right now when things were going so well between them. "I believe you could do the same, if you wanted to." He squeezed her hand. "Kari, I believe you're strong enough to do whatever you want to do."

She was beginning to believe she could, too. Up here in this remote area with this compelling man, she'd found the courage to stand up to her father. Soon she'd have to confront James Sinclair with that piece of news.

There was no getting around it, Dillon decided after they returned to the house. They needed supplies, and the roads were certainly clear enough for a drive into town. He peered into the refrigerator, the freezer, the cupboards, calling out items for Kari to write down. He checked the laundry room and added a few more things, then the bathroom. He'd already completed another list for the stock. Finishing, he put both in his shirt pocket.

"Are you sure you don't want to go into town with me?" It had been nearly two weeks since the night she'd fallen asleep in his truck. He'd thought she'd surely have cabin fever by now. But oddly, she showed no signs of it as she shook her head.

"No, you go ahead. Zeus and I will be fine here. I've started a mystery I want to finish." In truth, she'd love to have gone and checked out the town she'd never seen. But the remote possibility that someone would recognize her kept her from going. Tonight, after dinner, she'd tell Dillon and then decide what to do, whether to call her father again, or whatever.

"Okay." He grabbed his jacket from the peg. "Is there anything you can think of you need?"

Smiling, she shook her head.

Dillon walked over and kissed her soundly. "I won't be long."

"I'll miss you," she said, and found she meant it. Lord, when she fell, she *really* fell.

He grinned at her from the doorway. "Me, too."

Chet Baker owned the small supermarket on Main Street and did most of the work himself. A short, stocky man, he was friendly to a fault and had been known to help out more than one family when the weather had ruined their crops.

Standing at his counter, he totaled Dillon's purchases. "That pretty much do it?" he asked before ringing it up as final.

"That's it." Dillon felt good. Who wouldn't, after the morning he'd had in the hayloft, followed by a horseback ride to the river? Afterward, they'd eaten lunch, a great chicken salad Kari had made. He loved the way she tried new recipes, hardly ever making the same thing twice. A man wouldn't get bored with Kari around.

And he wanted her around for all time, Dillon thought as he reached in his wallet. He'd bought a few extra things—an angel food cake mix, ice cream, a bag of marshmallows. Things he'd never buy for himself, but he guessed she might like them. This thinking of pleasing someone else was new to him. But he kind of liked it.

Taking out several bills, he handed them to Chet, then spotted a stack of newspapers at the end of the counter. "Add a paper in, too," he said, shoving it into one of his bags. Pocketing his change, he pushed the cart out to where his truck was parked at curbside.

He'd already been to the feed store. Quickly, Dillon set two grocery bags on the passenger seat and two on the floor, then rounded the truck and got behind the wheel. The late-afternoon sun was still shining, and though it was chilly, there was a definite hint of spring in the air. Spring, the season of renewal and rebirth, of growing things. Of hope.

Grinning like an idiot, he started out, then had to stop at a railroad crossing two blocks along to let a train pass by. Waiting, he reached for the newspaper on top of the closest bag and unfolded it, glancing at the front page. His eye stopped at a double-column picture with the caption above it that read Where's Kari Sinclair?

Holding the newspaper closer, he gazed at the picture. Sure enough, it was Kari. Kari Smith, or so she'd said. His Kari. Only her name was Sinclair, not Smith. And damned if she wasn't the daughter of Senator James Sinclair.

Chapter Ten

Stunned, Dillon quickly scanned the article. "Not seen since a speech she gave at the Bonaventure Hotel in Phoenix two weeks ago...usually very visible...had been heavily booked on a north-south trip across Arizona stumping for her famous father...said to have the flu, but for two whole weeks?...the Sinclair camp tight-lipped about their youngest campaigner...charming spokesperson...no serious romances reported... Where was Kari Sinclair?"

The photo showed Kari laughing into the camera, her large, dark eyes dancing, undoubtedly enhanced by clever makeup. Her hair was long and curly instead of straight and tied in a ponytail, the way she usually wore it with him. It was a waist-up shot showing her wearing what appeared to be a well-cut business suit with a silky blouse. She looked lovely. Not better, just different.

The honking of a horn directly behind him had Dillon dropping the paper and moving forward, scarcely aware that the train had long since passed by. The truck shook as he crossed the railroad tracks, but he hardly noticed. One sentence kept replaying itself over and over in his mind like a terrible litany: she'd lied to him.

All right, so perhaps that first night she'd been confused and possibly a little frightened. After all, she'd been driven to the middle of nowhere by a perfect stranger, marooned in a snowstorm with him and his big dog. That would unsettle anyone.

But she'd been with him two weeks tomorrow and had endless opportunities to tell him the truth. Yet she hadn't.

She'd told him she'd contacted her father's office and no one would be looking for her because she needed time to think things through. Hard for Dillon to believe that a man as powerful as Senator Sinclair would simply say, "Sure, honey. Stay wherever you are until you get good and ready to come back." Very doubtful. That had to mean she'd lied to her father, too.

Why not? She apparently was good at it. Hadn't she suckered him into believing she was just taking a little time to get her head on straight? Hadn't he, after the slightest hesitation, decided she was on the up-and-up and opened his home to her? And, worst of all, hadn't he all but handed her his heart?

She was good. He'd give her that, Dillon thought as he turned onto the dirt road leading to his property. She'd wormed her way into his life with her good-natured attempts at being Susie Homemaker, cooking and washing and mending, then she'd completed the travesty by worming her way into his heart. He'd dropped his guard, and in no time he was kissing her, holding her, wanting her. Naturally, all that had led to the next step: he'd taken her into his bed.

Why hadn't she told him the truth? was the burning question. Why couldn't she have just been honest with him? What had she imagined he'd do, call out the Marines? When Lisa had sabotaged his ranch rather than confess she hated the country life, he'd spent many an hour asking himself why. Now, after vowing he'd never take another woman at face value, here he was again.

With a squeal of tires, he halted the truck on the apron in front of the stables. His mouth a thin line, he crammed the newspaper into the nearest bag. Every line of his big body was tense and furious as he slammed his way out of the cab and walked around to the truck bed to unload his supplies for the barn. His steps long and angry, he quickly dispersed everything, then scooped two sacks of groceries into his arms and headed for the house.

He hadn't rehearsed anything, because there was really nothing to say. She'd lied, when he'd told her, from day one, how much he hated lying. She'd probably lied about caring for him, too, and that might wind up hurting most of all. Shouldering the door open, he entered the laundry room, passing through to the kitchen.

Kari was removing a pie from the oven slowly and carefully, praying it had turned out all right. Cherry pie from a can she'd found in the pantry. And she'd thawed out two steaks for dinner. A man on a full stomach would listen more readily, she hoped.

Her face pink and warm from the oven, she slipped off the hot pad gloves and turned toward Dillon, a smile on her face. But when she saw his scowl as he dumped the bags of groceries on the kitchen table, the smile died. Nervously, she studied him, wondering what could have happened to shift his mood from warm and loving to cold and condemning in a couple of short hours.

"Get everything you need?" she asked tentatively.

"And then some," Dillon answered, his voice sounding weary and flat. Studiously ignoring the mouthwatering baking aroma, he shrugged off his jacket, hung it on the back of the chair and turned to her.

His blue eyes were as stormy as she'd ever seen them. Swallowing hard, Kari stood her ground, shoving up the sleeves of her sweatshirt. She had to know, though apprehension sat on her shoulders like hundred-pound weights. "What's wrong?"

Dillon grabbed the newspaper from the bag and held it out to her. "You tell me."

Edging closer cautiously, Kari saw the picture and the large caption over it, her heart sinking like a heavy stone. An involuntary gasp escaped from between her lips as her eyes flew to his. "I can explain."

He tossed aside the paper as if it had singed his fingers. "Really? What possible explanation could you offer for deliberately hiding the truth, for living a lie in my home for two weeks?"

She had to make him see, to make him understand. "Dillon, I wanted to tell you. Several times I started to, but…this morning, in the loft, I went up to tell you everything. You said we'd talk later. Remember?"

He remembered, all right. He remembered a woman who'd distracted him by pretending to care, by confusing his mind and body with sex. He was almost as disgusted with himself as he was with her.

Icy fingers of fear clutched at her heart despite the heat in the kitchen. His face was like a chunk of chiseled granite, hard, unbending, cold. "I never meant to hurt you. Please understand. At first, I was afraid to tell you because…because I didn't know you, and all my life I'd been warned about strangers. I couldn't trust you back then, not right away.''

He made a sound deep in his throat. ''*You're* talking about trust? Do you hear yourself?''

He was twisting her words, not really listening. ''By the next day, I knew I wanted to stay, at least for a little while. Life here was so peaceful and quiet, with no demands. You were so nice about everything—when I messed up with the washer and your underwear came out pink, when I burned your breakfast. I'd never met anyone so easygoing. And then, that first day you touched me, I knew I'd run across someone very special.''

Dillon jammed clenched fists to his waist and stood with that challenging air about him. ''So special you couldn't tell me the truth. You made a fool of me, Kari.''

''No! No. That wasn't my intention. But each day it became harder to bring it up, to confess. I was afraid you'd kick me out, that you'd throw me in your truck and take me right back home.''

He nodded curtly. ''It seems you read me well. Get your things. I'm driving you home tonight.''

All that she'd been afraid of was happening. Kari felt her heart break. She had to make one last effort. ''Dillon, please listen. I didn't lie outright, I just didn't tell you all of it.''

His eyes narrowed. ''I imagine you've heard of lying by omission?''

''Yes, but I would have told you. Probably tonight. I was feeling terrible about the lie between us. I love you, Dillon. You have to believe that.''

If possible, his face hardened even more. ''Who can

believe anything a liar says?'' He grabbed his jacket. ''I'll be out by the truck. Don't take too long. It's a long drive.''

The hot tears came then, as she heard the finality of the door closing behind him. He wasn't going to listen, to try to understand. With Dillon, when it came to lying, things were either black or white. She'd gambled and lost.

Slowly, each step painful, Kari made her way to the room she'd used when she'd first arrived, where she would change back into the clothes she'd arrived in.

At the side of the barn, Dillon stood splitting logs he'd stacked for firewood. He needed to work off some steam before he set off or he'd drive up the side of a telephone pole.

Swinging the ax high, he slammed it down on the wood chunk lying on the tree stump, listening to the satisfying sound of wood splintering. Tossing the two pieces into a growing pile, he placed another large chunk in position and raised the ax again.

''You picturing anyone special on that there log?'' Mac asked, wiping his hands on his checkered kerchief as he stepped out of the barn. ''By the look of things, you'd like to split someone's head open 'stead of that piece of wood. Am I wrong?'' He spit into the dirt, then shifted his chew to the other side of his mouth.

Dillon barely glanced at the old man. ''Maybe.'' Down came the blade and two pieces flew off the stump from the force of the blow.

Pushing his hat back just a bit, Mac studied his friend and employer. ''Anyone I know?'' he asked, his small eyes squinting.

Dillon drew in a deep breath, then blew it out, pausing with the ax head resting on the ground. "You know, Mac, you were right all along, and I should've listened harder. Women mess up your head real bad, then they think they've got you."

So that was it. Mac glanced over to the house, then back at Dillon.

"Who needs them?" Dillon went on, putting another piece of log in place. "We get along just fine without 'em. From now on, the only females allowed on this ranch are the four-legged variety." His angry eyes swung to Mac's face. "If I *ever* bring another woman here, you have my permission to hit me over the head with something hard and heavy." Raising the ax, he struck a mighty blow.

"That so?" Mac stuffed his kerchief into his back pocket. "Kari done something bad?"

"Yeah, you could say that." The pain of it twisted his insides.

Just then Kari stepped out. She was wearing a long raincoat he'd never seen on her, and she looked sad. Zeus was alongside her, looking oddly droopy. Animals sensed things. Anyone who worked with them knew that.

Mac turned to Dillon, who'd slammed the ax blade into the stump and was wiping his forehead with his hand-kerchief. "You sure this is the smart thing to do? She's not Lisa, you know."

Dillon pocketed his handkerchief. "No," he said, feeling his anger vanish in a wave of sadness, "she's an even better liar." Turning on his heel, he marched to his truck and got behind the wheel.

Mac stepped forward, watching Kari slowly walk over, the dog at her heels. When she was in front of him, she moved close and hugged him, holding on tightly for just a few seconds.

"Take care of yourself, Mac," she whispered, then bent to the big German shepherd. Leaning down, she hugged his head to her, fighting tears. Straightening finally, she climbed up into the cab of the truck.

Zeus barked twice as she shut the door, wanting in. "Stay!" Dillon commanded.

Mac caught a glimpse of Dillon's grim face as he swung the truck around and headed toward the road. Removing his hat, he scratched his head, then patted his thinning hair.

Closing the barn doors, Mac sighed as he hobbled toward his trailer. He'd best rest up. "C'mon, boy," he said to Zeus. "Ain't nothin' we can do now."

The ride to Paradise Valley northeast of Phoenix took place in utter silence except for Kari's brief directions on how to get to the Sinclair home. Dillon drove just at the speed limit, she noticed, but she could see he was anxious to dump his unwanted passenger, the sooner the better. The hands that gripped the steering wheel were coiled tightly, his profile hard and stony. He kept his eyes focused straight ahead. The tension in the air was almost palpable.

As for Kari, she just felt numb. She kept going over things, wondering just when and how she could have changed this whole scenario. There never seemed to be a right moment for a coward to confess, she supposed. In all her conjecturing of possibilities, wondering how Dillon would take the news, she'd pictured him angry at first, then maybe disappointed that she hadn't trusted him enough to tell him who she really was. But then, she'd gone on to envision him forgiving her, taking her in his strong arms where she'd vow to never keep anything from him again.

That had been a foolish fantasy. He'd acted out her worst fears, her worst nightmare. He not only wouldn't forgive, he wouldn't even listen.

It had grown dark as they made their way south. Alongside them on the divided highway was a minivan that captured Kari's attention out the side window. Two young boys were each seated by a back window flanking a car seat where a sweet-faced little girl slept, a pacifier dangling from her mouth. The young father was driving, the mother in the passenger seat talking to him. Suddenly they both laughed and she sent him a radiant smile.

Kari looked away, tears coming into her eyes. That was a family, loving and complete, happy together. For a brief few days, she'd envisioned a life like that. Not the kind of household she'd grown up in where politics and business ruled their every moment, where her father had been like a stranger, traveling a good deal of the time during her growing-up years. Not the sort of family where the mother, although a good person, loved the limelight, too, and was gone more often than not, leaving Clara, the housekeeper, to raise two daughters. One daughter, Dana, apparently wanted that same kind of life for her future. Kari most definitely didn't.

No, she wanted a family life like the folks in the minivan probably had. She'd dared to dream that Dillon would want her at his side, to work the ranch, to be his wife. She'd taken that dream a step further and hoped he'd want children—two or three—boys who were as strong and handsome as he, a little girl whose hair she could braid, someone to buy dolls for. They already had the vine-covered cottage; well, not exactly, but a cozy cabin that they'd have to add on to. They even had the dog. The ideal family.

But it wasn't to be. She hadn't told Dillon everything, and therefore was branded a liar in his eyes. All the good moments they'd shared, the nights entwined in each other's arms, the soft words of love—all forgotten over her dreadful infraction of Dillon's unwritten regulations.

Kari knew she had no one to blame but herself. He'd laid out the rules from day one, telling her soon after about Lisa, his mother, any number of others who'd lied to him. And knowing that, she'd kept silent. Her mistake. But she'd made a larger one.

She'd fallen in love with a man who'd never learned about forgiveness.

The old-fashioned globe streetlamps of the neighborhood where Kari had grown up were softly glowing as Dillon drove up the hilly road. Hadn't he guessed, even before he'd known Kari was a senator's daughter, that she would live in a place like this? Large rolling lots, manicured lawns, bougainvillea blooming in a riot of colors along stucco walls that hid the wealthy from the eyes of the prying peasants.

"It's the last one on the right," she said quietly.

Of course, the one on the highest hill, so the good senator could look down on the world from his secure vantage point. Dillon swallowed around a bitter lump in his throat as he pulled up to an iron gate with a large *S* scrolled on each half. There was a black box on the driver's side standing on a cement pillar.

"You have to press the security code for the gates to open," Kari told him. "It's 5-9-3-8-5."

Lowering his window, Dillon punched in the code and

watched the gates swing inward. How had he ever thought that Kari would be satisfied with a simple rancher, when she'd grown up with all of this? What colossal ego had made him think she would choose him over this obviously opulent life-style? Gritting his teeth, he followed the winding driveway toward the pillared entrance.

The grass was so green it looked artificial. Royal palm trees were artfully placed along the perimeter of a wrought-iron fence. Roses and hibiscus and poinsettias thrived in free-form flower beds. Two huge columns flanked the tall double doors. Dillon had the incongruous feeling he'd just arrived at Scarlet O'Hara's Tara.

He shifted into Park. She had no luggage, so there was no reason for him to get out and help her. She was home now, where there would be relatives and servants to attend to her every need. She didn't need him, that was for certain.

It was late, and Dillon was very tired. The thought of having to drive back all alone and then face his empty house was almost more than he could bear right now. But he'd be damned if he'd let her know how badly she'd hurt him.

He turned to her, saw she was dry-eyed but nervous, her hands twisting her belt. He couldn't let her vulnerability sway him. He'd have to play it tough. "Goodbye, Kari. It's been fun," he said, and saw the blood drain from her face.

Without a word, Kari opened the truck door and jumped down. Hurrying up the three wide steps, she didn't pause, didn't look back. She pressed the doorbell, heard the chimes echo inside and prayed someone would answer quickly. She needed to get away from Dillon's condemning eyes, to be alone so she could weep in private.

At last the door swung wide and Clara stood there in her white uniform, a surprised look on her round face. "Oh, Miss Kari. We've all been so worried about you." Taking her hand, she pulled Kari into a bear hug, holding her close to her ample body.

"I'm okay, Clara," Kari told her, gently stepping aside.

Clara stared uncertainly at the truck still by the door, the driver in shadow. "Is the gentleman coming in?"

"No, he's leaving." Kari shoved the door closed, then heard the roar of the truck's engine as Dillon zoomed around the circle. "Is anyone home?" she asked the housekeeper as she removed Norma's raincoat.

"Your father's in Washington, but he's expected back tomorrow. Your mother's playing bridge tonight and should be home in another hour or so. I'm not sure where Dana is." Clara slipped an arm around the young woman she'd known from childhood on. "Are you all right, honey? Could I fix you something to eat?"

"I'm not hungry, just tired." Giving Clara's hand a quick squeeze, she headed for the circular stairs. "If anyone asks, please tell them I'll talk to them in the morning. I want to take a shower and get some sleep."

"Of course." Clara went to the closet to hang up the raincoat, then walked to the phone in the library. James Sinclair had given her specific instructions that he was to be called immediately if Kari called or showed up.

Kari woke to the sun streaming in through two tall, narrow windows alongside her bed since she'd forgotten to pull the drapes across them last night. After her shower, emotionally drained, she'd fallen into bed and into a deep, restless sleep almost immediately. If her mother had stopped in after her bridge game, Kari hadn't heard her. But then, around three in the morning, she'd awakened and lain there, unable to go back to sleep, the events of the past two weeks playing over and over on the screen of her mind. It had taken her till nearly six to finally drop off again.

The bedside clock let her know it was eight, and above it, the date showed to be April 1. Kari stretched lazily, wishing she could ease her mind as simply as she'd rested her body. No matter how she tried to ignore things, the last few hours she'd spent with Dillon kept creeping to the forefront of her mind.

Where had she gone wrong?

Oh, honesty be hanged! She hadn't done anything so terrible, had she? All right, she'd masqueraded under another name, but how had that hurt him? She hadn't lied and gone drinking like his mother had. She hadn't sabotaged his ranching efforts with small, mean little tricks, then released his new horses into the wild. In every other way, she'd been totally up-front with him.

Including the fact that she loved him, which she was certain he no longer believed, either.

A sharp tap on the door drew her attention, then it was opened by a tall, robust-looking man with a full head of silver hair that had once been as blond as Kari's, and sincere brown eyes much like her own. "Hello, Dad," Kari said, pulling the covers up over her short sleep shirt and bracing herself for what she knew was coming. "I thought you were in Washington."

"I took the red-eye home when Clara called to tell me you were here." Wearing dark gray suit pants and a still-crisp white shirt with tie and jacket missing, James looked every inch the elder statesman as he sat down on the edge of Kari's bed. "Would you like to tell me now what you've been up to for the past fourteen days?"

His tone, the same one he used when he chaired his committees, always made Kari feel about ten years old. Determined to remember the changes she'd decided to make in her life during those two weeks, she met his unwavering gaze with one of her own. "I took a hiatus. I needed to think about the direction of my life." He was silent, so she went on. "As I said on the phone—I love you, Dad, but I'm not happy working for your campaign. I'm not sure what I want to do exactly, but I know it doesn't involve politics. That's your thing. I need to be my own person."

James crossed his legs, braced one arm on the bed. "All right, fine. I'm unclear on why you had to run off and frighten us all in order to come to this decision."

Kari sighed, knowing conversations of this nature with her father were never easy. "I didn't intend for things to happen the way they did." Then she told him about taking the two allergy pills after talking with him on the phone that night in the Bonaventure, about deciding to go for a walk, about growing sleepy and winding up in a truck bed, then the drive up north and the marooning snowstorm. She wasn't too specific because she didn't want to involve Dillon in any way, nor to have her father know where he lived. As protective as James Sinclair was, he just might order the man drawn and quartered.

James frowned. "Do you realize what a risk you were taking?"

"Yes, but it turned out all right." Up until yesterday afternoon.

Sinclair tried valiantly to keep a lid on his famous temper. If he was too insistent, he knew Kari would just clam up and he'd never get to the bottom of this escapade. "Who is this truck driver? Clara said he drove you home last night."

"He's a rancher, raises horses, breeds them, trains them and sells them. He…he was very kind and considerate, a gentleman."

"What about his wife?"

Kari watched her fingers fold a section of the comforter. No, she wasn't going to lie, not even by omission. Lying was what got her into this mess. "He doesn't have a wife, just an older ranch hand who lives on the premises and a stableful of horses and a German shepherd named Zeus." Which was more than she'd planned to reveal.

The senator's jaw clenched despite his best efforts. "Then you stayed in this horse breeder's ranch house, just the two of you?"

"Yes," she said, her voice steady, her eyes defying him to ask more.

James rarely disappointed. "Is there a possibility that you're pregnant?"

"That does it!" Kari threw back the covers and got up, anger causing her to tremble. "Are you aware, Dad, that I'm twenty-six, not sixteen? That question is way out of line. If you're unhappy with the way I conduct my personal life, then say so now. I can be packed and out of here by noon. You may recall, I do have money of my own." The inheritance from her grandfather was invested, and she hadn't touched it, but she knew it was there. A thought flashed into her mind and she went with it. "As a matter of fact, I plan to get a place of my own very soon, anyway. I was going to wait until after the election, but just say the word, and I'm out of here to-day.''

A good politician, and a good father, knew when to retreat to regain lost ground. James Sinclair loved his family, but he was aware that sometimes he was a bit heavy-handed. ''That won't be necessary. I apologize. I'm only trying to protect you, Kari.''

At the closet, she grabbed her robe. ''Well, stop. I don't need so much protecting. Give me a little credit, will you? I'm a grown woman capable of making my own decisions. You've got to let me do that, and if I make bad ones, then I'll have to handle that. You can't wrap me in cotton and keep me safe.''

''Yes, you're right. I'll try, Kari.'' He rose to his full six-three height, moved to hug her. ''I was just so worried.''

Kari felt the fight drain out of her. ''I know, and I'm sorry I put you through that.''

He leaned back, studied her face, noticed her eyes were just the slightest bit swollen. If that rancher hurt his daughter...

''This rancher, are you going to see him again? Do you care about him?'' He hadn't the right to ask, but he needed to know.

Kari pulled free, turned away. ''I don't want to talk about him or anything else right now.'' She glanced toward the door. ''Is Mom up?''

When she got that stubborn look on her face, James knew he wouldn't get any more answers from her. Sighing dramatically, he opened her bedroom door. ''Yes, she's in the breakfast room, and so's Dana. They let you sleep in.''

"If you're going down, tell them I'll be there in a few minutes." She disappeared into the bathroom.

"No kidding, Kari," Dana said, studying her sister's face, "you look different."

Swallowing hot coffee, Kari frowned. "What do you mean, different?"

Dana Sinclair narrowed her dark eyes and brushed back a lock of sable hair the exact shade of her mother's. "I can't put my finger on it exactly."

"Well, I'm not. I'm the same as before." *Except my heart's broken and I want to go back to DeWitt so badly I can taste it.*

"Actually, you do look a little pale, Kari," Dusty Sinclair said, nibbling daintily at a slice of dry toast.

Kari ignored that observation and poured herself more coffee.

Dana glanced through the archway. "All right, Dad's gone upstairs. Now tell us, what *really* happened?"

Kari didn't know whether to laugh or cry. "Nothing happened." Except that she'd fallen in love for the first time in her short life, and it happened to be with a man who didn't want her.

Dana waved her hand, her nails a vibrant red. "I don't believe you. Dad said you were marooned in a snowstorm in some remote little town with a cowboy for two weeks and you tell me nothing happened? Do you think I just fell off a turnip truck?"

Staring down into her cup, Kari shook her head. "He's a rancher, not a cowboy."

"Well, pardon me. I didn't know there was a difference."

"There is. He raises horses, not cattle."

Trying to be reasonable, Dana nodded. "Okay, rancher, then. What's he like?"

Kari looked up, saw her sister's curious eyes on her and her mother's concerned gaze. Enough was enough. "He looks like Mel Gibson, has a sense of humor like Robin Williams and a checkbook like Donald Trump's. Any more questions?" She shoved back her chair and picked up her coffee mug. "I'm going to get dressed."

Two pairs of brown eyes watched her leave the breakfast room, then turned to look at each other.

"She fell for him," Dana announced, smug in her knowledge of the ways of love.

Dusty Sinclair let out a ragged breath. "I'm afraid I have to agree with you."

Chapter Eleven

Lying in his bed in DeWitt, Dillon heard the mantel clock strike twelve. He'd been pounding the pillows a full two hours and he had to be up at five. Turning over, snarling at the twisted blanket, he swore inventively under his breath. On the floor alongside the bed, Zeus lifted his head and gave him a questioning look.

"Don't say a word!" he warned the innocent dog.

Shifting again, he scrunched the pillow beneath his head, arranging it just so, and took a deep breath. Suddenly he sat up straight, staring at the offending pillow. That was it, of course. He couldn't get to sleep because the pillows smelled like Kari, the sheets smelled like Kari, the whole damn room smelled like Kari.

Disentangling himself, he got up and yanked the sheets from the bed, pulled the cases from the pillows and tossed aside the blanket. In the hallway he flipped on the light and marched to the laundry room. At the washer he stuffed the bedding inside, bent to the soap box and scooped a generous cupful before sprinkling it on the offending sheets. Angrily he pulled the Start knob and watched hot water spurt into the machine.

That was the answer, to get rid of every trace of her scent that wound around him, twisting his insides. She was in the very air he breathed. Grabbing the can of air freshener, he walked back to his room and sprayed liberally. That sent Zeus hurrying to his fireside pillow. Returning the can, he paused, staring at the washer and dryer, remembering.

Remembering the day she'd put his red shirt in with the white load, turning everything pink. The hesitant way she'd shown him what she'd inadvertently done. The surprise on her face when, instead of getting angry, he'd laughed.

Why had she expected anger? he now wondered. Was it because she hadn't known him then or because, living in her father's house, she'd grown used to explosive men? None of his business any longer, Dillon reminded himself.

He wandered out to the kitchen, and the first thing he noticed was the cherry pie Kari had made with such care yesterday, still uncut, uneaten. Tomorrow he'd take it over to Mac's trailer. His appetite had fled, it seemed. Suddenly, eating alone held little appeal, when for years he'd eaten just that way, before Kari.

He couldn't help smiling at how pleased she'd been when he'd praised the chicken and dumplings she'd made, his favorite dinner. She'd hobbled about that night on a bruised ankle after the trap incident. That ugly thing

would have had most women screaming…crying. Kari
had only worried about upsetting him.

Strolling to the window, Dillon stared out at the quiet
night, a sliver of a moon up there somewhere. There'd
been a big moon out the night he'd hurried to the stable
with Kari to help Calypso give birth to a healthy colt.
He would never forget the wonder in Kari's huge brown
eyes as she'd watched the mother clean her son. The son
she'd named Cinnamon, the colt who seemed to be looking for Kari every time the stable doors opened.

That thought had him remembering the afternoon he'd
put Domino to Dixie in the paddock, the enthralled way
Kari had watched the entire mating, as if holding her
breath. That was the first night he'd carried her to his
bed and made slow, delicious love to her.

Dillon slammed a fist onto the kitchen counter, causing
Zeus to get up from his pillow to see what was up. He
was doomed to remember, it seemed. What good would
it do to erase all traces of her scent, to give away all the
food she'd cooked or all the items he'd bought for her
that day in the market? It was his memories he couldn't
erase.

More than a little irritated at himself, Dillon strolled
to the couch and sat down, staring into the still-glowing
embers of his earlier fire. Zeus came over, whined once,
then placed his big head on Dillon's lap. ''Yeah, I miss
her, too,'' he muttered to the dog, stroking his fur. To no
one else would he confess that, but Zeus wouldn't blab.

Since returning from driving her home, even Mac
seemed to censure him with every look, every gesture.
Tired of everyone's displeasure, he'd brought her up to
Mac earlier today, not going into details, but explaining
that Kari hadn't been totally honest with him. Mac had

listened in that quiet way he had, then scratched his head before throwing in his two cents' worth. "Ain't nobody perfect. Some would say even you. I think you made a mistake." With that, he'd hobbled out of the barn.

How had Kari managed to win over his ranch hand, his newborn colt and probably the mares as well, to say nothing of his own dog? In just two short weeks, she had everyone on her side.

All right, so she was charming. But she'd lied. He'd have let her stay if she hadn't lied. However, a nagging voice in the back of his head reminded him that he'd have driven her back as soon as the roads became passable again. A man doesn't keep a senator's daughter in some remote cabin if he doesn't want trouble. And that was the one thing she hadn't wanted—to go back. Still, it had come to that, hadn't it?

Getting up, Dillon scowled as he went back to his room. Quickly he remade the bed with clean linens and lay down. Hands under his head, he lay staring at the ceiling. The light from the barn spotlight drizzled in through the far window. He could no longer smell that marvelous female scent.

Now if only he could get her off his mind.

Kari smiled at the roomful of senior citizens gathered in the town meeting hall of Sun City West in Phoenix as they applauded her speech. The weather was warm for the first week of April, and she knew she looked fresh as a daisy in her yellow suit, her long hair recently trimmed to barely touch her shoulders. She had also put on makeup and had had her nails done after the manicurist had scolded her royally for allowing her hands to get in such dismal shape.

"Whatever have you been doing?" the woman had asked Kari. "Your hands look as if you scrub floors for a living."

Actually, Kari had wanted to tell her, she *had* scrubbed a floor or two recently. The laundry room floor, the day the washer suds had overflowed, and the kitchen floor, when she'd spilled cherry juice on her last day in DeWitt.

Sitting back down at the head table, Kari tuned out the mistress of ceremonies as she droned on about the senator's many virtues, letting her mind drift. Despite her declarations to the contrary, she was back on the circuit, campaigning for James Sinclair. To keep peace in the family, she'd agreed to follow through on her commitments until after his election. By then she hoped to have scouted out an apartment and made plans to move out of the family manse.

Everyone was trying to talk her out of the move, including Dana, much to Kari's surprise. To no avail, for she had to stick to her plans or she'd be sucked in to another year and another. This was a merry-go-round she needed to get off. Maybe she'd even move out of the Phoenix area. Some of the Northern Arizona suburbs were less populated, quieter, more peaceful. Now that she'd had a taste of country life, she found herself craving it.

Her father was once more his smiling self, and Kari thought she knew why. James had bought himself about six months till the election, six months to work on Kari to stay at home, to stay with his staff. She knew exactly how he worked. However, she would surprise him this time, as she wasn't giving in. She wanted her freedom, her own life, space to pursue her own dreams.

Whatever they were, Kari thought, joining in a burst

of applause for something the chairwoman had said, a smile ever in place. She would have to get a new dream, since Dillon had effectively slammed the door on the dream he'd awakened in her. She would not dwell on that, on longing for a man who was too pigheaded to listen to her explanation and too self-righteous to forgive.

The luncheon ended on a happy note, and afterward several guests came up to congratulate Kari on her talk, a few even requesting autographs. It wasn't until one of the guests, a man in a white shirt and bow tie, approached that anything of a personal nature was asked.

"Here tell you been out of touch for a spell," he said, studying Kari through thick bifocals. "So the papers say. You got yourself a fella, Ms. Sinclair?" His smile was impish.

Kari didn't realize her hands were trembling as her smile slipped a bit. She became aware that the buzzing conversations around her had stopped and that a reporter with poised pencil and pad was waiting for her reply. She checked the man's name tag. With difficulty she gave Elmer Watkins a big smile.

"I hear a good man is hard to find." She turned her smile on the tiny woman clinging to Elmer's arm. "Mrs. Watkins may have gotten the last one."

The couple smiled and chuckled, walking away pleased. Kari closed her eyes briefly, wondering if this day would ever end.

Why was it that time seemed to drag so, on these speaking trips, yet there hadn't been enough hours in the day on the DeWitt ranch? There'd been so much to do, three big meals a day to fix, which wasn't exactly a snap for someone who hadn't even read a cookbook until a few weeks ago. Then there'd been the visit to the barn,

a stop at the stalls of each of the mares as well as Henry,
a carrot or apple for the two rambunctious colts, then a
longer stay with Calypso and Cinnamon. The only one
she avoided was Domino, who snorted at everyone who
came near him, even Dillon. She'd thought that after that
energetic mating he'd be in a better mood.

After that, there'd been walks to take, time to practice
horseback riding in the paddock, coffee visits to Dillon,
laundry to do. She'd never been bored, never lain awake
at night unable to relax, sleeping for the first time in years
like an innocent babe. Now, she was constantly bored,
and sleep was a rare visitor to her bedroom. This morning
she'd had to apply concealer with a heavier hand to cover
the beginnings of dark shadows under her eyes. Any moment now someone from the press would notice and ask
her more questions.

With a smile Kari accepted another program for her
autograph, thinking that in five minutes she'd beg off and
leave, saying she had another commitment. She did, with
the ladies of the Sun City Garden Club. Glancing to the
back of the room, she noticed Norma with her ever-
present clipboard in hand waiting to whisk her to the limo
and the next appointment. Tony Baloney and Brunhilda
hovered near the door, trying to look inconspicuous and
therefore standing out even more in this crowd of retirees.
Since her unexpected two-week absence, they both
watched her like two hawks ready to pounce.

Stifling a yawn behind her hand, Kari checked her
watch as she handed the program back to the tall woman
wearing three strands of pearls. Four more minutes.

She hated having to call him. But Kari knew she'd
have to. Twice now, her father had asked her about her

amethyst ring, the one that had belonged to his mother. James knew she wore it all the time. She'd given him some vague excuse about having misplaced it somewhere in her room when in fact, she knew exactly where it was. She'd left it on the sink in Dillon's bathroom.

Seated at her desk in her room, she stared at the phone. It was evening, seven o'clock, an hour that usually found Dillon in the cabin. It would be too dark to work outside and, unless one of the horses had a problem, he'd have finished up in the stables a while ago. Maybe he was eating a late dinner or reading the newspaper. Or perhaps he was curled up on his big couch in front of a blazing fire with one of his many books. It stayed colder than Phoenix that far up north.

Deciding to bite the bullet, Kari picked up the phone and dialed the number she'd memorized. One ring. Two. He picked it up in the middle of the third, his voice sounding sleepy.

"Dillon, it's Kari. I hope I didn't wake you."

Standing at the kitchen phone, he ran a hand along the back of his neck, struggling with various emotions he'd thought he had under perfect control. "No, just finishing the dishes."

One cooks, one cleans up. Those are the rules. She pictured him at the sink, dish towel slung over one shoulder, his blue eyes wary as he wondered what she wanted. The mental picture was so strong it had her hands shaking.

"I'm sorry to bother you, but I seem to have left my ring in your bathroom. Did you find it?" A sudden thought struck her, that he might think she'd left it there on purpose, to have an excuse to call him. "It belonged to my grandmother," she added, hoping he would read between the lines and realize that she wouldn't have called except for a special ring.

"Yeah, I did." That same night he'd been brushing his teeth when he'd spotted the ring. He'd picked it up and held it for a long time, fighting the memories that washed over him.

"Would it be too much trouble to mail it to me? No rush. But the next time you go into town?" It was on the tip of her tongue to offer to pay the postage, but she stopped herself, knowing that would probably offend him.

"Sure, no problem." He wanted to ask her how she was, what she'd been doing, any number of things. But he kept still, not knowing how she would take his inquiries.

This was *so* hard, Kari thought, much harder than she'd thought as she blinked back tears. She wanted so badly to reach out to him, to ask him if, during these long, terrible days apart, he'd thought things over and decided to listen to her side of the story. She wanted to ask how his nights were, if he remembered lying with her, holding her, loving her, the way she did. But the silence stretched out and she remembered his cold, stony profile on the ride home. No, she wouldn't bring up anything personal.

"How's Cinnamon?" she finally asked.

"Growing." *Missing you, but not nearly as much as I do.*

Kari forced a smile into her voice. "That's good. Well, that's it, then. Take care of yourself."

Say something, anything, just keep her on the line a little longer. "Yeah, you, too." He held the receiver until he heard the click at the other end. Bowing his head, he closed his eyes and hung up.

Dillon wandered the house, thoughts racing around in his mind like mice in a maze. Should he have said more? If so, what? She'd sounded so damn good, so normal, so like Kari. He curled the hands that ached to hold her into fists.

Was he angry with her or himself? Dillon no longer knew. Had he been too hasty in dumping her back home like something he had no further use for? Did she think he'd tired of her and grasped at any excuse to get rid of her? Had she maybe learned her lesson about telling the truth, and this call was her way of reaching out to him to say she's sorry, that she's still interested? But then, could he ever trust her again?

He shoved a hand through his already-mussed hair. He still hadn't gotten that haircut. His fingers skimmed along his jawline, the beard he'd started to grow because Kari said she thought he'd look good wearing one. It was at the itchy stage, but he didn't have the energy to shave it off.

Why not? She would never see it now. She was back where she belonged, in her father's house, with servants and luxury everywhere she looked. He gazed around the main room of his cabin and wondered how he'd ever thought she would be content with so little when she'd been used to so much.

He didn't give a damn about her family's money. He hoped she knew that. But would her father ever believe it? Dillon was doing all right for himself, building his herd, his business, fixing up his spread, finally commanding some good-sized fees. Still, he was what he was—a country rancher, a horse breeder and trainer. Kari was the daughter of a United States senator, one who lived in a house larger than the DeWitt Library. One look at her and any fool could spot breeding. He no longer even owned a suit that fit.

But there was no denying his feelings, though he'd been trying to do just that. She was the first woman he'd truly loved, and he wanted her to be the last, the only. Love had sneaked up on him, catching him unaware. It had probably begun as far back as that first night when he'd come in out of the cold and seen her sitting in his rocker, her feet wet and cold, shivering all over, but not complaining.

Dillon had told himself after Lisa had gone that he didn't need a woman in his life, that relationships took too much hard work and energy. He had a business to build. He liked doing as he pleased, answering to no one. But recently, things had changed. Now, even the cabin he'd so lovingly restored, the one that had given him so much pleasure, mocked him with its empty rooms and silence.

He scraped a hand over his face. He never should have taken her back to her father's house. Hadn't she told him she was unhappy there? With him she'd been happy. No way had she faked that.

So she'd made a mistake. So had he, in not allowing her to explain, in rushing her home, in comparing her to Lisa.

I need to be my own person, she'd told him. And her father hadn't allowed her to discover herself. If things had been different, would he have? Trying to be scrupulously honest, Dillon thought he would. He wasn't a control freak. He believed everyone should march to their own drummer, something he'd tried to explain to his own father. Here, Kari would have had the freedom to be herself.

A moot point, he thought, for he'd lost her due, in large part, to his pride. Could he make things right? She'd sounded cautious on the phone, but not unfriendly. Should he risk having her turn the tables on him by rejecting him? Rising, Dillon squared his shoulders. He'd never considered himself a coward.

Rubbing his forehead, he walked to the medicine chest, reached for the aspirin bottle. He'd never been one for a lot of headaches.

Until recently.

He'd no sooner swallowed the pills than he heard a pounding at his front door. Who would be coming here at this hour? Frowning, he went to answer.

"Hey, Dillon." Reggie Bennett who owned the next ranch two miles over, stood on the porch, his soiled white hat in hand. "We got trouble."

"Come in, Reggie. What's the problem?" Dillon wasn't close friends with Reggie or any of the other ranchers, for that matter. But he belonged to the Arizona Ranchers Association and had met most of the other members. He'd also welcomed their help when he was shoring up the sides of his barn. In turn, he'd helped two others reroof their cabins. In the country, neighbors helped neighbors, even those they didn't know too well. It was the only way to survive, especially against nature.

In the entryway, Reggie shook his head. "Hennessy's flooding. Harry and Nate came to get me 'bout an hour ago. We got to get some sandbags together, get everyone we can to help. You and me, we're not in too much danger 'cause our ranches are up a fairly steep incline. But some of the men—their places are already getting runoff."

"Okay. Where are we meeting?"

"Over at the Nichols' farm. Got about a dozen guys so far, got a few more to enlist. We could use someone to direct the workers, you know. There's coffee set up."

"I'll get Mac and we'll be right there." Dillon knew if he overlooked the older man, he'd never hear the end of it. He'd make sure Mac didn't overdo.

"Thanks." Reggie headed back out. "You got any sandbags, bring 'em along, will you?"

"Sure thing." He closed the door and rushed off to get dressed.

It was dark as pitch as Dillon drove his truck along the rutted back road, only his headlights showing the way. Despite the bumps, it was faster this route than going all the way out to the highway and circling back toward the river. His four-wheel-drive could handle rough roads easily. Alongside him, Mac bounced up then down as they hit a small gulley.

"Hold on," Dillon told him. Mac absolutely refused to put on a seat belt. "Wouldn't want you to drop out."

"You just worry about yourself, sonny," Mac returned, not pleased to be routed out of bed, but knowing he had to help out. "I knew this was gonna happen. Rode out thataway couple days ago. Damn river was almost spilling over then."

"Yeah, I had a feeling with the early spring thaw that we'd have trouble." Dillon held on to the wheel as they rumbled along.

Mac took his chewing tobacco out of his jacket pocket, then decided to wait. "Hear anything from Kari yet?" He knew he was opening a can of worms, but he also felt that particular can needed opening. Dillon had been mean as a stallion with a burr under his saddle lately. "Coupla weeks now since she left."

Dillon knew exactly how long ago Kari had left. Two weeks, three days and six hours. But who was counting? "She called awhile ago."

"Did, eh? She comin' back?"

"Why would she? I made it clear she should go home." And had been living with the consequences of that impulsive reaction ever since. Dillon ground his teeth.

"Durn fool thing you did, you ask me."

"I don't recall asking you."

"Maybe not. Someone's got to tell you. That woman's crazy about you. I heard the two of you in the hayloft that day, and…"

Dillon's head swiveled toward the old man. "You what? You were spying on us?" The very thing Kari had feared.

"Hell, no. I got better things to do. I went in to check on Maisy's sore foot. Heard you both wrestling around up there. Seemed you were getting along just fine. I left soon's I realized what was going on. Only a durn fool would walk away from her, and I never known you to be a fool, Dillon. Not till now."

Dillon's lips thinned. "What went on between Kari and me is personal." The truck hit a rut so deep he nearly bumped his head, the jostle not improving his mood any.

"I'm not lookin' to know the details, but you're old enough to know there ain't many gals out there like that one. You let her go, you'll live to regret it. Mark my words."

Dillon let out a ragged sigh. Mac had given voice to his own thoughts. "Maybe you're right."

"Ain't no *maybe*s about it. That's all I'm gonna say."

"I certainly hope so." Dillon swerved the truck onto the path leading to the Nichols' farm. They had a job to do, he thought as he glanced at the swollen river. A big, important job. But after it was done, he'd go see Kari. Because if he didn't try to get her back, like Mac said, he'd live to regret it.

Kari sat at the kitchen table in the breakfast room sipping coffee and munching on a raisin bagel. She really hadn't wanted to get up this morning, though the sun was shining and it promised to be a beautiful day. April was one of her favorite months in Arizona, with the weather usually warm, rather than intensely hot like in the summer months. Still, she felt somewhat lethargic.

Of course, she hadn't gotten to bed until sometime after midnight, having attended a block party fund-raiser in Scottsdale with Dana. Yet this morning her sister had bounded out of bed around six and been on her way to a radio interview without so much as a cup of coffee. Where did the girl get her energy?

Taking another bite, she wandered across the kitchen and turned on the small television set that Clara had on a shelf above the counter so she could watch her afternoon soaps. The housekeeper was already at the market, her mother was out for the day, and her father not due back till around noon. She was scheduled at the Ritz-Carlton for a luncheon, but not until one. So, for now she had the house to herself for a change. Topping off her coffee, Kari sat down again, propping her bare feet on the adjacent chair.

Remote in hand, she did a little channel surfing, hoping for a news program. She'd been too busy of late to even read a newspaper. It wasn't until her second go-round that she spotted something that caught her eye.

The local newscaster with his sincere haircut and his direct gaze was talking about the terrible flooding in the vicinity of Flagstaff, Arizona. Sitting up taller, Kari turned up the volume. The man went on to say that the Hennessy River, badly swollen from melting snow coming off the mountains in the early spring thaw, was creating a serious problem for farmers and ranchers in the vicinity, especially around DeWitt.

Absorbed now, Kari forgot about her breakfast as the picture switched to a scene along the banks of the river, the voice-over explaining that neighbors were pitching in, hauling sandbags to shore up the rising water. As the camera scanned the shoreline, she saw men in work boots and others in hip boots wading in the water and stacking the bags. Already the bags were nearly waist high in some spots.

As she watched, Kari thought she recognized the very section that she and Dillon had visited on her last full day in DeWitt. He'd explained then about when he'd been a young man helping out his uncle and the neighbors during just such a flooding situation. The next shot was of the churning water, then a wide angle of the mountain some distance away with water flowing rapidly into the river. As they zoomed back to the shore, Kari squinted, trying to see if she could spot a tall, dark-haired man working shoulder-to-shoulder with others to prevent a further disaster.

She was certain Dillon was there, because that's the kind of man he was, someone to depend upon. Someone good and kind, someone honest and reliable. But then, she'd known that from the start.

Back to the newscaster in the studio. "As anyone can see, the residents of DeWitt and surrounding area are working against time to hold back the mighty river. No one knows exactly when it will crest, but the best guess is several days from now. That means more long hours for these hardworking farmers to try to save their crops from ruin.

"I've been asked to request volunteers to help these flood victims. Any able-bodied man or woman who has the time and energy to lend a hand would be greatly appreciated. More sandbags are needed, also, as well as food for the volunteers. If you can help in any capacity, please call the number at the bottom of your screen for more information and specific directions."

Getting up, Kari hurried to the drawer where she knew pads of paper and pens were kept. Quickly she jotted down the number, then sat down again, her mind considering possibilities.

Her father would be furious, her mother would worry, and Dana would definitely think she'd lost her mind. Even if she made the long trip, Dillon could very well refuse her help, though she doubted his neighbors would. She was certainly an able-bodied person, young and strong. She'd never hauled a sandbag, but she was willing to try. If not that, perhaps she could round up food for the tired and hungry volunteers, serve drinks, something.

It might look to Dillon as if she were pursuing him. And maybe she was. She only knew she had to go. Her heart wasn't here giving lackluster speeches, living a boring life with a family who truly didn't need her. Not like those people needed her. She belonged in DeWitt alongside the man she loved.

Even if he didn't want her.

Her excitement building, Kari dialed the number on the pad.

Chapter Twelve

She'd nearly worn a path in the living room carpet, waiting for her father to get home. Kari saw his pale gray limo pull into the circular drive behind her BMW and rushed out before the chauffeur had brought the big car to a full stop. Anxiety had her yanking open his door while he was still giving instructions to the driver on when to pick him up next. Thank goodness he was alone, she thought as James stepped out, a puzzled smile on his face.

"Well, well. To what do I owe this unexpected pleasure?" James bent to kiss the top of his daughter's blond head. "It's been a long time since you've come out to meet me."

"I need to talk with you, Dad," Kari said as they walked inside.

In the marble foyer the senator stopped when he noticed two leather suitcases he knew to be Kari's standing near the door. He turned to her, noticing that she was wearing a navy turtleneck sweater over jeans, and on her feet were something that could only be called hiking boots. "That's quite an outfit. I thought you had some appointments this afternoon? A luncheon at the Ritz-Carlton, wasn't it?"

"Dana's subbing for me." Kari had been elated when she'd tracked down her sister and Dana had agreed with very little persuasion. But she'd wanted to know why. When Kari had told her that she was going to the man she loved, there'd been a shocked silence. Then Dana had said, "Go for it, honey. We only go around once."

Kari trailed after her father into his study, hoping he wouldn't make this too difficult for her. She'd waited to explain in person, knowing James would have been hurt by a letter or phone call. "I've cleared the rest of my calendar, too, Dad." She watched him sit down at his desk, lean back and raise his eyes to study her. She had his full attention now.

"I see. Care to explain why?" James kept his features even, but it was an effort. He loved his younger daughter, but he had a great deal of trouble understanding her.

Kari sat down in the low cane-back chair opposite her father, her voice steady and sure. She wanted his blessing on what she was about to do, but with or without it, she was going. "Dad, you once told me you knew when you were in your early teens that you wanted to go into politics, that you belonged in the public eye. Do you remember telling me that?"

Here we go again, James thought. Why couldn't Kari be more like Dana, who would likely wither up out of the limelight? "I'm sure I did say something like that," he said patiently.

"Well, it took me a little longer to know just what *I* want to do, but I finally know."

The senator reached into his vest pocket and removed a cigar he'd been saving to help him relax during a tense moment. He was certain this moment qualified. "And that would be?" He rolled the tip of the cigar along his tongue, savoring the taste.

"I'm in love with a rancher up in DeWitt, and I'm going back there to help him and his neighbors through a crisis."

James all but spit the cigar across the room. It took him half a minute to be able to speak. "That's the cowboy you were marooned with in that snowstorm?"

"Rancher, not cowboy. Horses, not cattle. And yes, it is." Her eyes softening, she leaned forward, trying to reach him on another level. "Dad, I know how much you love Mom. Well, I love Dillon and I want to be with him. Here, I'm just going through the motions, not really living, just existing. I *need* to be with the man I love."

"But you came back, you didn't want to talk about him. I gathered you'd quarreled and…" He slowed down, realizing he was all but sputtering. "What kind of name is Dillon, anyway?"

She smiled at that, at how flustered he'd become. "It's Irish. His father, by the way, is as stubborn as you are."

James frowned. "It's not a matter of stubborn. It's a matter of protection. How in the world can the Secret Service protect you up in some godforsaken little town living in a little shack with cows roaming all over?"

Kari let out an exasperated sigh. The man never listened, never heard what she said. "Horses, not cows. The town has around three thousand residents and the house is well built and cozy, not a shack. And I don't want the Secret Service to follow me. I won't need them. Dillon is very protective.'' She remembered the shotgun alongside the fireplace, the way he'd rushed to her aid when Rich had her cornered. "And so's Zeus.''

James's frown deepened. "Who the hell is Zeus?''

"A big German shepherd who hardly ever left my side.'' She glanced at her watch, realizing time was rushing on and she'd wasted enough waiting for him. "I wanted to tell you in person, but I can't wait for Mom since Clara tells me she's not due home until this evening. But I've already spoken with Dana. You'll have to explain things to Mom.'' She stood, shoving up her sleeves, anxious to be gone.

"Now, hold on just a minute.'' The senator drew in a deep breath, reaching for the calm he knew was there somewhere. "I can't let you go traipsing off to some vague place with some man I've never met. Kari, you're not just an ordinary woman. You're a senator's daughter, a kidnap risk, a way for some nutcase to get to me. I can't allow you to—''

"No, you hold on. I'm not going to live my life according to your plans just because you're a political figure. You could very likely be in the senate for the next twenty years, or run for higher office. Dad, I won't put my life on hold while you get to live yours just as you please. And I already told you, Dillon won't let anything happen to me.'' Of that she was certain. If he took her back at all, he'd guard her better than Tony Baloney and Brunhilda ever could. If he didn't take her back...well, she'd cross that bridge when she came to it.

James's busy mind was considering several other arguments. "What is the big rush, then? Why can't this Irishman come down here and meet your family, get to know us, like everyone else does?"

"You mean so you can interrogate him, get the CIA to check out his background, find out his political leanings and see if he's good enough for me? I wouldn't put anyone I cared for through that. You'll get to meet him one day, hopefully when this crisis up there is over."

"What crisis?"

Kari pointed to the newspaper on the corner of his desk. "It's all over the papers and on television. There was a lot of snow this past winter in the mountains and this early spring has melted it all very quickly. The Hennessy River runs near Dillon's ranch. It's threatening to overflow, if it hasn't already. All the ranchers and farmers in the surrounding area are working together to haul sandbags to the shoreline to hold back the water. I need to go there and help them."

The shocked look on her father's face would have had Kari laughing if the situation weren't so serious.

"You plan to go up north and haul sandbags? Kari, have you lost your mind?"

"No, Dad, I think I've finally found it. Please don't try to talk me out of this."

He saw that he was getting nowhere, so he switched tactics. "Look, I can make a couple of calls and have a dozen men there in no time with all the sandbags they'll need. I can—"

"That's fine, but I'm still going. Try to understand, *please.*"

Slowly James got to his feet. "Believe me, I am trying. This is just a bit of a shock, that's all. Not only does my daughter tell me she's in love with someone I've never met, but that she's leaving her family behind and going up to some remote town. That's enough to shake up my world."

Kari moved to his side, slid an arm around his waist. "It shook up my world to fall in love with Dillon. I didn't go looking for him, or for a relationship. But I couldn't help myself. I love him, Dad."

Finally, he nodded. "It happened like that to me, too, the first day I saw your mother. I couldn't have stopped it any more than I could have held back a runaway train."

Blinking back tears, Kari smiled at him. "I knew if you'd hear me out that you'd understand."

Arm in arm, they left the study and walked together toward the front door. "You're not just going to move in with him, are you? I mean, what about marriage and all that? Your mother will be hurt."

Kari didn't believe that for a second. As usual, James was thinking of how such a thing would affect his campaign. "Marriage is certainly something I'd like, if he wants me."

James snorted. "*If* he wants you! Who does this cowboy think he is that my daughter wouldn't be good enough for him?"

She let him blow off steam, as always. "I didn't say that. We have some things to work out."

At the door the senator decided to give it one last shot, perhaps his best. "Kari, be honest. Aren't you going to miss being around men of power?"

Slowly she shook her head. "Dad, I'm going to answer you with a totally melodramatic statement—power, like beauty, is in the eye of the beholder. I find Dillon, a man who gets out of bed when it's still dark outside, works eighteen hours a day at something he loves, even though it's hard, dirty, sweaty work, every bit as powerful as you. Actually, you might even like him."

James wasn't convinced of that, but he knew he was fighting a losing battle. Placing both hands on Kari's arms, he turned her toward him. "You're sure this is the right thing you're doing?"

"Absolutely."

"But if something goes wrong, you'll call me? You know you always have a home here?"

She moved into his embrace then. "I know that, but thank you."

He kissed her then, feeling suddenly older than when he'd walked in. Picking up her bags, he followed Kari to her BMW parked in the circular drive and waited for her to pop the trunk. Finished stowing the luggage, he pulled her to him for another fierce hug, finding his vision suddenly blurry. "You'll take care of yourself, not take any foolish chances?"

"I promise. Please don't worry. Pinocchio will be just fine." Kari prayed she was doing the right thing.

At the sound of their special code name, he nodded again. "I want you to call me often." James Sinclair prayed he wasn't making a mistake letting her go. But then, what choice did he have? Kari had never been headstrong, not until now. Love did that to a person, he well knew.

"I'll call. I'm not sure when, but I'll call."

He nodded, watched her get behind the wheel and closed her door for her. He was no longer certain he could trust his voice.

"Please explain to Mom and Dana," Kari said, starting the car. Slipping into gear, she waved to him as he stood on the bottom step. "I love you, Dad," she called out as she drove away.

"I love you, too, honey," the senator whispered, then went inside, his steps slow and hesitant.

She had to put on her headlights as she reached the center of DeWitt. She'd only glimpsed the Main Street from Dillon's truck the evening he'd driven her home. No one was around except one old man walking a skinny dog. Even the one grocery store was closed. Was everyone at the river?

Driving carefully, Kari peered out into the growing darkness. She wasn't sure just where the cutoff was to Dillon's ranch, the dirt road leading in. The only way she knew to reach the river was to follow the path from the cabin to the stream, where they'd gone on horseback that day.

Finally she spotted an opening that seemed slightly familiar and turned in. Her little car bounced along the uneven path for what seemed like a long way. Just when Kari was thinking she'd made a wrong turn, she saw the cabin directly ahead. Her heart lurched at the sight.

A light was on in the living room, though Dillon's truck was gone, and Zeus was nowhere in sight. The barn looked achingly familiar, but before she could get tangled in memories, Kari turned left along the rutted path they'd traveled on horseback.

Darkness seemed to descend here like a thick blanket, with dense trees on one side and the gurgling stream on the other. Her headlights were the only bright spots keeping her on the rugged trail as she gripped the wheel tightly. Automatically she slowed so that the small car wouldn't get damaged in the many potholes. She hoped her memory hadn't failed her and that this was the right way. Lord only knew where she would wind up if it wasn't.

Then, with one window still open, she could smell the river, just as she had the last time she'd visited the area. There was also a subtle sound, like the swishing of water. Not a roar, more like a murmur. Bouncing about as she hit a big rut, Kari held on to the BMW's wheel and kept going, certain she was on the right road now.

The path wound around slightly, and as she went past the bend, she could see lights in the far distance. Slowing even more, she could hear voices carried on the night breeze and over the large body of water. It wouldn't be much further.

Minutes later she saw the shoreline just ahead, the sandbags piled up along one side. Kari estimated about twenty people just ahead working to add more bags to the piles, men and women, young and old. Off to the left was a sloping path leading to a farmhouse, where nearly a dozen trucks were parked every which way. Lights had been strung up overhead, and a long table was laden with food dishes and two huge coffee urns.

No one seemed to pay much attention as she found a space alongside a mud-splattered silver truck and parked. The night air was chilly. Kari rolled up her window, shrugged into her denim jacket and locked the car, pocketing the key. Walking toward what seemed to be Control Central, where a very tall, redheaded man with a clipboard was giving orders to a couple of teenage boys who'd also just arrived, she scanned the crowd for a familiar face.

But she couldn't spot the tall, broad-shouldered, dark-haired man her eyes sought. Not discouraged, she moved closer, sure she'd find Dillon somewhere.

"Can you use another pair of hands?" she asked the redheaded man who seemed to be in charge.

"Sure can," he said even before he swung around to see who'd asked. His eyes narrowing, Bob Nichols looked over the young woman with the lush blond hair tied back with a piece of yarn, the designer denim jacket, the pressed jeans and brand-new hiking boots. "You're new around here." Bob felt silly stating the obvious, yet sure he'd have remembered this gal if he'd met her before.

"I'm a friend of Dillon Tracy's," Kari said, hoping that much wouldn't offend her past host. "And I'm stronger than I look. Where can you use a hand?"

"Over there," he said, pointing to a truck bed where two men were unloading sandbags. "Just grab a bag and carry it on over to the shore. There's a couple of men there in charge of where they're needed to go. Dillon's one of 'em, if you haven't seen him yet."

"Thanks." Zipping up her jacket, Kari walked to the truck and approached the first man hefting a sandbag. "Can I help?"

The man's tired gaze seemed to perk up as he looked at her, and he automatically sucked in his stomach. "Yeah, sure. Think you can carry one of these?"

"I can try." Kari took the bag from him, realizing it wasn't filled to the brim but was still a heavy load. "Got it."

"Okay. Take it to the shore." He watched her go for a minute, making sure she was able to walk and carry the bag, then turned back to unload more.

Arriving at the water's edge, Kari saw where several

men were instructing folks to stack the bags. What looked to be a half-mile length of the river bank had already been braced. No telling how far along they'd have to pile them up before they could be sure the river had crested. Carefully, she eased the bag onto the lowest stack, then turned around, heading back for another.

"You're a sight for sore eyes," Mac said, walking gingerly toward her. Then, hurriedly dumping his sack, he grimaced from the pain shooting through his shoulders.

Kari was immediately sympathetic, but knew she'd have to be careful not to hurt his pride. "Mac, it's good to see you. How long have you been at this?"

"I dunno. Hours. We got here about two in the morning." He was no longer sure which morning. Taking off his hat as they walked back toward the truck, Mac wiped his damp head with his kerchief.

"The redheaded man in charge over there said I was to tell some of you who've been working for hours to take a break." She touched a hand to his bony shoulder. "Want a cup of coffee?"

Each step a pain, Mac decided to take her up on the offer. "Might could use a cup. How about you?"

"I just got here."

He stopped just short of the truck being unloaded. "Why'd you come back?" he asked, his eyes squinting into her face.

"Because I couldn't stay away, not when I found out what was happening up here."

Damn fine woman, Mac thought. Only a couple of women out here dragging the bags, and they were farmer's wives with a lot at stake. Kari had just come back on a hope and a prayer. "You seen Dillon?"

"Not yet." She paused, wondering if she should ask, then plunged in. "How is he?"

"Stubborn as a damn mule." Mac put his hat back on, adjusted it just so. "But he's comin' around." And the old man meant to see to it that Dillon made it sooner rather than later.

Coming around. Well, she did know Dillon wasn't exactly the impulsive type. Still, she had no idea how he would react when he finally saw her. "I'll get back to it, Mac. You get that coffee." Smiling at him, she hefted another bag.

Mac ambled over to the grub table, thanked the woman who handed him a cup of steaming coffee, then made his way back to the front line, looking for a dark head that stood out above most others.

Kari lost track of how many trips she'd made from the truck to the riverbank with the heavy bags. One truck pulled out and another backed in with its load of stacked sacks. The workers scarcely skipped a beat as they trudged back and forth, trying to beat Mother Nature.

Everyone was friendly, she thought, which helped. A short man who'd been watching her tapped her shoulder and handed her a pair of heavy leather gloves. She smiled her thanks. A woman she'd never seen before pressed a plastic cup of coffee into her hands on one trip, and Kari accepted it gratefully, remembering she hadn't eaten since her morning bagel. Her hiking boots were soon muddy, her jeans damp, her jacket soiled from the dusty bags. She sneezed nearly every trip from the dust swirling about, but determination kept her going.

These people didn't know her, Kari was aware, but she wasn't the only nonresident helping out. The farmers and ranchers along with their families were pleased to have the volunteers, smiling their thanks, clapping shoulders and shaking hands when time permitted. No one asked who they were or why they were there. It was as if all of them were united against the threat of the mighty river.

"What are you doing here?" a deep, familiar voice said from behind her, nearly causing Kari to drop the bag she'd just hefted.

Gripping the sack, she turned around to gaze into blue eyes still incredible, still suspicious. "Exactly what I want to do, putting some meaning into my life." She walked toward the river, needing to set down her burden.

Dillon followed. He'd been watching her thoughtfully for several minutes ever since Mac pointed her out. All through the long night and day, he'd done the mindless, back-breaking work and thought about Kari. He recalled every detail of her beautiful face, that gorgeous body, those warm brown eyes. He remembered all they'd done together and had experienced a wave of longing that had nearly toppled him. Then he'd thought about the things he'd said to her, the things he'd done to be rid of her. And he felt ashamed.

He wasn't an unfair man, just a distrustful one. Twice burned made a man hesitant, wary, prudent. But he'd judged her and found her wanting, without so much as listening to her side of things. He'd decided on the way there last night that as soon as this necessary work was done, he'd rest up and go to her. He'd been restless, anxious to get going.

Then Mac had pointed to someone and asked him to look. And there she'd been, like a vision he'd conjured up. Golden ponytail flying behind her as she trudged along, tired, dirty and magnificent. He'd never seen a more beautiful sight.

Taking her arm after she dropped the bag, Dillon drew her aside, walking with her to the back of a thick pine tree. "What did you mean by that?" he asked.

Kari let out a ragged sigh. "Just that I went back and told my family I'd stick it out until after Dad's election. But I couldn't do it. My heart isn't there and hasn't been for a long time. I can't handle that scene anymore. I was miserable. You should know what I mean. You walked away from a new law practice to do something you believe in. Well, I'm doing the same thing."

Hope and doubt mingled inside Dillon, confusing him, scaring him. "But why here?" he asked, wanting to know. *Needing* to know. Could it be that she really meant what she said?

The weariness seemed to drop from Kari's features as she met his steady gaze. He had a dirt smudge on one cheek, and his hair was windblown and still too long. On his face was the start of a wonderful beard. The shoulder of his jacket had a jagged rip, and his boots looked as if he'd waded through ankle-deep mud. She'd never seen anyone she wanted more. "Because here is where *you* are."

"Hey, Dillon," came a shout from close by, "want us to start up the hill or go check the far end for leaks?"

It was as if he hadn't heard a word except the six little words she'd uttered. All of his doubts vanished in that one simple statement. All of the people, the muddy river and the surrounding night disappeared for Dillon. All he could see was the woman who was the other half of him. One long step took him close, as he dipped his head and took her mouth.

There it was, Kari thought, the wild flavor she'd been missing, the head rush she'd longed to feel again, the heating of her blood with just a touch of his lips. Every-thing forgotten, she pressed herself against the broad strength of him and kissed him back as if there were no tomorrow.

"Dillon? Are you back here?" The persistent voice came closer until Reggie Bennett stopped in his tracks, staring at Dillon Tracy kissing the blond woman every-body had been wondering about as if he'd never let her go. "Oh, sorry," he said, and began backing away.

Neither Kari nor Dillon noticed. Long moments later he finally eased back and stared into her misty eyes. "Can you hold that thought while we finish up here?"

"Mmm, I've been holding that thought for weeks now. I guess a few more hours won't matter." She stepped back, aware that she was trembling, not caring. *He wanted her again*, her heart sang. Dear God, Dillon wanted her again.

With renewed vigor, Dillon hurried back to the men along the bank, ignored the few comments and raised brows, and got everyone organized and working. "C'mon, guys. Let's get this done."

"Yeah, boys," Reggie said with a grin, "let's go. Dil-lon's got more important fish to fry than a mere little river to hold back." Amidst a chorus of chuckles, every-one went back to work.

Slowly Kari emerged from behind the pine tree and caught Mac's eyes. He winked broadly and held up one crooked thumb.

Smiling, she answered with a thumbs-up in return.

Around about one in the morning, there was a large shout that arose along the banks of the Hennessy River. The water had crested finally and was beginning to recede. The hundreds and hundreds of sandbags, the hours and hours of back-breaking work, had done the trick. Not a single home had had water come close enough to do serious damage.

Tired to the core, the Nichols family packed away the foodstuffs remaining on the grub table and bade their friends and neighbors farewell as truckloads of farmers and ranchers and even a few strangers wound their way along the rutted road back to the highway, heading home for some well-earned rest.

"Damn near twenty-four hours," Mac commented as he and Dillon bounced along somewhere in the middle of the exiting caravan of vehicles. "I think I could sleep standing up."

Equally as tired, yet too revved up to think about sleeping just yet, Dillon only grunted a reply. His eyes on the rearview mirror, he watched Kari's little convertible following directly behind him. Hadn't he just guessed she'd have chosen some sporty little number like that? He'd be lucky if he could afford that car in ten years, even if he wanted one, which he didn't.

But that wasn't important. He wasn't going to think about her money, her assets. He wanted to concentrate on what she'd said. She'd come to DeWitt after seeing the plight of his neighbors on CNN to pitch in. She was no hothouse flower, as she'd once told him. She'd worked alongside big, burly farmers and strong teenagers and ranch hands who could hardly keep their eyes off her. They were sure she was a misguided visitor, not one of them. But he knew better.

She fit in because she'd earned the right to be here. And she fit him like a custom-made glove. To hell with her family, her money, their differences. She hadn't lied

about who she was to hurt him, but because she knew it
was the only way he'd let her stay. And in the process
she'd fallen in love with him, which had surprised her as
much as him.

Why had she come? Because this was where he was.
Whither thou goest, I will go, he remembered from his
youthful Bible studies. She'd followed him because she
wanted to be with him. That was all he needed to know,
all he *ever* needed to know.

"So, Kari's back to stay, is she?" Mac asked into the
silence.

"Damn right she is," Dillon said, grinning at the old
man.

"'Bout time you came to your senses." Mac's final
word.

The teeth-jarring ride home seemed to take forever, but
at last Dillon pulled his truck up close to the barn. Only
once during their lengthy ordeal had he taken an hour
and gone home to check on his stock, to water and feed
them. Otherwise, he'd left Zeus in charge. He could hear
the big dog barking now as he jumped down from the
cab and watched Kari park behind him.

"Okay if I leave it here?" she asked, dragging her
weary bones out.

"Yeah, fine." Moving a bit slowly himself, Dillon
opened the stable door and released Zeus. The dog
sniffed at him once, then bypassed Mac, who'd managed
to step down, before sailing straight for Kari.

"Hey, boy, it's so good to see you." She stooped to
let him lick her face, to pet his big head, to let him know
she was back.

"See you two tomorrow, not early," Mac muttered as
he made his painful way to his trailer.

"You did a hell of a job tonight, Mac," Dillon called after him.

Too weary to answer, Mac just raised a hand in acknowledgement and trudged on.

Straightening, Kari unlocked her trunk. "I brought some clothes, just in case I'm invited to stay."

Moving to her side, Dillon leaned down to kiss her lightly. "You're most definitely invited to stay for the next, oh, hundred years or so." He lifted the bags out and swore he could hear his shoulder muscles groan out loud.

Smiling, Kari followed Dillon to the back door and inside to the laundry room where she stepped out of her muddy shoes while he struggled out of his boots, and they hung up their dirty jackets.

"I desperately need a shower," she commented unnecessarily. "But it's your house so you go first."

"Didn't you hear on the news that we have a water shortage up this way?" Setting her bags in his room, Dillon took her hand and led her to the bathroom. "We've been given strict instructions to shower in pairs."

"Is that so?" she asked, noting the mischief in his eyes. Oh, Lord, but she'd been so afraid, and here he was, laughing, looking so wonderful. "Funny, I must have missed that broadcast."

He tugged her sweater over her head, dropped it to the floor, then leaned in to turn on the water. By the time they had each other undressed, steam had filled the small room. Stepping under the spray, Kari just stood there, letting the heat ease her achiness and fatigue. She ducked her head under, let the stream wet her from top to bottom.

Watching her take the soap in hand, Dillon knew he

couldn't wait another moment. Picking her up, he stroked her back as she wound her legs around his waist while his mouth came down on hers. The kiss was long and breathtaking.

"I...I thought you were really tired," Kari said when he finally let her up for air.

"Honey, there's tired, and then there's tired," he answered just before lowering his mouth to her breast.

Later, much later, lying in bed together, Dillon raised himself on one elbow and studied her in the glow of a dim lamp. "Are you sure this is how you want to spend the rest of your life, Kari? You only saw a small sample so far. Ranching is hard work, and I'm going to be honest with you. I'm doing all right, but it could take years for me to see a really decent profit. I believe now that I can convince my dad this ranch is a good investment and a growing business, but I'll never be able to give you all that your father has given you."

She frowned up at him, annoyed. "Do you think I care about my family's money? I wouldn't be here if that was all that was important to me. I don't mind hard work, if I can be with you—I think I held my own out there to-night. It's much harder for me to do something every day that I hate to do. Which is what I've been doing for years now."

She was saying all the right things, and he desperately wanted to believe her. "What about your father?"

"I had a long talk with Dad before driving up. I think he finally understands that I have to do what pleases me. And what pleases me, Mr. Tracy, is you." She stared up into eyes still not certain, still hesitant. What more could she say? "I love you, Dillon. I have from the start. But maybe I was wrong to come back."

Zeus picked that moment to put two large paws on the bed, stretching to lick her hand.

"No, you were absolutely right to come back, although I have to tell you that I'd made up my mind I was going to drive to your place to try to persuade you to come back right after we finished with the river." He saw Zeus licking her hand, then watched her pet the big dog who looked at her adoringly. "We were both lost without you. I love you very much. Welcome home."

Zeus wasn't very happy about being locked out of the bedroom right after that. But how else could Dillon show Kari exactly how happy he was to have her back where she belonged?

* * * * *

Silhouette Books is delighted to alert you
to a brand-new MacGregor story from
Nora Roberts, coming in October 1998,
from Silhouette Special Edition. Look for

THE WINNING HAND

and find out how a small-town
librarian wins the heart of elusive,
wealthy and darkly handsome
Robert "Mac" Blade.

Here's a sneak preview of

THE WINNING HAND....

The Winning Hand

There was something wonderfully smooth under her cheek. Silk, satin, Darcy thought dimly. She'd always loved the feel of silk. Once she'd spent nearly her entire paycheck on a silk blouse, creamy white with gold, heart-shaped buttons. She'd had to skip lunch for two weeks, but it had been worth it every time she slipped that silk over her skin.

She sighed, remembering it.

"Come on, all the way out."

"What?" She blinked her eyes open, focused on a slant of light from a jeweled lamp.

"Here, try this." Mac slipped a hand under her head, lifted it, and put a glass of water to her lips.

"What?"

"You're repeating yourself. Drink some water."

"Okay." She sipped obediently, studying the tanned, long-fingered hand that held the glass. She was on a bed, she realized now, a huge bed with a silky cover. There was a mirrored ceiling over her head. "Oh my." Warily, she shifted her gaze until she saw his face.

He set the glass aside, then sat on the edge of the bed, noting with amusement that she scooted over slightly to keep more distance between them. "Mac Blade. I run this place."

"Darcy. I'm Darcy Wallace. Why am I here?"

"It seemed better than leaving you sprawled on the floor of the casino. You fainted."

"I did?" Mortified, she closed her eyes again. "Yes, I guess I did. I'm sorry."

"It's not an atypical reaction to winning close to two million dollars."

Her eyes popped open, her hand grabbed at her throat. "I'm sorry. I'm still a little confused. Did you say I won almost two million dollars?"

"You put the money in, you pulled the lever, you hit." There wasn't an ounce of color in her cheeks, he noted, and thought she looked like a bruised fairy. "Do you want to see a doctor?"

"No, I'm just…I'm okay. I can't think. My head's spinning."

"Take your time." Instinctively, he plumped up the pillows behind her and eased her back.

"I had nine dollars and thirty-seven cents when I got here."

"Well, now you have $1,800,088.37."

"Oh. Oh." Shattered, she put her hands over her face and burst into tears.

There were too many women in his life for Mac to be uncomfortable with female tears. He sat where he was and let her sob it out.

"I'm sorry." She wiped her hands at her somehow

charmingly dirty face. "I'm not like this. Really. I can't take it in." She accepted the handkerchief he offered and blew her nose. "I don't know what to do."

"Let's start with the basics. Why don't you take a hot bath, try to relax, get your bearings. There's a robe in the closet."

She cleared her throat. However kind he was being, she was still alone with him, a perfect stranger, in a very opulent and sensual bedroom. "I appreciate it. But I should get a room. If I could have a small advance on the money, I can find a hotel."

"Something wrong with this one?"

"This what?"

"This hotel," he said. "This room."

"No, nothing. It's beautiful."

"Then make yourself comfortable. Your room's been comped for the duration of your stay—"

"What? Excuse me?" She sat up a little straighter. "I can have this room? I can just…stay here?"

"It's the usual procedure for high rollers." He smiled again, making her heart bump. "You qualify."

"I get all this for free because I won money from you?"

His grin was quick, and just a little wolfish. "I want the chance to win some of it back."

Lord, he was beautiful. Like the hero of a novel. That thought rolled around in her jumbled brain. "That seems only fair. Thank you so much, Mr. Blade."

"Welcome to Las Vegas, Ms. Wallace," he said and turned toward a sweep of open stairs that led to the living area.

She watched him cross an ocean of Oriental carpet. "Mr. Blade?"

"Yes?" He turned and glanced up.

"What will I do with all that money?"

He flashed that grin again. "You'll think of something."

When the doors closed behind him, Darcy gave in to her buckling knees and sat on the floor. She hugged herself hard, rocking back and forth. If this was some dream, some hallucination brought on by stress or sunstroke, she hoped it never cleared away.

She hadn't just escaped her life, she realized. She'd been liberated.

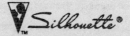

Take 2 bestselling love stories FREE

Plus get a FREE surprise gift!

Special Limited-Time Offer

Mail to Silhouette Reader Service™

P.O. Box 609
Fort Erie, Ontario
L2A 5X3

YES! Please send me 2 free Silhouette Special Edition® novels and my free surprise gift. Then send me 6 brand-new novels every month, which I will receive months before they appear in bookstores. Bill me at the low price of $3.96 each plus 25¢ delivery and GST*. That's the complete price, and a saving of over 10% off the cover prices—quite a bargain! I understand that accepting the books and gift places me under no obligation ever to buy any books. I can always return a shipment and cancel at any time. Even if I never buy another book from Silhouette, the 2 free books and the surprise gift are mine to keep forever.

335 SEN CH7X

Name _____ (PLEASE PRINT)

Address _____ Apt. No. _____

City _____ Province _____ Postal Code _____

This offer is limited to one order per household and not valid to present Silhouette Special Edition® subscribers. *Terms and prices are subject to change without notice.
Canadian residents will be charged applicable provincial taxes and GST.

CSPED-98

©1990 Harlequin Enterprises Limited

Bestselling author
Joan Elliott Pickart launches
Silhouette's newest cross-line promotion

with
THE RANCHER AND THE AMNESIAC BRIDE
Special Edition, October 1998

Josie Wentworth of the oil-rich Oklahoma Wentworths knew penthouse apartments and linen finery—not working ranches...and certainly *not* remote, recalcitrant ranchers! But one conk to the head and one slight case of amnesia had this socialite beauty sharing time and tangling sheets with the cowboy least likely to pop the question....

And don't miss The Daddy and the Baby Doctor by Kristin Morgan, when FOLLOW THAT BABY! continues in Silhouette Romance in November 1998!

Silhouette Books

Available at your favorite retail outlet.

Silhouette Romance
celebrates the joys
of first love in
VIRGIN BRIDES

September 1998:
THE GUARDIAN'S BRIDE
by Laurie Paige (#1318)
A young heiress, desperately in love with her
older, wealthy guardian, dreams of wedding the
tender tycoon. But he has plans to marry
her off to another....

October 1998:
THE NINE-MONTH BRIDE
by Judy Christenberry (#1324)
A widowed rancher who wants an heir and a prim librarian
who wants a baby decide to marry for convenience—but will
motherhood make this man and wife rethink their
temporary vows?

November 1998:
A BRIDE TO HONOR by Arlene James (#1330)
A pretty party planner falls for a charming, honor-bound
millionaire who's being roped into a loveless marriage. When
the wedding day arrives, will *she* be his blushing bride?

December 1998:
A KISS, A KID AND A MISTLETOE BRIDE (#1336)
When a scandalous single dad returns home at
Christmas, he encounters the golden girl he'd fallen
for one magical night a lifetime before.

Available at your favorite retail outlet.

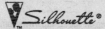

Available October 1998
from Silhouette Books...

World's Most
Eligible Bachelors

DETECTIVE DAD
by Marie Ferrarella

The World's Most Eligible Bachelor: Undercover agent Duncan MacNeill, a wealthy heir with a taut body...and an even harder heart.

Duncan MacNeill just got the toughest assignment of his life: deliver a beautiful stranger's baby in the back seat of her car! This tight-lipped loner never intended to share his name with anyone—especially a mystery woman who claimed to have a total memory loss. But how long could he hope to resist succumbing to the lure of daddyhood—and marriage?

Each month, Silhouette Books brings you
a brand-new story about an absolutely
irresistible bachelor. Find out how the sexiest,
most sought-after men are finally caught.

Available at your favorite retail outlet.

Silhouette®

Silhouette®

SPECIAL EDITION™

COMING NEXT MONTH

#1201 FATHER-TO-BE—Laurie Paige
That's My Baby!
When Celia Campbell informed honorable Hunter McLean she was carrying his child, he was stunned! He couldn't recall their impulsive night of passion, much less envision playing daddy the second time around. He knew that getting married was the right thing to do, but could he open his heart to love?

#1202 THE WINNING HAND—Nora Roberts
MacGregor Series
Sweet, unsophisticated Darcy Wallace was feeling very fortunate! After winning the jackpot, she caught dashing and dangerous millionaire Robert MacGregor Blade's eye. But she would need more than luck to convince this confirmed bachelor of her dreams to gamble on a future—with her....

#1203 FROM HOUSE CALLS TO HUSBAND—Christine Flynn
Prescription: Marriage
Heart surgeon Mike Brennan had a gentle touch, a soothing voice—and, boy, did he look sexy in his scrubs! But nurse Katie Sheppard had vowed *never* to marry a doctor—particularly one who was her best friend...and best-kept secret crush.

#1204 THE RANCHER AND THE AMNESIAC BRIDE—Joan Elliott Pickart
Follow That Baby!
Josie Wentworth of the oil-rich Oklahoma Wentworths didn't know the first thing about working ranches—or grumpy, gorgeous cowboys. But a case of amnesia had the socialite princess riding the range—and yearning for a lifetime of lovin' with the man least likely to say I do!

#1205 PARTNERS IN MARRIAGE—Allison Hayes
A housing shortage in Turtle Creek? Whatever was Shelley Matthews to do? First, the schoolteacher moved in with devastatingly handsome Blue Larson. Then, despite her misgivings, she offered to be the Lakota Indian's partner in marriage. Dare she trust in happily ever after again?

#1206 THE BODYGUARD'S BRIDE—Jean Brashear
Women To Watch
In the name of justice, Jillian Marshall vowed to avenge her sister's murder. Nothing stood in her way—except for dangerously attractive bodyguard Drake Cullinane, who had an agenda of his own. Only he could soothe the pain paralyzing her heart, but how much would she sacrifice for love?